PLAYING WITH DANGER

HOLLOW POINT
BOOK 2

RILEY EDWARDS

Playing with Danger
Hollow Point Book 2

Cover design: Lori Jackson Designs

Written by: Riley Edwards

Published by: Riley Edwards/Rebels Romance

Edited by: Kendall Black

Proofreader: Julie Deaton

Book Name: Playing with Danger

Paperback ISBN: 978-1-951567-60-6

First edition: September 1, 2024

To my family - my team – my tribe.
This is for you.

CONTENTS

1

"SOPHIE, ARE YOU LISTENING TO ME?" my mother snapped.

Nope.

Not even a little bit.

Often times I stopped listening to my mother three minutes into our conversations. This was because it took her approximately three minutes to get through the pleasantries before she started in on my lack of...fill in the blank...motivation, ambition, drive...those were her favorites but she had others that included the lack of... a man in my life, or social life, or a country club membership—and yes, that was a real complaint. That was where a woman of my age should go to find a man.

My age was thirty-seven, not sixty-seven, so I was hardly getting ready to die an old maid.

Though if I didn't end this conversation soon I might die of boredom.

And, wow, that made me sound bitchy or like I was a horrible daughter. I wasn't. I loved my mother. But she was a mother, not a mom. Plus she was a good mother, so really I shouldn't complain—even mentally—that I wanted to poke my eardrums with ice picks when she started on a rant.

"Sorry. I'm at the grocery store."

"Grocery store?"

She sounded like I'd just told her I was at a female mud wrestling match and I was the main attraction.

"Yes, Mother. I need to eat."

"On a Friday night?"

"Yes, Mother. I tend to eat every night of the week."

"Bless. So much cheek."

The woman couldn't decide if she was a Southerner or British.

Side note: she wasn't either. She was born in England but moved to Kansas when she was five. That's where she met my father—not when she was five, when she was twenty. He was in the Army. According to her they had a whirlwind courtship, got married, and she followed him to Georgia when he PCSed. A year later I was born. She denies it, because a dignified woman didn't have sexual intercourse before marriage—insert eye roll—but her math didn't add up. She was pregnant with me before they'd made it to the altar. Not that it mattered because when his enlistment was up, which was two years after I was born, he took off to parts unknown, never to be heard from again. By then my mom had fallen in love with

Georgia, or so she says, but really I think it's because she didn't get along with her very stuffy, stuck-up parents who were British.

Now, that's not a dig on Brits. I'd been to England; I loved it there and the crap about the stiff upper lip stuff was total BS. The time I'd spent in London I found Londoners to be the opposite of everything I'd heard—most of it coming from my mother who was again five when she left and had only been back for visits since then.

So all of that to say, my mother was a complex and confusing woman who loved me. But damn if she didn't ride my ass.

How her husband put up with her ranting I'd never know.

Now, Nathan, he didn't rant and drone on. He was neither confusing or complex. Too bad she only met him seven years ago and got hitched to him two years ago. My childhood would've been much warmer.

"Excuse me."

That didn't come from my mother.

That came from next to me.

The voice smooth like velvet but with a hint of grit.

"Sorry."

I quickly grabbed what I wanted and stepped away from the boxes of linguini I'd been rudely blocking while chatting with my mother.

Why I perused I'd never know. I always got the same brand. I liked what I liked and I didn't deviate.

One could say I lived a narrow life.

One could also say I had zero situational awareness as well. This became embarrassingly apparent when I promptly collided with a black-clad chest.

"Holy shit. I'm sorry." I quickly stepped back, where I hit the display of Kraft grated cheese, knocking some of the thankfully plastic containers off the top. Only to step forward again and slam back into the man in an effort not to knock down the entire display.

"What's happening?" That was my mother.

"Are you alright?" That was the black-clad chest.

I pulled my forehead off the very hard, muscular chest, and tipped my eyes up to find the hottest man I'd ever seen in my life staring down at me.

"Someone kill me," I breathed.

"Do I need to call 9-1-1?" Again, my mother.

"No, Mother, please don't call the police. I'm fine but I have to go."

Without waiting for a response, I pulled my phone away from my ear. On my way to shoving my phone into my pocket my hand brushed the man's forearm and hip.

"I promise I'm not trying to be weird and feel you up. I'm just afraid if I move I might do something else embarrassing like say, trip and fall into the jars of spaghetti sauce. And red's not my color."

Oh my God.

What was wrong with me?

Red's not my color?

The man smiled.

It was dazzling and friendly and holy hot potato I wanted to ask him if I could take a picture. Not to do anything weird like pull it up later tonight while I was playing hide the dildo with my vibrator for extra stimulation—the plug-in kind, since I hadn't had a real penis in so long I'd forgone batteries.

What's better than one toy?

Two.

Two was always better.

But not two in the vagina at once...that was a little too kinky for me. Like double-penetration toy-style.

What the hell is wrong with me? I screamed in my head.

"Sorry, God, I'm sorry."

I slowly backed away from the man. When I was far enough away I noticed he was in those black pants that police officers wore with the pockets on the sides, and black combat boots.

Of course he was a hot cop.

He could have a whole IG page dedicated to his hotness.

"Nothing to be sorry about."

Before I made a bigger fool out of myself, I smiled and dashed away.

It wasn't until I paid for my pasta and garlic and I was safely in my car that I bust out laughing.

A week later, it was again Friday night, and I was again going home alone to make dinner for me, myself, and I when it happened.

It went something like this...

"We meet again."

Oh, God, I knew that voice.

Only this time I was not in the grocery store. I was at the liquor store.

This could be dangerous.

"There are glass bottles all around me. I think perhaps it's safer if I stand still and let you grab what you want."

His hand went to my hip, his chest pressed against my back, and he reached around me to grab a bottle of red wine.

I might've moaned.

He might've heard, if the way his fingers twitched on my hip was anything to go by.

"Thought you didn't like red," he said close to my ear.

His warm breath fanned over my neck. The smell of male sweat, and outside, and maybe a hint of tobacco invaded my senses. Then there was his voice.

Sweet baby Dolly I was having a mini-orgasm.

My sad, narrow, lonely life had come to this.

A sexy stranger giving me an orgasm in the wine aisle.

I might as well buy five cats, three birds, and start an alone-and-under-forty knitting club.

I had been reduced to voice orgasms.

My mother would say, 'I told you so.'

"I'm Valentine," he said, still close.

"Sophie."

"Nice to meet you, Sophie."

Oh yeah, totally having a vagina spasm.

"Nice to meet you."

That was as far as we got before all hell broke sideways.

And gunshots rang out all around us.

"Down!"

Hot Cop didn't need to tell me twice.

I was on my hands and knees staring at a black pair of combat boots when I heard, "This is a stick up," accompanied with a round of pops, whizzes, and whistles.

Did people really say that in real life?

"Get the hell out of here!" someone shouted.

"Dumbfuck!" someone else yelled.

"I hope your daddy whoops your ass when you get home!" a third bellowed.

"Don't move." That was Valentine, then his boots were gone.

I waited a few moments, then I moved. Actually I crawled. Not far, just to the end of the red wine aisle to peek around the display. The cashier was behind the counter looking fit to be tied. Three very irate patrons stood holding their booze. Shattered glass littered the floor, red pooled next to the broken bottles.

No Valentine.

Movement to my right caught my attention. I turned from the checkout area and my breath caught in my lungs. The rest happened fast. Too fast. I caught a man tugging down a black mask and he caught me staring. For a long moment our eyes stayed connected. A moment that would prove to be a mistake. I scurried back, the now-masked-man lunged. He reached down, grabbed a handful of hair, and yanked me to my feet.

Pain, sharp and swift, radiated from my scalp down to my neck, making me cry out. And with that the strangest thing happened—it was like I woke up.

Not in the sense I suddenly realized I was about to become a hostage in a robbery.

It woke me up—full stop.

With bright blinding clarity my narrow life came into focus. My whole life I played it safe. I made lists. I went about my day checking off the things I'd accomplished but none of them were worth much. I didn't venture outside of my comfort zone. I didn't take chances. I set goals that were easily attainable instead of dreaming of the impossible. For God sakes, I bought the same brand of spaghetti noodles because why bother trying something new. I was stuck and had been for years, maybe all my life. I hated my job but stayed. I told myself that was what adults did. Further, I lied to myself and gave myself a gold star for toughing out a shit situation because that made me someone with a good work ethic. I had one real friend; the others were leftovers from a time in my life when I put up with mean girl gossip and catty behavior because having someone meant I didn't have anyone.

My life was going nowhere, but that didn't mean I didn't want to continue to live it.

That was what likely made me snap.

I didn't want to die.

With a rebel yell and my nails bared, I attacked. I scratched and kicked and thrashed until me and the masked man were on the floor with the endcap full of buckets of margarita mix on top of us. The black knit cap was askew so I clawed the side of his face. My knee was close to his groin so I jacked it upward as hard as I could. Unfortunately some of the buckets broke open. I slipped around in sticky, sugary syrup. I ignored the sharp stabbing pain digging into my side and enjoyed the would-be hostage-taker's howl of pain.

That was as far as I got before a pair of hands went under my armpits and hauled me off the hair-pulling asshole who wanted to use me as a real-life shield. I hadn't lifted my eyes from the man now cupping his gonads when a pair of black boots blocked the view of my handiwork.

The rest happened as fast as it had started. Valentine rolled the robber to his stomach, yanked his arms behind his back, and pinned him face down on the sticky lime-coated linoleum—or was it lime-coated laminate? Either way the man wasn't moving. Neither did Valentine, except to turn his head and give me a full-body scan, which made me want to shiver under his heated gaze.

"You're bleeding," he gruffly noted.

Against my better judgement I glanced down at my shirt. Sure enough the peach blouse was stained red.

The roaring in my ears started first. The whooshing in my belly that always accompanied the unfortunate soundtrack in my head that told me I was going down started next.

Christ on a cracker.

Not now.

"Told you red wasn't my color."

Then it was lights out.

2

WHO KNEW AN ATTEMPTED robbery and a kid throwing firecrackers at a liquor store clerk would be such a time suck?

Okay, so, maybe the long slice that nicked the side of my boob and traveled down my side six inches also took some time to be looked at, cleaned, and bandaged by paramedics. Or I should say, one paramedic called Delilah. She was sweet, but I figured that was an act since she turned into the devil when she figured out that contrary to her best efforts to get me to go to the hospital, I wasn't going to waste the rest of my afternoon that would bleed into my evening sitting in the waiting room of the ER. I think she purposefully used more alcohol swabs than necessary to clean my cut—that thankfully wasn't deep, just long and bleeding like a son of a bitch. She had grimaced and apologized when the germ-killing solution burned its way down to my soul, causing the sting to bring tears to my eyes. So maybe she wasn't the devil, just thorough even though she was unhappy I'd refused her advice.

Whoever said getting cut by a shard of plastic didn't hurt just as bad as being sliced by glass had obviously never been stabbed by a party bucket before. Stabbed might've been a little dramatic, but it was the story I was sticking with. God knows my life being as boring as it was I needed a good story to spice it up.

Coupled with my near-death experience, the stabbing would be my claim to fame. Not that I had anyone to tell but my roommate who would call me out for my theatrics like he always did when my impressive skills of overexaggerating a story took a turn into the unbelievable.

Now I was the proud wearer of a sticky, bloodstained blouse with an over-the-top bandage under my shirt. I'd given my statement to the police—that would be three of them who let me tell my story then asked follow-up questions to their follow-up questions. I was exhausted and ready to go home, drink a bottle of wine, where at such time I'd finally allow myself to stop using humor as the crutch I always relied on and freak out that I'd almost been taken hostage in a robbery attempt.

I was almost to my car when I heard my name, then I was stuck in a mental conundrum—pretend I didn't hear Valentine calling after me or stop and face the man. I wish I could say my problem was due to exhaustion, but I was running high on adrenaline that was quickly wearing off and I wanted to be alone when the crash hit. Alone where no one could witness my unravelling.

Unfortunately in my hesitation the choice was made for me.

"Sophie, wait up."

Damn.

Okay, I could do this. Surely the man had more important things to do than hang out in the parking lot of a crime scene talking to a stranger. It hadn't taken long for my first impression of him to be confirmed—he was a cop. With his brethren still crawling all over the store he wouldn't have much time to waste on me.

I slapped a fake smile on my face before I turned to face the very handsome Valentine.

"I think the universe is telling us something," I quipped. "First, near disaster in the spaghetti aisle, now this. Seems dinner *and* drinks are out for us."

The frown that pulled his brows together was my first indication he didn't find me amusing. The way his gaze dropped to my chest area was not due to my superior breasts—not that I'd ever had a man zero in on my B cups before and now clearly wasn't going to be the first time—but it was another clue Valentine wasn't enjoying my attempt at humor.

"It looks worse than it is," I started. "Apparently a little blood mixed with lime juice makes for one hell of a stain."

At that his eyes traveled up, taking a long time to meet mine.

"Do you need a ride to the hospital?"

Even if I'd been planning on going to the ER both my arms still worked and I hadn't lost enough blood I couldn't operate my car.

"Delilah patched me up," I told him then added, "The paramedic."

"I know who she is, but you should still get checked out."

Not this again.

"You might know who she is but obviously you're unfamiliar with her kickass field dressings."

"I'm acutely aware of how good the woman is at her job," he fired back as his hand lifted. He dropped it back to his side short of its intended target, which looked as if he were aiming for his stomach. "You still should—"

"I don't mean to cut you off but I'm fine. I don't need to go to the hospital for a scratch."

Again his eyes dropped to my shirt. He accompanied this with a pinch of his lips.

"Right," he forced through a frown.

"Thanks for—"

This time he cut me off. "I didn't do anything. By the time I got back you'd successfully taken out the threat." He paused and ever so slightly shook his head. "I shouldn't've left you back there by yourself."

Ah. His unhappy frown wasn't about me kicking bad guy ass before he could. He felt guilty he left me unprotected.

"And deprive me of practicing my self-defense moves?" I teased.

When those lines bracketing his mouth got deeper I figured now was the time to get serious.

"Listen, Valentine, there's no reason for you to feel guilty or any sort of way about leaving me the way you did. You had a job to do. You were seeing to that. You had no idea someone was going to come into the back."

The man still looked unconvinced.

As much as I wished it wasn't the truth, there was nothing I could do about that. Especially with the impending freakout I wanted to have in private.

Instead of trying to do the impossible I asked him, "Are *you* okay?"

My question seemed to take him off guard, or maybe it was surprise I'd flipped the script and was asking after him—the big, tough cop. And I didn't mean that snarky. The dude was big; he towered over me with broad shoulders and a muscular frame that I'd already dreamed about after our first meeting, so naturally I'd lust after him again even if I was covered in sticky blood and he was grimacing. The tough part was merely an educated guess.

"Valentine!" a uniformed police officer called out. When Valentine craned his head to look over his shoulder the cop went on shouting, "We need you for a minute!"

Without answering—or perhaps the dip of his chin was an answer—Valentine turned back to me. He looked like he wanted to say something, probably something along the lines of an unnecessary apology.

So I let him off the hook. "Thanks for checking on me. I promise I'm fine. See you around."

I turned to leave but halted when he said my name.

"Yeah?"

His stare morphed into something different. The change was miniscule but unmistakable. His gaze heated even as his features softened. Then it was gone so fast I wondered if I'd imagined it. And when his guard went up to what I'd call a cop mask giving nothing away, he dipped his chin, followed by, "Drive safe home."

"Thanks. You, too."

I didn't stick around to see if he had more to say. I could feel the anxiety of the day seeping in. On my way to my car I checked my watch, grateful Hayden would already be gone.

The closer I got to my complex the more the pressure built. By the time I pulled into the lot my chest felt heavy. When I made it into my apartment my breath was coming in short, choppy pants. But it wasn't until I made it to my bed and curled into a ball did I let it sink in.

And not just what had happened that day.

Everything.

The way I lived my life.

The way I allowed people to treat me.

The way I'd stumbled through life taking scraps instead of reaching for more.

The way I tolerated the constant nagging from my mother.

The way I'd brushed off growing up with the knowledge my father had abandoned me.

The way I'd let everything get so out of control.

I was on a merry-go-round.

I wanted off.

I wanted more.

I wanted to try a different brand of spaghetti noodles, dammit.

I'd give myself this—one night to feel the despair of living half a life when today could've been it.

Lights out, never to wake up again, all over, the end.

Tomorrow I would figure out what I was going to do with the rest of my life.

3

MY HEAD THROBBED, and not from the one glass of wine I'd allowed myself last night after my crying jag. It was from lack of sleep. My body ached like I'd gone five rounds with a heavy weight. Four tablets of Motrin and the hot water from the shower was doing nothing to alleviate the soreness in my muscles. Though showering with a plastic grocery bag duct-taped over the bandage Delilah had told me not to get wet wasn't exactly conducive to a relaxing shower.

I was in the middle of rinsing the conditioner out of my hair, mentally bemoaning the pain I knew would accompany the removal of the silver tape that held the bag in place, when it happened. My breath seized in my lungs as freezing cold water smacked me in the face, leaving me sputtering.

"I hate you!" I grunted and moved fully under the warm water to stave off the chill.

"No, you don't!" Hayden yelled back. "You love me."

"It's official. I'm breaking our marriage pact."

The water pressure changed and I knew Hayden was refilling his bucket.

"We don't have a marriage pact, goof."

"If you throw another bucket—"

Icy water rained over the curtain and doused me again.

"Asshole!"

"Out, Soph, or I'm picking the restaurant."

Saturday brunch.

This was what Hayden and I did. It was the one afternoon we set aside to connect.

"You're going to feel like a total tool for giving me an ice bath when I tell you about my day yesterday."

"Please, tell me the reason you're killing the planet and using all the hot water for the building is because you had crazy monkey sex last night and pulled a hamstring."

I wish.

"When have I ever had crazy monkey sex?" I asked as I finished rinsing my hair.

"Never, that's why I'm out here crossing my fingers for you."

I turned off the water, pulled the curtain aside just far enough for my arm to reach out. I wiggled my fingers and demanded, "Towel."

A towel was shoved into my hand. "At your service."

I seriously loved Hayden.

Unfortunately, that love was in a friends-only way.

It wasn't that Hayden was unattractive; he was extremely good-looking. It wasn't that he wasn't funny, or smart, or ambitious, or any of the things that made a man dating material. It was because Hayden had been my ex-boyfriend's best friend, now ex-best friend since I got Hayden in the breakup. That was because Hayden was a good, decent man who was hurt and pissed off that Oakley had cheated on me. Not once, but twice. Not that I knew about the first one until I found out about the second, then all his lies came out. Hayden had been enraged. I had been crushed. He gave me three months to nurse my broken heart before he called me and asked me to lunch. It was then Hayden told me he'd kicked Oakley's ass and broken off the friendship.

He didn't seek me out to be a creep. During my year-and-a-half relationship with Oakley, Hayden and I had become friends. Not the lie-in-wait male friend who was secretly bidding his time until he could lure you into bed. Genuine friends. So, me and Oakley broke up. Hayden and Oakley broke up. And Hayden became my best friend. That was five years ago and we moved in together as roommates two years ago when his last roommate moved to Arizona.

Truth be told, sometimes I secretly wished I was attracted to Hayden. Life would be so much easier. But the one and only time I stared at him while we were binging old *Law & Order* episodes wondering what it would be like to kiss him, my lip curled up and my vagina promptly hung a 'Do Not Enter' sign in my panties. Incidentally my feet had been in his lap and he was giving me an over-the-sock foot massage since feet were gross and that was the only way I'd allow him to touch them. Meaning if there was ever a time I'd be open to the idea of kissing him it would be while he was doing something sweet and generous after I'd had a long day.

It should also be noted Hayden was not attracted to me in anyway either. Zero boners from him in regard to me. Not even an, oops it's morning and I can't control my erection as you're running to the only bathroom we have in the apartment and you're only in a t-shirt and undies. Zip. Zilch. No tent popping in our apartment.

"Now that you're done I'm leaving."

That was totally Hayden. He'd pour ice water over my head while I was in the shower. He'd sit on the toilet seat and talk to me. But as soon as the water went off and he'd handed me my towel, he vamoosed to give me privacy.

I did the same to him, though I rarely got the bucket over the railing before he'd yell that he knew I was in the bathroom. That took most of the fun out of it but I still got mine back.

He'd also sit and binge old TV shows and eat popcorn with me. He'd also come home from a date, tell me all about it—sometimes more than I wanted to know—and razz me about my horrible sex life. Read, nonexistent sex life. There were times he'd get serious and tell me he was worried I wasn't happy. The man was good at a heart-to-heart but over the years with the kind of mother I had I'd perfected the art of hiding my unhappiness. Or more to the point—lying.

Meaning, I wasn't as fired up as I was yesterday when the rush of what had happened was still fresh to tell Hayden what had happened. Mainly because he'd be pissed I hadn't called him right away.

That meant I took my time getting out of the shower and peeling back the duct tape I'd stupidly used. I also took my time getting ready. By the time I made my way out to the living room, finding Hayden sitting on the couch with his tablet in his hands, dread had taken over.

4

"HAYDEN?" I prompted when he didn't say anything.

"Quiet," he snapped.

I was sitting opposite of Hayden, my ass on the edge of one of the two papasan chairs that normally sat to the right of the couch in front of the window that had a bird's eye view of the pool and clubhouse. I'd dragged one in front of the TV so I could face him while I explained yesterday's doings before we left for lunch.

Now I was regretting telling him.

Hayden had never snapped at me.

But then I'd never shared with him I'd been caught up in a would-be robbery. Further from that, I'd never shared with him I'd been in a physical altercation, and that was only because before yesterday I'd never actually hit anyone. Moving on from that I'd never had the plastic shards from a broken bucket of margarita mix slice into me.

Yesterday's plan to use humor and dramatics to tell my story died a fiery death three sentences in when Hayden's eyes glittered with fury. It was then I'd changed tactics and gave him only the facts without commentary that would lead him to believe I was a badass heroine who took down the bad guy.

I did my best not to fidget in the silence but when Hayden broke eye contact and glanced down to my wringing hands in my lap I knew I failed miserably.

"You know," he started conversationally with a hint of disdain. "I blame your mother for this."

Of course he would. He blamed her for everything.

"Hay—"

"No, listen to me, Sophie. I'm serious."

He didn't just look serious—he looked ser-*eee*-ous.

Damn.

"I've been around your mom a lot, been around you longer. Knew you when you were with Oak and I was friends with him then, so I heard all about her before I met you. Pretty much the only thing I'll side with that douche on at this point is how he felt about your mom. She's cold. Not only that, she acts like you're an inconvenience while at the same time she inserts herself in your life in unhealthy ways. She has no respect for the boundaries of others but she'll butt her nose into whatever she wants. So, I get it, why you wouldn't call me while I was at work, tell me what happened. Because you knew I'd bag work and get my ass home to make sure you were okay. She taught you that. She taught you to make yourself small so you wouldn't bother her if she was otherwise occupied. That's not just fucked-up, that's the very definition of fucked-up."

I had nothing to say; he'd pretty much summed up my relationship with my mother. Which was another reason why Nathan marrying my mother was a crime against nature. They didn't fit. Not in the slightest. Something I never understood. Though since she'd gotten together with him she had changed—a little. So, as right as Hayden was, he didn't know she used to be worse. I didn't offer up an explanation for my mother's behavior, mainly because I never understood her or why she did and said the things she did.

"I'm pissed as shit," he went on. "That last night while I was working at the bar, slinging drinks, you were at home alone freaking out."

I hadn't told him I'd been freaking out. But he knew me, so it was a good guess.

"It also pisses me off you were attacked by an armed—"

"I don't know that he was armed," I cut in. "I never actually saw a weapon, and after when I was questioned by the police they didn't say if he was or wasn't."

That got me a deep scowl.

Eek.

"The part that doesn't piss me off is that you kicked his ass."

Well, that was something.

"Don't get too excited, Soph. I'm back to pissed you didn't go to the hospital."

"It's a scratch. Delilah the Devil cleaned it and taped me up. I didn't even need superglue. Though I will admit sometime in the middle of the night it started to throb, then the rest of me started to ache and my calf muscles cramped so bad I now have to tell you you were right and I should've gone to the gym with you all the times you asked because...damn, I'm out of shape."

I took in a big breath and focused on my friend. "I was scared. Not during but after when I realized what had happened and how much danger I was in."

"Christ," he grunted.

"I actually think it was good it happened."

Hayden gave me an incredulous look that clearly said he didn't agree.

"It shook something loose," I rushed out. "When faced with the possibility of becoming a hostage with an uncertain ending I realized I didn't like my life all that much. And that's what spurred me on to attack. I didn't want to die thinking about how unhappy I was."

"Sweet—"

"I'm quitting my job on Monday," I announced. "You know I don't like it much; what you don't know is I hate it. My boss is an asshole. The women I work with are catty and grown-up mean girls and I only put up with it because I'm afraid if I stand up and state my opinion they won't be my friends."

"How *exactly* is Henry an asshole?" he asked.

Another reason to love my best friend. The dude was not only protective of me but had serious issues with men being assholes to women.

"The kind I can handle. He's a run-of-the-mill asshole who has to remind everyone he's the boss. And he has to do that because he sucks as a boss and no one respects him. I don't like the work I do, so quitting to rid myself of him isn't a problem. I have plenty of money saved so even if it takes me months to find something else I got my half of the bills covered."

Hayden's eyes narrowed into slits.

"I don't care about the money. And don't dip into your savings. I'll cover the bills until you get a new job."

That wasn't going to happen but right then I wasn't going to argue with him. Hayden and I lived together because we were both saving to buy houses. Though I figured Hayden might already have enough saved but he knew I didn't so he stayed living with me.

"I'm also going to...try new things," I went on. "And have a talk with Nathan. I'm not copping out; I just need his direction."

Hayden didn't look convinced Nathan would be able to lead me anywhere.

It wasn't so much that Hayden didn't like my stepfather. He did, but he was firmly on my side with the crime against nature that Nathan had married—then remained married to—my mother. Thus to Hayden, he was suspect or was with her for possible nefarious reasons—like he was a serial killer who needed a cover and a crazy, overbearing wife would do the trick.

"What new things will you be trying?"

"Well, I figured I'd start out small, like try a new brand of oatmeal."

"Pass," he denied. "There's only brown sugar Quaker Oats allowed in this house. Try again."

And he called *me* dramatic.

"Fine. I'll try the Indian place you're always begging me to try."

"Seriously?" He looked shocked.

"Yes," I pushed out because I wasn't sure if I was serious. But now that I said it I had to follow through.

My intestines were already forming a picket line.

"You're really okay?"

"Yeah, I'm really okay. I had my cry last night." I paused to suck in a lungful of oxygen and blew it out. "But, yeah, I'm good. I think I needed something to shake me up and get me to open my eyes. Nothing says 'wake up' like a masked man yanking you to your feet by your hair."

Hayden frowned.

I smiled.

"Too soon?"

"Way too fucking soon," he groused. "But since you're already making jokes now seems as good as any to tell you to put your shoes on. We're getting Indian."

It was my turn to frown and his to smile.

"Don't worry, Huxley, we'll start you out with Tandoori Chicken and ease you in."

I wasn't sure I wanted to be eased into anything.

I wasn't even sure if I was ready to start my life as a tryer of new things.

"Rightyho, Winslow."

I was almost to the short hall that led to the bathroom and two bedrooms when he called my name and I looked back at him.

"Yeah?"

"Proud of you, Sophie."

Not for the first time I hoped Hayden found someone worthy of all the goodness he had to give.

"You know with my newfound badassery you should start warning your babes they should think twice about yanking your chain or they might get a beatdown."

"Right, Rambo Sophie. I'll be sure to warn them."

That meant I was smiling when I got to my bedroom door. It was also when the craziest thought popped into my head. I wondered what Valentine would think of the nickname Rambo Sophie. I bet he'd think it was funny.

5

A MONTH LATER...

I was running late.

I should've already been on my way to my mother's house. Tonight was the night I was going to talk to my mom and tell her... shit, I didn't know what exactly I was going to say but an invitation to dinner seemed like the perfect opportunity to hash a few things out even though I hadn't found time to talk to Nathan.

Not because I was avoiding the situation.

I'd been busy.

I'd quit my job!

My plan was to take a week, search job listings, revamp my resume, then start to apply for new positions. But during my week off I started to wonder why I was going back to work for someone else instead of starting my own business. I had some money saved; if I struck out on my own and failed, my 'Save for a House Fund' would take a hit but I wouldn't starve. Now I was taking freelance jobs building websites and copywriting. My first three jobs I did for free to start a portfolio. That paid off huge and those three people referred me to their friends. I wasn't making enough to pay all my bills but when I cut out my going-out-to-eat budget, and takeaway coffee, and wine I was already halfway to a full-fledged self-employed boss who could live off her earnings.

Something else that had happened was I'd tried to nicely back away from the outside of work semi-friendships I had with my coworkers. Which didn't turn out to be nice but not for lack of trying on my part. It was just that when I'd agreed to meet Sydni for lunch after declining the first two invitations, she'd immediately started in commenting about the other patrons. I stayed quiet like I normally did in times like these. Not because I condoned or agreed with what she was saying but confrontation gave me a rash. Like literal red splotchy patches on my chest and cheeks. Thus I avoided conflict. But since I disagreed with all the snide comments, I was stewing under the surface. When Sydni called our server fat after she took our order I could take no more. Rash be damned, it was time I started to stand up for myself and others around me.

Perhaps me yelling at her in the middle of a crowded café wasn't the best way to go but I was a fledgling badass, so when my temper flared I didn't hold back. That was when the whole restaurant learned what a bitch Sydni was and what she'd been saying about the people around us.

Or maybe that was the right call. Maybe if more people stood up in the middle of crowded restaurants and called their 'friends' out on their horrible behavior the world would be a nicer place.

Or maybe in the future I needed to choose better friends who don't call people fat or make comments about how shiny a man's bald head is, or how skinny the woman across the room is. Actually, there was no maybe about that. I needed better friends—full stop.

So there I was at thirty-seven sorting through my life, making changes, happy with the progress I'd made. And I'd learned a few things, Tandoori Chicken was delish, Naan bread even better, different brands of spaghetti noodles didn't taste any different, not working for an asshole boss was rad, and starting from scratch on the friend front—save Hayden—wasn't difficult.

Now all I needed to do was change out of the slacks I'd worn to meet with the lovely owner of Hot Java into a pair of jeans so I could face my mother. Of course she'd love me showing up in slacks. That was why I was going to wear jeans. Petty—sure. Was I behaving like a rebellious teenager—yes. Did I care—no. I was well beyond the age where my mother had a say in my wardrobe.

I stopped short at the mouth of the hallway.

The shower was running.

Perfect.

I booked it back to the kitchen, found my Super Big

Gulp cup, and filled the forty-four-ounce plastic cup to the brim with cold water.

As late as I was, I was never running late enough to dole out some payback.

I tiptoed down the hall even though Hayden thought I was going straight to my mom's after my meeting. I tried the door handle and smiled when it turned. This oversight on his part was again because he thought he was safe. Normally I'd have to use the baby flathead screwdriver I kept in my room to pick the lock.

Sucker!

As quietly as I could, I slipped inside the steam-filled bathroom and wasted no time dumping the cup of water over the curtain.

"What the fuck!"

The shower curtain swung open.

And...

That was *not* Hayden.

Nope.

Standing in front of me gloriously naked—wet *and* naked—was absolutely not my roommate.

My eyes roamed over so much defined muscle I had to be hallucinating. Either that or the steam billowing was playing tricks on my eyesight because...*damn.*

Perfectly formed shoulders, pectoral muscles that looked to be bigger than my boobs, smooth skin over ridges of cut abdominals, a perfect V that led to...

I vaguely heard my name but that vague was *vague.* My attention was riveted on something else, and that something else was way more interesting than my name.

Holy shit.

Hoe-lee-shit.

And to make matters worse, it twitched.

"It" being the massive penis.

Massive.

Huge.

"Wha...what is...what is *that*?"

Then, it started shaking because the body it was attached to was shaking.

"What the fuck?"

Now *that* was Hayden. I couldn't be sure since he was behind me but I was fairly certain he, too, was talking about Valentine's very large penis.

"I didn't know they came in that size," I mumbled. "It's hanging mid-thigh. And the girth..."

"You mind putting your baton away, brother?"

"Shush, Hayden. I'm in the middle of discovering a bodily phenomenon—"

"Sophie," Hayden growled.

Unfortunately, Valentine slapped the spigot and turned off the water. Then he was reaching for a towel.

"You could give the man some privacy," Hayden grunted.

"And miss his—"

"Swear to God, I already need eye bleach. And if you say another word I'm gonna to have to find a therapist and you're paying the bill."

Under normal circumstances I'd gladly pay for Hayden's therapy but I had a business to get up and running.

"Good to see you again, Sophie," Valentine said as he wrapped the towel around his waist.

"Wait—" Hayden started.

"Don't speak to me," I cut off Hayden to declare. "We're in a verbal timeout until I can get that... visual out of my mind. No, we're in a verbal timeout forever since that is burned into my brain and I'll never be able to look at you again."

"How do you know Sophie?" Hayden inquired.

"I've seen her around a few times. We met at the grocery store—"

"Valentine's Hot Cop?" Hayden asked.

Someone kill me.

Though after I'd just ogled the man's gigantic penis, him knowing I called him Hot Cop was the least of my concerns.

"Hot Cop?"

Was that a smirk I heard in Valentine's voice?

I wouldn't know since my eyes were still glued to the area between his legs.

What? Sue me, it was *that* big.

"Should've called him Hot Cock but who would've guessed he was packing—"

"Out," Hayden commanded.

To punctuate his demand he pulled me out of the

bathroom and slammed the door behind us. Then he continued to shuffle me down the hall into the living room.

"What are you doing here?" he asked when he stopped us.

"I live here."

"You're supposed to be at your mom's."

"Well, I'm not, and you were supposed to be in the shower," I accused. "Now my life is ruined."

Hayden sighed and ran his hand through his sweaty hair, making it stand up in different directions. He was used to my drama but that didn't mean I didn't tax his patience.

"How am I supposed to find a man now?" I went on. "The next penis I see will be miniature by comparison. I'll never be able to have sex again without thinking about Valentine and his—"

"Sophie."

"Are they normally that big?"

"Seriously," he grunted.

I had questions, so many questions.

"Oakley's wasn't—"

"I do not want to know the size of Oakley's dick," he professed.

"Well, it wasn't that big," I told him. "Or even half that size."

"Please God, stop talking about dicks."

"Fine," I huffed. "But just so you know when I get

home from my mom's I'm doing internet research and if that lands me in some weird place I'm blaming you."

Hayden's gaze went to the side, mine followed, and there he was—Valentine in my apartment fully dressed in uniform.

"Jesus fuck, now she's having a cop fantasy to go with her frankendick one."

Valentine chuckled.

I didn't.

Reality hit and when it did my cheeks heated and I was ready to flee.

"I should..."

Shit. What should I do besides embarrass myself more and run to my room and crawl under my bed?

"I should," I started again. "Go change."

I heard Valentine chuckle again and it dawned on me he might think I needed to change my panties after I saw him in all his glory. And it was glorious.

"I didn't mean—"

"Stop talking," Hayden thankfully cut me off again.

"As much as I'd love to stay, I really got to hit the road," Valentine mercifully announced.

I wanted to die a thousand deaths.

"Sophie, it was good seeing you again."

"Yep," I said to his feet, which was where my eyes were firmly planted.

"You doing okay?" he softly asked.

Gah.

"In general? Yes. In the immediate I want to die," I told him honestly.

"The shock wears off."

My eyes shot to his.

"Eventually," he added.

"Is that what you tell the women you bed?" I fired back. "Because if it is I hope you also supply detailed instructions on what to do with *that*."

"She's normally not like this," Hayden defended me.

"See you around, Sophie." Valentine smiled at me, jutted his chin at Hayden, and was out the door before I could further embarrass myself.

My shoulders sagged in relief.

"What was that?" Hayden asked.

"That's what I've been asking. What was *that*?"

"That was my friend taking a shower after a basketball game when he was paged to go into work."

Oh, well that explained why Valentine was in my shower, but did not explain his extra-large dick. Though I figured Hayden was done discussing the largest penis in the world.

"Is there a Guinness world record—"

"Enjoy dinner with the She-Devil. I'll talk to you when you get home."

With that he stomped toward the hall.

"You're testy," I called out. "I'm sure it sucks having to roll that thing up in his boxers to walk so don't be too jealous."

"Goodbye, Huxley."

Now I was seriously late.

Not that I minded. I'd gladly take a lecture from my mother about punctuality if it meant seeing Valentine again.

6

"I'M VERY CONCERNED," my mother said through the sound system of my car as soon as I answered.

I didn't have to ask what she was concerned about. It was the morning after the dinner where I told her I had quit my job and I'd put out my shingle and was giving this self-employment gig a shot. I also didn't have to ask what she was concerned about because she'd already voiced her concern.

"Good morning, Mom," I returned, choosing to ignore her rude opening.

"Now's not the time, Sophie."

One could say my mother only listened to parts of conversations she wanted to listen to. She discarded the rest and did what she wanted. Nathan, on the other hand, had looked proud as I stumbled my way through an awkward ramble explaining to my mom I didn't love the way she was always nagging and in my business. Of course I didn't use those words. I used nicer words. Now I was seeing the error of my ways. Much like what happened with Sydni, direct was the way to go. My problem was I didn't care I was never going to see Sydni again, and my mom was my mom. As strained as our relationship was I didn't want to go the rest of my life not speaking to her. Obviously I needed to find another way.

"You could just tell me you're proud of me," I whispered.

"Proud of you?" she asked back like the concept was foreign.

And that got me thinking; had my mother ever told me she was proud of anything I'd ever done?

"Or you could tell me that it'll be a lot of hard work to get my business going but you know I can do it," I offered.

"Lying to you to make you feel good doesn't actually do you any good. I'm your mother, not one of your friends."

I stared unseeing through the windshield of my car as my mom's words penetrated.

Lying to you...

So she wasn't proud of me and she didn't believe I could own my own business and make it successful.

"You're almost forty. It's time you start thinking about your future. You live in an apartment with a roommate. No job. No financial security. No retirement..."

I stopped listening when I saw Valentine jump out of

his truck and watched as he walked across the parking lot toward Hot Java. Which reminded me; with my mother's call I'd yet to go in and get my coffee.

As if he sensed someone staring at him, Valentine scanned the cars in the lot until his gaze landed on me. He changed directions and I continued to watch his now purposeful strides bringing him to me.

God, he was beautiful.

And the last person I wanted to see.

"Are you listening to me?" my mother scoffed.

"No."

"No?"

Now she wasn't sneering. She was screeching.

Sigh.

Did life have to be this complicated?

"No, Mother, I stopped listening when you started your usual refrain about what you feel are my shortcomings. Though I admit I wasn't really listening after you told me you weren't proud of me and didn't believe in me."

"I said no such thing, Sophie."

Yes, she did. But there was no point arguing about it. Nonetheless, it was worth noting she sounded affronted I'd suggest such a thing.

Valentine was fast approaching and I wanted this call to be over for more than one reason. Mostly due to the fact my mother hadn't listened to a word I'd said last night. But also because even though my windows were rolled up I didn't want to chance Valentine hearing my conversation.

"I have to go."

"We're not done, Soph—"

She might not have been done, but I was and proved that by ending the call.

It almost felt good hanging up on my mother. So good in fact I wondered why I hadn't done just that anytime she decided to lay into me about what she felt were my poor life choices.

I wasn't in debt. I had a savings account. I didn't gamble, steal, cheat. I paid my taxes. I owned my car outright. I didn't do drugs, never had tried any, and only drank responsibly. I'd never been arrested or had any run-ins with the police. I'd been an obedient daughter. I'd never snuck out of the house, taken her car for an underaged joyride, thrown wild parties. Sure, I'd talked back as a teenager—on occasion I'd been what my mother called cheeky—but I'd never been disrespectful and I'd been a good student.

Yet, I still wasn't good enough.

With my mind full of my mother I'd missed Valentine stopping at the side of my car but I didn't miss him tapping on the window.

After my embarrassing run-in with his penis and my mother spreading her joyous love, I wasn't in the mood to face Hot Cop.

His head tipped a fraction, his eyes roamed my face, and for a moment I wished I knew what he was thinking as he studied me. That wish was granted when he, uninvited, opened my door.

"What's wrong?"

Before I could answer Valentine—not that I was planning on telling him a single one of the many 'wrongs' that were swirling in my mind—his gaze shifted from me to the interior of my car.

"C'mon, honey, let's get you your coffee."

I didn't get a chance to answer that either, since he reached in, hit the stupid button that all new cars had to shut off the engine (sidenote: I missed a regular key in the ignition start) unbuckled my belt, grabbed my purse off the passenger seat, and pulled me out of the car.

"Key in your purse?"

I nodded.

"Will it lock automatically?"

I nodded again.

After that I was walking hand-in-hand with Valentine while he carried my hot-pink Valentino crossbody with gold chains and buckle I'd bought from TJ Maxx during a seriously great sale. After speaking to She-Devil, that being after I spent the night in her home sharing a meal, then going back to my apartment and spending the rest of my night bitching to Hayden about her, meaning it had been a She-Devil bitchfest until late into the evening. Further meaning I'd spent a lot of time thinking about my mother which was never fun. Thus I was surprised when I smiled.

Hot Cop Valentine carrying my hot pink Valentino.

At this point in my life it was the little things.

I was holding onto anything and everything I found amusing. If I didn't I would lose my mind.

It wasn't until we were next in line when Valentine asked me what I wanted.

"Coffee," I told him.

"Right. Anything special?"

"Does coffee come with extra caffeine and a splash of GFY?"

Valentine's smile said he knew what the abbreviation stood for.

"Not sure about the go fuck yourself but I can hook you up with extra caffeine," he said quietly.

The man in front of us stepped to the side. Valentine shuffled me forward and I was met with a beaming smile from the barista who had helped me yesterday.

"Hey, Valentine. Hey, Sophie," she chirped. "Your usual?"

"Hey, Crystal. Make it two, extra shot in Sophie's."

Her eyes widened comically.

"Oh, boy, hope you're not planning on sleeping tonight, girl," she mumbled.

Valentine handed her his card, tossed a ten spot in the tip jar. I'd waited tables in my twenties, my best friend was a bartender, I was a generous tipper, and while I couldn't math in my head that quickly by my calculations that was a seventy percent tip.

"What did you order me?" I asked.

"Extra caffeine."

"I think I need you to expand on that. Are we talking clean-my-house-and-do-all-the-laundry caffeine or are we talking run-a-full-marathon caffeine?"

Those sexy lips twitched.

"Somewhere in the middle."

He took his card back, thanked Crystal, I did as well, and we stepped out of line.

"And you're sure there's no GFY in there?" I asked as Valentine led me to a small two-top by the window.

"Depending on if you can handle your caffeine you might find some go fuck yourself in there."

Drat.

I could handle my caffeine.

"Bummer."

"Who pissed you off?"

I glanced around the busy coffee shop and took a deep breath. Yesterday when I was here to speak to the owner about rebuilding her website the smell of fresh-baked cinnamon rolls and coffee beans excited me. Today not so much.

"How long have you known Hayden?"

The corners of Valentine's mouth hitched up. If that wasn't sexy enough—which it was—when his smile dissolved into a knowing smirk my panties nearly caught fire. My guesstimation they were only slightly simmering instead of outright blazing was only because I had firsthand knowledge he was lugging around a monster in his pants and quite frankly it scared me.

"I met him when he started volunteering at the Hope Center."

Interesting.

So they'd known each other a while, but *that* long?

It seemed my roommate had been holding out on me. I made a mental note to give Hayden shit for not telling me about Hot Cop sooner.

"I heard about the fire."

Gone was the good-natured guy who was letting me change the subject.

"Sorry, I—"

"Nothing to be sorry about," he said. "A good friend of mine, Phoenix's boy was trapped in that fire."

"The news said everyone made it out. He's okay, right?"

"Yeah, he's good."

If I remembered right the news had said that the fire set at Hope Center was arson. I couldn't remember the details beyond the building had been condemned. Which was a blow to the community. The Hope Center offered free services sponsored by donations for programs like after school tutoring, big brother / big sister opportunities for at-risk youth, sports, and such. Hayden went to the center twice a week to play basketball with the teenagers.

Thinking on it now, why hadn't I ever volunteered? I had free time. I could give up Saturday lounging on the couch to help out. Word was the director of the center was always trying to find new ways to engage the kids the center served. I didn't have an abundance of skills but I could help someone with homework or a school project—as long as it wasn't math. Hell, what kind of a person did it make me that I'd never even dropped off supplies from their Amazon wish list?

"You know your eyes give you away," Valentine noted. "You're back to pissed."

"Well, this time it's at myself, for being selfish instead of at my mother for being—" I snapped my mouth shut.

Damn, I had a big freaking mouth.

"Ah, trouble with the 'rents."

"What adult says 'rents'?"

"The kind who plays basketball and baseball with a bunch of teenagers. I'm hip on all the lingo."

A harassed-looking Crystal stopped at the side of our table and dropped two coffees in front of us.

"I want you to know, you're the only person I personally deliver coffee to. Not even your fellow brethren in blue get table service. And that's not because I don't appreciate all of you protecting and serving. It's just, they actually listen for their names being called."

"Sorry, Crys."

The woman smiled at Valentine then turned to me.

"Good luck."

With that she hustled away.

"What in the world is in this?"

"Don't ask, just drink."

Sophie from a month ago would've demanded to know every ingredient. No way would she try something new without knowing if she was going to like it. Heck, she'd refuse it outright since she didn't try new things.

What a narrow and stupidly boring life I had led.

With a tentative sip I did what I was training myself to do—explore new things.

It tasted like strong coffee and vanilla syrup.

"Well?"

"It's good."

Which meant I didn't understand what was with the 'good luck'.

"Good. Drink up, then you can tell me why your mother is pissing you off."

That wasn't going to happen.

"I mean no offense, but I don't know you."

I was slurping back more of my vanilla drink, which was actually better than good, it was amazing, when Valentine announced, "You've seen my cock."

The ramifications of the reminder was vanilla-flavored coffee coupled with saliva drenching his black t-shirt.

"I take it you're a spitter."

My momentary shock ended in an eruption of laughter.

Valentine let this go on for a long time, which was good since I couldn't get myself under control. It was like all the stress, worry, and uncertainty of the last month had finally bubbled up and made me loopy.

But his softly spoken, "you have a great laugh" made

the stress, worry, uncertainty, and the crap my mother pulled melt away.

I ended my laughter on a smile. To which he said, not in a soft murmur but in his normal rough voice, "And you have a great smile."

That was sweet.

Unbelievably sweet.

"I'll tell you about my mother if you promise never to mention your..."

"C'mon, Sophie, you can say it," he teased.

My lips pinched to stop my smile and I shook my head.

"I'm not sure if I should be offended or smug I've rendered you speechless."

"Neither. I'm not speechless, I'm flabbergasted penises come in that size," I corrected.

His lips curved up like he thought I was amusing. As much as I liked his mouth and as much as I liked seeing his smile, I needed to veer the conversation away from his penis before my curiosity got the best of me and I asked to see it again. (Strictly for research and verification purposes, of course.)

"My mother is opinionated."

Understatement.

"Right."

"And she's vocal about her opinions."

Valentine picked up his coffee, took a sip, and waited. I knew he was giving me time to parcel out the information I wanted to give him. That was again sweet. So I made the decision and decided this was the perfect opportunity to get an outsider's perspective. I knew what Hayden thought, but he was my best friend and his opinion was skewed.

"After the liquor store...incident, I quit my job. I hated it, I wasn't happy, but I stayed because I hated change more than I hated my boss. As you know I live with Hayden. I have low overhead. I have a healthy balance in my savings account so I decided to invest in me and start my own business."

He had something to say to that. "Congratulations, Sophie. Takes guts to go out on your own."

I couldn't help but to stare.

That right there was all I'd needed from the woman who'd birthed me. Just that. Simple. Nice. Thoughtful. Affirming.

"By the look on your face I take it your mother's not happy for you."

Another understatement. This time a gross underestimation of what my mother was.

"No. She has *concerns*," I told him. "Loads of them, actually. Which translates to disapproval."

"Did you borrow money from her?"

"No."

"Do you owe her money?"

"No."

"Does she pay your rent? Car payment? Cellphone bill?"

"No."

"Then why the fuck do you care if she disapproves? It's your life. If she's not financing the decisions you make, then why does she have a say?"

Good question.

Instead of answering, I picked up my coffee, glanced at Valentine over the rim, and silently begged him not to speak while I was drinking so that we didn't have another spitting incident.

"I knew you had it in you," he said through a smile after I swallowed.

"Yeah, well, don't get too excited—" I stopped abruptly, thankfully remembering at the last second, I didn't know Valentine well enough to make inappropriate jokes. "Sorry. It's arguable who has more off-colored jokes, me or Hayden. And I'd argue it's me."

"Need I remind you, we're friends. And friends joke with each other, off-color be damned."

We weren't friends. He was Hayden's friend.

While I was coming up with a proper response to his friends declaration his phone shrilled with three long tones. Or at least I thought it was his phone until he pulled a pager out of his pocket.

When his attention came back to me he was frowning.

"Sorry to cut this short. I have to get to work."

"Of course. Sorry to hold you up."

"Sophie?"

He was no longer frowning but the seriousness on his face gave me pause.

"Yeah?"

"You didn't hold me up. I asked you to coffee, so don't apologize for giving me the gift of your time."

He hadn't asked. He'd dragged me inside and bought me coffee. I didn't get a chance to remind him, and not only because he was standing. The full weight of what he'd said hit me. It was heavy, it was kind, it was all kinds of sweet, and it was something else. A feeling I couldn't place. All I knew was it felt good and warm and I wanted more of it. I wanted to snuggle under the heaviness and stay awhile.

"Have a good day, babe."

"You, too, Valentine. And be safe out there."

That earned me a smile and the warmth grew.

"Careful with that latte. There's enough caffeine in there to turn you into an over-energized honey badger."

"I make no promises."

I watched him walk out of Hot Java, thinking he had a really great ass.

Two hours later I was bouncing around my apartment with more energy than any one person should have. The kind of energy that made it impossible to concentrate on any one task. In the middle of loading the dishwasher I noticed the windows in the living room were dirty. I stopped loading dirty dishes to clean the windows. In the middle of wielding the Windex I noticed the bottom sill was filthy. I abandoned the glass to clean the sill. Then I went on to check the sills in my bedroom but as soon as I entered the room I saw the dirty piles of clothes I'd separated earlier and decided I should throw in a load. And if I was doing that, I should grab the towels and floormats in the bathroom. That led to me to noticing the ring of soap scum in the tub. So I attacked the bathroom with a bottle of Soft Scrub, forgetting about the laundry.

I'd done no work and hadn't completed a single task.

I was going to kill Valentine.

7

"JACKED UP ABOUT THAT KID," Shiloh Marcou grumbled from beside me as we walked through the precinct.

Sunny wasn't wrong, it was fucked up Brian Hamilton was beat to shit and in the ICU.

"But it was cool of Ethan to keep Cap up to speed on the case."

It was cool but I knew Ethan Lenox didn't brief our captain out of the goodness of his heart. The detective had better things to do, namely tracking down the person responsible for beating a fifteen-year-old kid. Further from that, Ethan had no obligation to keep Cap up to date on an attempted robbery case that didn't involve SWAT. However, it involved me, and Ethan being a friend and Cap being the type of man who was all about keeping his finger on the pulse of his team, he gave us an update.

"Not a coincidence Ackerman gets bonded out and within hours the kid's beat to shit," Sunny went on as we hit the back exit of the station.

She wasn't wrong about that either.

Dale Ackerman was Lenox and Jase Taylor's prime suspect. He was also in the wind.

I swung the key ring looped around my finger, catching the key to the SUV in my palm as I spotted today's ride.

"You're awfully quiet today," Sunny noted. "You're not still pouting I kicked your ass during quals are you?"

It was cute she thought grown men pouted.

"That was a week ago and we're all used to you showing off," I told her, purposefully evading her comment. "Though not all of us have twenty-four-seven access to Triple Canopy."

"Please. I outshot you before I met Luke."

That was the damn truth, not that I'd admit it and stop giving her shit about her husband. After all, the team and I had years of ribbing to make up for. Gone was the woman I'd met who'd made an art out of being close to the team while at the same time holding herself distant. Shiloh Kent only allowed you so close before she unleashed Killer Frost. Shiloh Marcou was entirely different—warm, friendly, and fully engaged.

"I have no recollection of that," I lied.

It didn't matter what her last name was, the woman was a damn fine cop and the best marksman we had on our team for two reasons. The first, the result of her being raised by her brother Echo who had drilled into his siblings a code of honor, integrity, and service. The second, the product of her feeling the need to prove she belonged on a SWAT team. The first was nothing short of a miracle considering who her father was. The second was unneeded.

"What gives?" she asked as soon as her ass was planted in the passenger seat.

It had been a while since she'd met and married Luke, but not long enough that I was used to this new Sunny who poked her nose into other people's business. Prior to Luke she would've happily ignored anything beyond work. Actually, she would've run a mile if any of us started talking about anything personal.

"I'm worried about Sophie."

"Sophie? The woman who took down Ackerman?" I didn't miss Sunny's proud smile for a sister who bested an asshole.

No, the woman who I hadn't been able to stop thinking about.

"Yeah."

"You think Ackerman's gonna go after her?"

Hearing my concern voiced out loud made my neck stiffen. That was the second time that morning I felt that twinge in my neck. The first time was when Cap had told us about Ackerman roaming the streets and Brian being in ICU and my mind had immediately gone to Sophie. It bore contemplation why upon hearing a fifteen-year-old was nearly beaten to death my first thought was if that was Sophie laying in that hospital bed, I'd lose my motherfucking mind in a way that would be life-altering.

Riddle and Mereno climbing into the SUV parked next to me pulled my attention back to the task at hand.

We had a search warrant to serve.

A warrant that had cut my time with Sophie short.

"Well?" Sunny prompted.

"Well, what?"

"Do you think Ackerman's gonna go after that woman?" she reiterated slowly.

Again I said nothing, too busy dealing with the itch on the back of my neck and burn in my gut to express my thoughts on Ackerman going after Sophie.

"You know she'll be notified he was bonded out. But if you're worried, you should talk to Ethan."

I'd do more than talk to Ethan. I'd talk to Dylan Welsh and ask him for a panic fob Sophie could carry, and call in a marker to have him monitor the device.

"I'm gonna call Dylan," I informed her.

"You're calling in a marker for this woman? You know Ethan will take care of her."

I wasn't going to think about why I was cashing in a favor with Triple Canopy when those were not something any cop would squander. TC owning a marker was gold.

"I know he will."

I felt Sunny's eyes drilling into the side of my head. Thankfully, Riddle pulled out of his parking spot before she could continue pressing me for answers I didn't have.

"SERIOUSLY? BOTH AT THE SAME TIME." Sunny feigned irritation.

I glanced up from adjusting the straps on my thigh holster and caught sight of Echo and Phoenix Kent making their way to our huddle. The men were easy to spot; they stood head and shoulders above most of the officers gathered in the staging area. The only family resemblance Sunny shared with her siblings was her blonde hair and blue eyes. Though the brothers had different shades, when all four Kent siblings were together you knew they were family.

"And you're surprised, because?" Riddle voiced my exact thoughts.

Our team was serving a search warrant for the drug unit. Echo being the lead of the investigation on the house we were hitting, he would conduct a secondary brief with our team before we headed out on The Beast. And where there were drugs there were guns. Seeing as Phoenix worked the gun task force neither was it shocking he was there.

Not to mention if one of Sunny's brothers were present before she kitted up to kick in a door they always made it a point to see her. But right now, the eldest Kent was sporting a frown and giving his sister a hard look.

I glanced back to Sunny just in time to see her wince.

They had a strict, no bickering policy before any of them went to work. All of the Kents were cops. The second oldest, River, had moved to Idaho but a change of location didn't mean a change of career. He was now married with a kid and a detective in his wife's hometown, Coeur d'Alene.

But Echo looked like he had something to get off his chest.

"You good?" I quietly asked.

"Yep," she answered too quickly.

"Why don't I believe you?"

"Should you be here?" Echo boomed as he approached.

Riddle and Mereno stepped closer to Sunny. Echo transferred his scowl to Riddle before he pinned his sister with a furious look.

"Echo—" I started but Sunny got to him before I could finish.

"Don't you dare," she issued her own warning.

"You're late," he growled.

Late?

We weren't late.

"Don't," she snapped.

"Do they know?" Echo went on.

"Echo, brother, you know the rules," I reminded him. "Whatever this is can wait."

That scowl deepened, a big meaty paw lifted, a finger came out, and he pointed at me.

"You watch her back."

What the fuck?

"Seriously, whatever's going on not only needs to

wait but you saying that shit to me when you know we always have her back and each other's is uncool."

"Yeah? Well, it's not every day my baby sister might be carrying my niece or nephew in her body when she's strapping on a vest. So I don't give a fuck what's cool. All I give a fuck about is, you keep her safe."

With that, Echo turned and stalked off, leaving Phoenix to clean up the mess he'd made.

"He might be a big, dumb idiot with zero sense but we love you and he's worried. Just be careful, baby sister," Phoenix softly said then followed his brother.

Now it was my turn to scowl.

"You're pregnant?"

"Maybe."

"Maybe?" Riddle asked. "How are you *maybe* pregnant?"

Sunny's eyes flashed with blue fire as she narrowed them on our teammate.

"We don't have time for me to explain menstrual cycles to you, Riddle."

You're late.

Oh, fuck.

"Sunny—"

"Don't you dare suggest I sit this one out," she interrupted me. "Even if I am pregnant the baby is the size of a pea and protected. I will decide when I step away from the team. Not you, not my brothers, not anyone."

I glanced around the men. Riddle, Mereno, Chip, Gordy, and Watson all tipped their chins in silent agreement. Whether she liked it or not, she just got six guards who would not let one thing happen to her or the baby.

"Right," I muttered. "Let's get this brief down so we can get to business."

TWO HOURS later after successfully serving the warrant, clearing the house so Echo, Phoenix, and their teams could go in to execute the search, and taking three subjects into custody, we were back at the station. Technically we weren't on shift and only came in because Bravo team was already out on a barricade situation so everyone split as soon as we got back. I was waiting to see if I could catch Ethan before I stopped by Triple Canopy. Then I was going to Sophie's apartment to talk her into carrying a fob that would track her location and double as a panic button. It was an invasion of privacy and one I doubted she'd agree to. I was prepared to fight my corner and if I felt I was losing, I'd enlist Hayden. It was a dirty play bringing in my friend—her roommate—but I'd get down in the mud and fight as dirty as I needed to, to make her see reason.

I pushed into the locker room to grab my wallet and keys out of my locker and stopped dead. Sunny was standing in front of her locker with her forehead resting on the metal door.

"Sunny?" I called out.

Nothing.

"Shiloh?"

Still nothing.

"Kent!"

She didn't lift her head but she did mumble her correction, "Marcou."

"Wanna grab some lunch with me?"

She shook her in the negative against the door.

"Sunny?"

"I'm not pregnant," she announced and extended her hand to the side holding a white plastic stick.

"Okay," I said cautiously.

"I don't know if I'm sad or happy."

Christ, where was Gordy? He was a husband and a father. He and Sunny were close. He was a fatherly figure to her and the only one out of any of us who was qualified to talk Sunny through this.

I could understand the sad part so I focused on the other.

"Happy?" I inquired.

"Do you want kids?"

"Let me take you to lunch," I dodged the question by asking.

She lifted her head and turned her red-rimmed eyes in my direction.

"I don't know if I'm ready to have kids."

Panic rose fast.

"What if I'm a terrible mother? Today clearly proved I'm too selfish to even think about—"

"Stop. Nothing you did today was selfish."

"I could've been pregnant and I still went into a dangerous situation. That doesn't say good mother, Valentine. That says selfish bitch—"

"Shut it," I interrupted her. "Like you said, even if you were pregnant it's a pea. I'm not particularly educated about a woman's body." I paused when Sunny smirked. "Reproductively I mean. What I'm trying to say is, a woman's body is made to protect that little pea. Not to mention, you had all of us there. Nothing was going to happen to you. We're not on shift for another two days so you could've waited to take that test. But you didn't wait. You took it as soon as you got back. That doesn't say bad mom or selfish, Sunny."

Her jaw clenched and she blew out a breath.

"My mom left us," she whispered.

Sheer panic moved through me and I felt my pits get sweaty. I could be first in the door with nothing but a shield between me and a bullet and keep my cool. I could break a window and climb through into an unknown situation and not break a sweat. Hearing the terror in Sunny's voice sent me spiraling. I was not the right person to give anyone advice. I could down a few beers, shoot tequila, or sip a whiskey depending on what a friend needed while they unloaded. I could buy Sophie a coffee with an extra shot and be a shoulder when she needed to blow off steam about her mother.

But actual advice? Wisdom? No.

And Sunny didn't need a few beers or a shot of tequila. She needed someone like Gordy or Riddle or better yet one of her brothers. They'd know what to say.

"How can I be a mom when I don't even know what one is?"

That was a good question.

One I didn't know how to answer since I no longer had a mom and my dad checked out when I was thirteen and never checked back in.

Oh, fuck yeah, panic had set in.

"What if I bail—"

"Woman, what the hell are you talking about? You would never bail on your child."

"How do you know?"

"Shiloh, you're one of the best women I know. Fuck, one of the best people—man or woman—I know. There is no way in hell you'd abandon your child. Or your husband. Maybe instead of thinking about all the shit your mother didn't teach you, you should start thinking about the things she did."

She met my response with narrowed eyes and pinched brows.

I was terrible at this shit.

Where the hell was Gordy, goddammit? I was screwing this up and Sunny needed someone better than what I could give her.

"That woman taught me nothing," she seethed.

"Wrong, Shiloh. She taught you the most valuable lesson you could ever learn. She taught you everything you never wanted to be. Men look to their fathers and they either want to be them, so they idolize and emulate, or they want to be nothing like them and they make moves to change everything about themselves to make sure there's nothing left of their father inside of them. I suppose women are the same. You had a shit mother, but she gave you something. You won't be a damn thing like her because you aren't anything like her. I'd say Echo, River, and Phoenix had a hand in that, but even if you didn't have them, you'd still be you. You'd still be the woman you are today because, Sunny, that's just who you are. Grit and determination and good to your core."

When I was done, she was no longer frowning but her eyes were filled with tears.

Christ.

How much more could I fuck this up?

"Sunny—"

"You're right." She sucked in a breath and swiped at her eyes. "Sorry for freaking out on you. I don't know why I'm so emotional. I just...I was late and Luke was excited and so was I. Then...I don't know...I just freaked out."

"Honey, did you stop to think that you freaking out about what kind of mom you'd be was your first clue you'll be a damn good mom?"

Her mouth twisted into a smile and she shook her head.

"No. I didn't think of that at all."

Right.

Crisis adverted.

"Thank you, Valentine. I needed to hear that—all of it. And thank you for not blowing sunshine and saying it straight."

"Like I'd ever try to pull shit over on you," I teased.

"You know what I'm saying," she said softly.

I did know.

Sunny worked hard at being genderless. She didn't want to be treated like 'the girl on the team.' She just wanted to be respected as a member of the team. Something that honestly was hard for the rest of us to get used to. Not because she wasn't skilled and could hold her own. She was the best on the range—that went for both our team and Bravo. She more than carried her weight on every callout. She earned respect as a cop then as a SWAT officer. The difficulty was fueled by instinct. Every man on our team shared a common belief—women and children were to be protected at all costs. We could pretend Shiloh wasn't a woman and just a valued teammate but the bottom-line truth was, any one of us would move to protect her if it came down to her or a man on the team. I would never forgive a teammate for saving me over her. And none of them would forgive me if I made the call to save them and let her swing. In no other way did any of us treat her differently. And she'd be pissed as shit if she knew we had an unspoken pact—Shiloh Kent, now Marcou, above all others.

"I know what you're saying," I confirmed. "Now, are you just gonna stand there the rest of the day holding that stick you pissed on, or are you gonna toss it and get home to your husband?"

"It is pretty gross, isn't it?" She laughed.

"Disgusting," I corrected.

"Luke's at work and if I go home I'll be tempted to call Echo and ream his ass, something I can't do because I know he's neck-deep in a case. Which means my next choice would be River to complain about what a loud-mouthed asshole his brother is. But I can't do that because he'll turn the tables and ream *my* ass for not telling him my period was late—"

I held up my hand to stop her.

"Can you do me a favor and never again discuss your period with me?"

"Please tell me you're not one of those men who are afraid of tampons."

"Nope. I have a box in my locker. They make excellent barrel cleaners."

Speaking of lockers. I made my way to mine and started in on the combo while I added, "Now, those diapers with wings? Yeah, no."

"So you're saying if your wife needed you to go to the store to pick her up pads you wouldn't do it?"

There would never be a wife.

I yanked open my locker, grabbed my wallet, and slammed it shut.

"I just added a new line item on the dealbreaker list."

"I don't know if I should tell you you're dumb or you're an asshole."

"How about you say nothing and instead throw the pee stick away, wash your hands, and follow me to TC? You can see your man, I'll talk to Dylan, then we'll throw a few down range and blow off some steam."

That was when Shiloh Marcou blew my mind.

She slowly made her way to me—with the piss stick still in her hand—and stopped in front of me. With a look I'd never in my life seen on her face—which was to say I now understood why Luke fell so fast and hard—she rolled up onto the toes of her boots and pressed a kiss to my cheek.

"Thank you for knowing exactly the right thing to say and exactly the right thing I needed."

When she rolled back down she thankfully headed to the trash can. Then she disappeared back into the bathrooms, leaving me wishing all women were as simple as Sunny.

My mind went to Sophie and I wondered if she'd be down with straight talk followed by shooting high-powered weapons at mannequins.

8

I WAS SWEATING.

I blamed Valentine for that.

With more force than necessary, I lifted the corner of my mattress near the wall to tuck the bedsheet's elastic edge under it. You know the one corner that's a huge pain in the ass because the wall and the nightstand is in the way and you have to pull the fitted sheet with all your might since the other three corners are already done? Yeah, that last pain-in-the-ass corner. That wasn't why I was sweating—okay, it was part of the reason. But the bigger part was I'd had a minor incident in the bathroom and had to open up all the windows and prop the front door open to air out the apartment. And since I loved planet Earth I turned off the AC since all the windows were open. Not to mention, electricity was expensive. Though it was more about the planet than the bill.

I dropped the mattress back in place and banged my wrist on the nightstand.

"Fucker," I muttered, then stared at the mattress and added, "I hate you."

"Good. You're putting all that GFY to good use."

I whirled around to find Valentine in my bedroom doorway.

"You!" I pointed at him. "This is *all* your fault."

He glanced around my bedroom with a smile on that criminally Hot Cop mouth.

"All of it?"

"I almost died today because of you."

"Come again?" he grunted as he did a top-to-toe visual search of my body.

I ignored the tingle that gave me, picked up the flat sheet off the floor where the rest of my clean bedding lay in a pile, and shook it out over the mattress.

"I've answered one email today. *One*. How am I supposed to build my empire when my ass isn't in a chair in front of my computer working?"

I tugged the sheet into place and folded down the top. When I felt I'd given him enough time to answer and he remained silent, I glanced over my shoulder.

"Well?"

"I'm waiting for the 'almost died' portion of this explanation before I comment. I'm also waiting for an appropriate time to chew your ass out for leaving your front door open for any whack job to walk in."

"The building is perfectly safe," I defended, and picked up a pillowcase.

"Me standing here is proof it isn't. And what the hell are you wearing?"

I glanced down at my once-white-but-now-dingy Justin Bieber concert tee with a very faded picture of the man himself circa the early 2000s, then down to my cut-off cleaning sweats and looked back at Valentine in confusion.

"You don't like The Biebs?"

"Baby." His voice was vibrating with humor. "No self-respecting grown man is a Bieber fan."

He was probably right.

Moving on…

"I'm in my cleaning outfit," I told him. I tossed the now cased pillow on my bed.

"I'm talking about what's on your head."

I lifted my hand to my head and encountered plastic.

Shit.

"Oh my God. I forgot!" I dashed across my room, stopping at the doorway when he didn't remove his big body from blocking my path and pointed up at him. "This is your fault, too."

"You wearing a shower cap is my fault?"

"Yes," I hissed and pushed past him.

I stomped my way to the bathroom but paused in the doorway to sniff the air. Once I ascertained I was no longer going to die from fumes, I marched in and tore off the cap, avoiding the mirror so I wouldn't expire from humiliation. I didn't need the baby blue with bright yellow rubber duckies visual as a reminder of my ridiculousness. I was bent over the tub with my head shoved under the spigot when I heard Valentine's voice muffled by the water. Yet I still heard his question.

"No, my hair's not going to fall out!" I shouted back.

Thank God I'd chosen to deep condition my hair this afternoon and didn't get a wild hair and decide today was the day I was going to bleach my brown hair blonde.

The conditioner had been in for no less than two hours.

I'd be bald otherwise.

Could you imagine?

"Then what exactly is my fault this time?"

I waited until all the conditioner was rinsed out before I twisted an arm back and wiggled my fingers.

"Towel."

Valentine shoved a towel into my hand. I twisted my hair up in the towel, got to my feet, and whirled on him.

"You saw my rubber duckie shower cap," I accused.

His brows went up. His expression went straight to he thought I had a screw loose, and he waited.

"*On*. You saw my rubber duckie shower cap on."

"And that's a problem?"

Now I was staring at him like he was the one who had a screw loose. Unfortunately I didn't get a chance to educate him on all the ways he'd ruined my day, because Hayden was home.

"Please tell me this isn't a role reversal and she's in there naked."

Valentine looked to the side and smiled.

"I'm fully clothed!" I yelled to Hayden.

"Is there a reason the two of you are reenacting the bathroom scene with the front door propped open?"

Valentine's smile got wider.

"All my lady bits are covered," I reminded my roommate. "And I didn't bring a cucumber in here to reenact Mr. Meat Stick Penis exposing his private parts to me."

Valentine's gaze sliced back to me. His grin faded into a smirk and he shook his head.

"Did you just call my cock a meat stick?"

"Yes! One of those salami sticks you buy in the deli section. Not to be confused with the Slim Jim ones you buy at a gas station."

"Thanks for clearing that up, baby."

I rolled my eyes to the ceiling and when I rolled them back Valentine's sexy smirk was still in place.

"Seriously," Hayden groused. "For the last time can we please stop talking about this?"

"Sure," I magnanimously agreed.

"Great. Now can you explain why I'm coming home from work and the front door is wide open and the two of you are in the bathroom?"

"Shoo." I waved my hands in Valentine's direction, needing him to back up so I could keep my distance. He looked way too good grinning at me and a girl could get ideas with all that sexiness aimed in her direction.

It was best if I stayed no less than six feet away from him at all times.

Valentine backed out, turned, and started making his way down the hall. My gaze dropped to his perfect ass. I'm not above admitting I stayed where I was and stared until I lost sight of it when he disappeared into the living room. When I came out of my trance and Hayden came into focus I knew I'd been caught.

Whatever.

I was a healthy woman who hadn't had anything but self-induced orgasms for a very long time and besides it wasn't my fault Hot Cop had the best ass I'd ever seen. Not to mention he also had the biggest dick I'd ever seen. I had yet to do my internet research to know if he was abnormally large or if I'd gotten shafted in the sex department and had only been with under-average men.

"Soph," Hayden called.

Right.

No more thinking about Valentine's perfectly formed penis.

"I needed to air out the apartment," I explained as I walked down the hall.

"Why?" Hayden asked.

"Because Valentine tried to kill me," I announced when I made it to the living room.

The man in question was lounging in one of the papasan chairs. I didn't want to notice how comfortable he looked or how much I liked seeing him in my living room. But there it was; he looked fabulous in my home. Though he looked better hanging in the doorway of my bedroom.

Hayden's attention went to Valentine.

"How'd you try to kill her?"

It must be noted Hayden didn't sound alarmed at this news. Nor did he ask Valentine about his attempted murder in an accusatory tone.

"No clue, we haven't gotten that far," Valentine informed Hayden. "All I know is everything is my fault. That everything includes her being unable to run her empire and wearing a rubber duckie shower cap. Beyond that, I got nothing."

Hayden nodded like that sounded about right.

"You staying for dinner?"

Dinner?

At Hayden's question I looked at my watch. Holy shit, it was after seven. I glanced out the window behind Valentine. It was no longer bright but still light out. It didn't get dark out until closer to nine. Such was summer in Georgia.

I'd lost a whole day.

"El Cabrito?" Valentine shot back.

"Soph? Seafood fajita burrito? Extra guac?" Hayden gratuitously asked.

He knew my order from El Cabrito never changed.

"Yep," I said and flopped down onto the couch, suddenly exhausted from all my frantic cleaning.

"Is it safe to shut the door and windows and turn the AC back on?"

"Do you still smell Liquid Plumr and Soft Scrub mixed together?"

"Jesus," Hayden clipped.

"Told you he tried to kill me," I mumbled, my energy waning fast.

"How is this Valentine's fault?"

I shifted just my head on the couch and flicked my gaze up to look at Hayden.

"It's his fault because this morning he ordered me a special concoction of caffeine, vanilla, copious amounts of sugar, and some sort of poisonous ingredient that temporarily gives you a wicked case of attention deficit disorder that makes it impossible to concentrate or sit still or remember you poured drain cleaner in the tub which means you forgot to flush the drain before you dump Soft Scrub in and the chemical reaction to that is smoke. This special coffee blend also gives you a serious case of the jitters and a dose of false ambition."

"A vanilla Red Eye with three shots."

I watched Hayden's eyes round at Valentine's explanation. Mine didn't round; they narrowed as I shifted to look at the sexy caffeine pusher.

"Three shots of *espresso*?" I demanded to know.

"Yup."

"So you were trying to kill me today by giving me a heart attack."

"The drama with this one never ends," Hayden mumbled.

He wasn't wrong, but still... my poor heart.

Seeing as my antics no longer fazed Hayden and I'd run out of steam I listened as he sorted dinner with Valentine. Then I listened to them talk about some basketball tournament that was coming up to raise money for the Hope Center while my eyes drooped, and it began taking longer and longer to open them between blinks.

My eyes were closed and I was almost snoozing when I heard, "What's going on with you and Soph?"

As interested as I was in Valentine's answer, his delay meant I was drifting back to sleep when his response yanked me back to consciousness.

"Didn't have her number so I came by to talk to her about the liquor store incident."

A disappointment I had no business feeling washed over me. In my tizzy I hadn't thought of why he was there. But if I'd been in my right mind, I would've thought to ask. However, I was in an altered caffeinated state and had not been clear headed the whole day. That included me leaving Hot Java convincing myself I'd had a third pseudo-date with a hot cop who didn't seem to mind I was a tad bit on the crazy side.

"Why do you need to talk to her about that?"

"The guy Sophie took down was bonded out. The same day the kid he was using as a distraction was beat to shit. Could be a coincidence but the detectives on the case can't find Ackerman to question him."

Cold suffused my body.

"Is Sophie in danger?"

My eyes came open, and when they did they immediately locked with Valentine's.

"No."

"How firm is that no?" Hayden went on to ask.

Valentine kept his stormy blue gaze on me when he rumbled, "Firm." He went on, speaking directly to me, and unfortunately he said, "But just to say, to make that so, I called in a favor and got you a device that looks like a key fob, but it's a panic button with a built-in tracking device. Until Ackerman is found, I want you carrying it with you."

Panic button?

Tracking device?

"So she's *not* safe," Hayden growled.

Valentine's gaze shifted back to Hayden.

No words were exchanged but still Hayden grunted, "Right."

When nothing further was said I asked, "Right, what?"

"Just being cautious, Sophie."

Cautious was good. No, it was great. I loved cautious but I still didn't understand.

"Cautious entails me carrying a panic button and being tracked?"

"In this case, yes."

"I need more than that before I agree to being tracked."

"I get that," Valentine conceded. "You can say no but I'd feel better if the guys at Triple Canopy monitored your location and you had a tool to call for help if needed."

"She's not saying no," Hayden answered for me.

Okay, hold on a minute.

I straightened out of the cozy ball I'd curled myself into in the corner of the couch, sat up, and glowered at my roommate and best friend. He at least had the decency to shift on the bar stool he'd pulled into the living room but other than that, showed no outward remorse he'd crossed a line he knew he'd be crossing by answering for me.

My mother did that to me.

All the damn time.

Hayden knew this and knew how much I hated it.

"Soph, we're talking about your safety."

"I know what we're talking about and I'm not saying no to the panic button. But before I say yes I need to fully understand what's going on and who exactly will have my location."

"What's going on is Valentine is trying to take care of you," Hayden snarled. "And with this you're going to let him."

Whoa.

Hayden had never, in all the years we'd been friends, lashed out at me.

"Hayden, be cool," Valentine warned.

Don't ask me how I knew it was a warning but I did.

His voice was smooth and low but there was a bite to it that screamed 'back off.'

"I'll be cool when she says yes," Hayden bit, then narrowed his eyes on me. "A kid was beat to shit by the man you took down. If there's even a fraction of a chance he'd come after you, either you take what Valentine's offering or I'm taking leave from work and I'm your new shadow."

That seemed excessive.

"Hayden—"

"You know I love you more than I love my sister. You know I'd lose my shit if someone took a fist to you. Valentine would not be here offering what he's offering nor would he have called in a favor with the guys at Triple Canopy, some of whom I've met, and they're known to be the best at security in Georgia and the surrounding states, if he didn't want you safe. Not a little safe. Not maybe safe. *Safe*, Sophie, as in the safest he can make you without moving in and being your personal bodyguard."

That was a lot to digest. And it wasn't that Hayden loved me more than Marybeth. I already knew that. Hayden's sister was a bit of a drag and a whole lot bitchy when he didn't loan her money. And he didn't loan it; he gifted it since she never paid it back.

The parts I was having trouble processing were many. First, Valentine wanted me as safe as he could make me—that was understandable; he was a cop. But the *safest?* Add to that he'd asked people who were the best in security for a favor to make that happen? We were strangers. I was nothing more than a friend of a friend to him.

I had yet to come up with a proper response to Hayden when there was a knock on the door and he excused himself to get our food delivery.

That left Valentine to answer the question that was preying on my mind.

"Why?"

"Why what?"

"Why are you going through all this trouble? A panic button? Asking friends for a favor? That seems like a lot for someone you don't know."

The man looked downright uncomfortable. Actually, he looked so uncomfortable that if his answer wasn't so important to me I would've let him off the hook.

"I can't answer that. I just know my first thought when I heard about that kid being in ICU and Ackerman being in the wind, was you. My second thought was if he got to you and it was you beaten up and lying in that hospital bed, I'd kill him. I know it's a big ask. I know it's intrusive as hell and I have no right to ask, but I'm still doing it."

That was more than enough for me.

"I'll take the fob."

Valentine visibly relaxed.

The sting of my earlier disappointment evaporated.

He'd come over here to talk me into accepting his offer.

He wanted me safe.

It wasn't the same as him coming over to ask me out for another coffee or offer me a night of wild, crazy, monkey sex that would ruin me for all other men, but it was something.

And that something meant more to me than a coffee date ever would.

9

I HEARD my phone ring on the bathroom counter. I finished rinsing the soap off my face before I checked my watch.

Seeing it was Sophie I answered, "Hey, everything good?"

"I have a question for you," she launched in. "How much time would I serve for progenitorcide?"

"Say what now?"

"Mothercide. Parentalcide. Creatorcide. Homicide of the woman who birthed you. Take your pick but be fast about it. I need to decide if the crime is worth the time and do you think if I explain to a jury all the ways my mother drives me batshit crazy I could get off on a technicality or extenuating circumstances? All I need is one sympathizer for a hung jury, right?"

Christ, she was cute.

"First tell me you're okay and safe then I'll explain to you why you don't want to commit a felony."

There was a stretch of silence long enough for me to twist my wrist to make sure the call hadn't disconnected.

"Where are you? You sound like you're in a car wash."

"You're on my watch and I'm in the shower."

"The shower," she repeated on a breath and I knew what she was thinking about.

My cock jerked at the memory. The way her eyes had roamed and lingered as she'd openly taken me in. Blatant interest she hadn't bothered hiding, or if she had tried she failed. The way she covered that interest with humor. It wasn't lost on me women enjoyed certain parts of my anatomy more than other parts. Over the years I'd had a lot of reactions; lust, fascination, shock, excitement, and when that happened I ceased to exist and it became all about my dick and getting them off. But not Sophie. She'd taken me in and immediately started giving me gruff. It was cute. It was funny. It was refreshing in a way I didn't understand until I saw her at the coffee shop and she hadn't had a personality transplant—that being turning overtly flirtatious and angling to get me into bed. I was still me and she was just her. I was the one who joked about her seeing me naked, purposely bringing it up to see what her reaction would be but also to tease her out of her heavy mood.

That had backfired, in more ways than one. The first being my reminder meant I'd gone to work wearing her coffee on my shirt. The second served only to reinforce what I'd felt the first time I'd run into her at the grocery store—a spark of interest. The third part of that was more complicated; it was nothing more than a feeling and one I couldn't explain. Which meant I wasn't real thrilled I couldn't place the feeling. The only thing I knew was it felt good and right and almost inevitable. A feeling of being drawn to someone for no reason other than it was unescapable and impossible to ignore.

"Baby, not that I mind taking a shower with you on the phone but I can't convince you homicide isn't the way to go if you don't talk to me. And just to point out you still haven't confirmed everything's okay."

"I haven't left my house this morning," she said like that was an answer and bad shit didn't happen to people in their homes. "And everything was perfectly fine until my mother called me to tell me she was on her way over. She didn't say, but she didn't have to because I know her. This visit won't be a friendly mother-daughter sharing a cup of coffee in order to catch up with each other. She's coming over to shove her opinions down my throat since she failed to convince me to give up on my business and go get what she calls a real job. But that's actually not why I'm calling, though I was slightly interested in the penalties one would face for strangling their mother."

I had no experience with overbearing parents. When my mother was alive she and my father had been supportive but not domineering. My dad had been firm in his guidance but only when it came to how he believed a man should behave—that being respectful, chivalrous, loyal, protective, and above all else trustworthy. However, it wasn't a lesson in morality or duty. Neither of my parents had ever pushed their wishes or dreams onto me or my sister.

Now since my mother's death, all guidance had ceased. I could tell my father I'd quit my job, sold all my belongings, donated the proceeds to charity, and planned to live under a bridge somewhere for the rest of my life and I doubted he'd bat an eye. He certainly wouldn't give fatherly advice.

But I didn't need experience with it to know her relationship with her mom was jacked.

"You could not answer your door when she arrives," I offered as a solution. "And there's this setting in your phone that prevents people from calling or texting."

"She's my mother."

Now that I had experience with.

No matter how many times I told myself I was giving up on my father I always went back.

"I get it."

"You do?"

This was not a shower conversation and not because it wasn't something I discussed—*ever*—it was well and truly not a topic to discuss when I couldn't give it my full attention.

"I do. So if you weren't calling to tell me your mother's coming over for an uninvited chat why are you calling?"

"Last night I forgot to say thank you."

I stood there for a second that led to two then three before I allowed the fullness of her gratitude to hit. It wasn't the words, it was the way she said them. The sincerity that was tinged with vulnerability. She wanted me to know me keeping her safe meant something to her and she wanted it to mean something to me, too. Not a cop doing his job, but as a man who would look after her.

My first inclination was to make an indifferent comment that wouldn't give any indication how much her gratitude meant to me. A simple, 'no problem' or 'it's my job.' However, as ever with Sophie I felt that unexplainable draw. A connection that had felt predestined now just felt real and absolute.

"My pleasure, baby."

"Well...I should... let you get back to your shower."

I felt myself smile at her sudden shyness.

"Didn't think you had that in you."

"Had what in me?"

There was a hint of affront sneaking into her tone. She thought I was making fun of her thanking me.

"You being shy."

"I'm not shy."

"No shit. I got that when you stood in the bathroom wide-eyed while I was buck-assed naked instead of turning around or leaving. But I knew before that when you groped me at the grocery store saying you didn't mean to do it when we both know you did."

"I didn't grope you at the store. I turned and you were

standing in my personal space. It's not my fault you have a huge chest and it got in the way when I was pulling my phone away from my ear."

"We'll agree to disagree."

"I'd argue that but my mother's knocking on the door."

Well, fuck. I thought I'd have time to get to her place before her mother showed. Either she lived close or Sophie had waited a while before she called me.

"I'll let you go, Soph, but only after I remind you, you don't have to take anyone's shit. Not even your mother's."

"Yeah."

I didn't like the defeat I heard only a little less than I liked her facing off with her mother without someone at her back.

"See you soon, baby."

Before she could respond I disconnected the call on my watch and finished my shower.

By the time I got to Sophie's my hair was still damp and only twenty minutes had elapsed. But when she opened the door the hurt in her eyes said twenty minutes was twenty minutes too long for her to be alone with her mother.

"What are you doing here?" she softly asked, then peeked over her shoulder before turning back to me whispering, "My mother's here."

My hand went to her chest, I gave her a gentle shove back into the apartment and walked in.

"Valentine?"

"No."

"No?"

I gave a long, assessing look and found I'd been wrong. In the twenty minutes since her mother had been in her home, she was hurt *and* angry.

That shit was not on.

"No, you're not taking another minute of this shit."

Sophie's eyelids slowly lowered. They were slower to open. Which made any indecision I had butting into her business vanish.

"Baby?" I called and waited until she focused on me. "I'm gonna make you as safe as I can, yeah?" Her chestnut eyes flashed. "I'm also gonna make sure a brother in blue doesn't get a call out for a progenitorcide or alternately my team doesn't get called in on our day off to handle a hostage situation."

Her lips pinched before they curved up into a smile.

"It'd suck they got called in on their day off," she returned.

Thank fuck she was onboard.

Right time to move this along.

I grabbed her hand, her fingers threaded between mine, and I didn't miss the way they fit. Like they were meant to notch into place—not too small, not too fragile.

Just right.

A perfect fit.

"Come on. Let's introduce me."

The very short hallway was nothing more than an architecture necessity delineating the bedroom to the right and the kitchen to the left. With me and Sophie holding hands the space was cramped yet I made no move to let her go.

I had a point to make.

When the kitchen table came into view I saw a woman sitting there with a bright yellow mug in front of her with a glittery cartoon smiley face decorating the front. Boldly in block letters it read Don't Yuck My Yum. I didn't attempt to hide my smile.

I knew Sophie had purposefully given her mother that mug as a GFY.

Petty.

Brilliant.

And something I could fully get behind.

"Mother, this is Valentine," Sophie introduced us.

I reckoned the ambiguity was on purpose—not expounding on our relationship, leaving her mother to guess if Sophie and I were friends or something more.

Again, brilliant, especially seeing as her mother's gaze had locked on our hands.

"Valentine, this is my mother, Lorelai."

"Ma'am."

Lorelai's eyes tipped up as she gracefully stood with a beaming, bright smile.

I instantly didn't like her.

"Sophie, why didn't you tell me you've found a suitor?" There was a tinge of disbelief that curled around the woman's purr.

"Oh, we're—"

"New," I butted in.

Sophie's hand convulsed in mine.

"Please, won't you join us? My daughter and I were just discussing the job market in Savannah."

Savannah was an hour's drive without traffic. It wasn't unheard of for the residents of Hollow Point to work in the city, especially the citizens who lived in the wealthier neighborhoods. But if you could find a job without the headache of a commute and traffic most people worked local.

I glanced from mother to daughter, took in Sophie's reddening cheeks, and shoved down my initial response that would go over like a ton of bricks, and opted to turn the tables instead.

"That's great, baby. I didn't know you were already branching out to pull in more clients from the city."

"Clients?" Lorelai spat like the word tasted foul. "We were discussing future employment."

Sophie went stiff beside me.

Dislike shifted to disdain.

"That was not what we were discussing, Mother. *You* were demanding I close my business *right this second* and apply to the jobs *you* found in Savannah that *you* feel were properly suited for *me*. *I* was explaining to you that wasn't going to happen and *you* were in the middle of telling *me* why it was when Valentine knocked on the door."

"Sophie Lynn Huxley, that was incredibly rude," Lorelai huffed.

Oh, yeah, I didn't like this woman at all.

"Rude or not, it's the plain truth."

Without another word out of Lorelai she swiped an expensive looking clutch off the table and swanned—yes, the woman swanned like she was making a grand entrance into a gala in her honor—only stopping when she circled the table to make her exit.

Then, unfortunately she spoke.

"It's time you grow up, Sophie, and come to realize your financial stability is on the line. One day you will thank me for not giving up on you."

Giving up on her?

Was this woman for real?

I didn't get a chance to ask.

We stood in silence as Lorelai let herself out of Sophie's apartment. As soon as the door clicked shut Sophie's body relaxed.

"Thank you for the rescue," she mumbled. "I couldn't get her to leave."

I twisted my hand out of hers and brought it up to her face to cup her cheek and to tilt her head back. Once I had her full attention, which meant her warm brown eyes gazing into mine, my mind went blank and my blood heated.

Fuck, she was pretty.

Sophie's eyes dropped to my lips so I watched those lips form the question, "What's happening?"

"No clue."

Her gaze flicked back to mine. The disappointment was easy to read.

But in what I was learning was true Sophie fashion, she laid it out.

"So you're not going to kiss me?"

Her invitation was sweet, made sweeter by her honesty.

"I didn't say that."

"Then what are you waiting for?"

That was a really great fucking question.

Though Sophie was already rolling up, meeting me halfway, so when our lips crashed together, they *crashed.* There was no slow build-up, no tentative touch of tongues. Sophie kissed like she lived—bold, out there, nothing held back. And fuck but I liked that. Too much. But it wasn't until her hands were under my shirt exploring my back, I had a hand on her ass, her tits pressed against my chest, and my dick painfully hard that I broke the kiss.

Sophie's lids fluttered open. Those deep brown eyes tipped up, and Jesus fuck I shouldn't have kissed her.

Not yet.

Not when I didn't have myself straight about the shit I was feeling.

"Wow," she breathed.

She was rolling back up for seconds. Something I wished I could give her but couldn't.

"Baby?"

"Hm?" she hummed, lips coming closer.

"Right now, I need you to step away and go grab your shoes, purse, keys, whatever it is you need so we can get out of here."

Those goddammed eyes hazy with a look I really fucking liked widened before the shutters slammed closed. Gone was the glassy fog of lust. In its place was hesitation and embarrassment.

As much as I needed to get out of this apartment and someplace public I couldn't let that stand. Especially not the embarrassment.

My hand still resting on her cheek slipped farther back. My fingers slid into her hair. The need to gather all those silk strands in my fist was damn near overwhelming—another reason we needed to bolt before I took hold of all that long, gleaming hair and took more than her mouth.

Using my hand on her ass I pulled Sophie closer, pressed my hips deep so she couldn't miss exactly what her kiss had created.

"That is why we need to move this to someplace public."

Her eyes flared as confusion and curiosity leaked in.

"Or this is going to go a lot further and faster than I suspect you're ready for."

"You'd suspect wrong," she volleyed.

"Okay, how about this? After that kiss I need to leave now before I find a way to get you on your knees to find what else you can do with that mouth of yours."

That eye flare turned auspicious and seeing that set my blood burning and my dick throbbing.

"The first time I have your mouth wrapped around my cock and my face buried in your pussy will not be right after you have a fucked-up drama with your mother. And that's exactly what's going to happen if you don't stop staring at me with those gorgeous eyes while my cock is so hard I can feel my pulse thumping in it."

"Maybe you should sit down. With all the blood flowing below the belt I wouldn't want you to pass out," she teased.

If she wasn't on point I would've smiled.

"Baby, me sitting down means you'll be on your knees in front of me."

"I see your dilemma."

She was being cute but that didn't mean she knew jack shit about the problem she was causing. And not just with my zipper imprinting on my cock. The woman was fucking with my head.

"So help me out, yeah?"

"Sure, but I want it known I'm leaving this apartment under orders, not because I want to. My mother is who she is. Her drama and insults are not new. I've lived with them my whole life. And just to add, you coming here, riding to my rescue, putting her in her place and watching her storm out is totally worth a blow job."

"Good to know. But I didn't say what I said to your mother for a payback blow job."

. . .

THE CUTE WAY Sophie's brows pulled together while her eyes narrowed wreaked havoc on my cock. But the way she snapped, "I was teasing," then tacked on, "I wouldn't actually blow you as payback" made me want to kiss the sass right off her tongue.

"Just to note, you talking about giving me a blow job —payback or otherwise—isn't helping."

"You know what would?" she fired back with a smile.

She was teasing again and she knew exactly what she was doing.

I unfortunately didn't.

I was tempting fate.

"Yeah, Sophie, I know exactly what would help."

My cock jumped at the idea of me getting with the program.

Her head twitched and those goddamned eyes sparked.

What the hell is it about her eyes?

She felt it.

Not that she could miss anything with our lower halves pressed together.

When her lips tipped up into a smile, I braced.

Fortunately, her phone rang before she could say more. Also fortunate—it was across the room, which meant I needed to let her go so she could answer it.

"Get that, baby," I encouraged. I removed my hands and stepped back.

A grin that looked a helluva lot like a smirk tugged at her mouth as she stepped away.

Seeing that, my sanity snapped. My hand shot out, wrapped around her biceps, pulling her to a stop.

But I waited until my mouth was at her ear before I promised, "If you're not careful, one day I'm gonna fuck that smirk off your pretty lips."

Sophie being Sophie was completely unflustered.

I was totally fucked.

All from a kiss.

No, not a kiss—a really great kiss. And pretty eyes, and a bold and confident attitude that turned me inside out. Add in her ass and a heavy dose of drama and I was a goner. Totally and completely in over my head.

So, yeah, I was fucked.

10

"WHAT'S GOING on with you and Valentine?" Hayden asked.

He was going for nonchalant but I knew him better than to fall for the uninterested tone.

"Nothing."

"Soph..."

It was my turn to unload the dishwasher. A chore that was not my favorite so I often times procrastinated until as late in the day as I could. Hayden, on the other hand, always unloaded in the morning before he left to go to the gym, or a run, a game of basketball, or whatever else it was that Hayden did with his mornings after he dragged his ass home from working late into the evenings at the bar.

To further procrastinate or perhaps evade my roommate's prompt for more, I changed the subject.

"Why don't you ever sleep in?"

"Because there's life to live and shit to do and I don't like sleeping my life away no matter how late I get in. You know this. Now, what's the deal with Valentine?"

Arrg!

"Nothing."

I knew he was watching me from across the room. I felt his best-friend-bullshit-meter laser focused on me as I was shoving a stack of plates into the cabinet.

"It didn't feel like nothing the two times he was here," Hayden noted.

It didn't feel like nothing the third time Valentine was in the apartment and Hayden wasn't and he laid the single best kiss of my life on me. If that wasn't enough, just hearing Valentine tell me we had to leave before his face was buried in my pussy had made my vaginal walls clench. And when he told me if I wasn't careful he'd fuck the smirk off my lips, I nearly orgasmed. What I hadn't done was wipe the smirk off my face in hopes he'd make good on his threat.

Sadly, he didn't.

After I dealt with a work call that had interrupted us, we'd gone and grabbed bagels and a coffee and he asked me more about my mother.

"I told you, he came over and dealt with She-Devil. We shared a coffee, he brought me home, walked me to the door, and that was it."

Now nothing.

It had been a week, and except for a bunch of text messages and a few phone calls, I hadn't seen him.

Incidentally I hadn't heard from my mother at all in that week, either, but I had heard from Nathan telling me that my mother loved me dearly and was just worried about me as it's a mother's right. I should give it some time and let him know when I was ready to come over and have dinner.

In other words, he wanted to try to play peacekeeper on this latest issue even though it hadn't worked during our most recent dinner, the one which had led to my mother ambushing me. Or all the other dinners besides. He was too good of a guy to give up, and whatever it was that he saw in my mother—and God knows he had to look really deep to find it—made him love her. And by extension me. It was weird—not him loving me, because we got along great—him and my mother. That was weird and strange and I never got it and likely never would.

"You think I don't know when you're lying?"

I glanced across the room and scowled in mock affront.

"I'm insulted," I lied.

"No, you're not. You know I'm right."

Of course he was, but I wasn't going to admit it.

"He's your friend. Why don't you ask him?"

"I have."

At that I perked up and put down the silverware basket on the counter.

"You asked him?"

Why was my voice pitched so high and why did my stomach just erupt with butterflies?

"You really suck at this," Hayden returned with a knowing smirk.

Which of course made me think about Valentine's sexy threat, yet again. I seriously needed to start dating —*stat*. Or at least find a good diversion to distract me from thinking about Valentine every five seconds.

"Whatever, Hayden, just tell me what he said."

"Nothing."

"Nothing?"

"He said there was nothing going on, the two of you were just friends."

Damn. That hurt way more than it should've.

"Told you."

I went back to shoving the silverware into the proper slots in the drawer. Hayden let the topic drop and went back to doing whatever he was doing on his phone. The silence only allowed my mind to wander to all sorts of places it shouldn't go.

Sure, Valentine was hot. The times I'd been around him he'd been sweet. Well, that was when he wasn't naked or kissing me. He wasn't sweet then. Those times his sex appeal had ratcheted off the charts and made my vagina weep with need and my nipples tingle. I really needed to get a hobby or a man. Something, anything, to make me stop thinking about a man who very obviously wasn't interested in me.

"Explain to me why you haven't asked him out."

Asked Valentine out? Was he nuts?

"He's not interested," I pointed out.

"How do you know?"

Because he kissed the ever-loving hell out of me, made some whispered dirty promises, dragged me out of the apartment, then firmly friend-zoned me.

"A girl knows."

"That's bullshit, Soph. You don't know because you haven't asked. It's not always up to the man to make the first move."

Suddenly this felt less like me and Valentine and more like him and a woman.

"Are you waiting for a woman to ask you out?" I carefully asked.

"Nope. Just trying to light a fire under your ass. Valentine's a good guy. I like him. I like him for you. But if it's not him, fine. But it's time for you to get back out there. Oakley was a supreme douche but not all men are cheaters and assholes."

His words felt like a blow to the sternum.

"I'm not still hung up on Oakley and you know that."

"I know you're not. You're hung up on what he did to you. It's time, Sophie. Again, if it's Valentine, cool. But it's time."

I had no idea where this was coming from. I'd dated plenty in the last few years. That was, I'd had a lot of first dates, a few seconds, and only a couple that lasted a few weeks. And only one that had made it to the six-month mark before I broke things off.

"I date," I defended myself.

"Sure you do. If you call interrogating a man over dinner a date."

There might've been some truth in that. But only because I didn't see any reason to get involved with a man if we didn't share the same values.

"Why are you being such a dick about this?"

Hayden stood, skirted the coffee table, and faced me. Belatedly, the look of concern registered.

"Because I love you. Because you've been living behind a wall for a long time. And as much as it makes me physically violent thinking about what happened in that liquor store, it woke you up. You're coming out of hiding and it's time for you to open your eyes, look in the mirror, and see you are a beautiful, smart, funny woman. You need a man. And not for the reasons your mother thinks you do."

Jesus, the blows kept coming.

"I need a man?"

"Right. You skipped right over the you're beautiful, smart, and funny."

Wait.

"Do you want to move out?"

Hayden's mouth twisted and his eyes narrowed.

Clearly that was the wrong thing to ask.

"You know, I don't know who I hate more," he weirdly started. "Oakley for being such a monumental prick and because of that you're now afraid to put yourself out there, or your mother for making you feel like you're not what you are. And that's a beautiful, smart, funny, loyal, kind, and loving great friend. Being all of those things, it's a waste you not finding a man to give all that to. But mostly it's a fucking tragedy you don't find one to give all that back to you. And it seriously fucks me that after all these years of you being my girl you'd ask me something so fucked up."

With that very successful parting shot, Hayden stormed out of the apartment before I could apologize.

Damn.

He was right; my question wasn't cool. I knew him. I knew that if he was ready to move out he'd tell me. He wouldn't do what I'd accused him of doing.

Double damn.

I finished unloading the dishwasher and cleaning up the kitchen, giving both of us a few minutes to cool off before I went into my room to grab my phone. That scene wasn't fun but it was far from the first tiff we'd gotten into and it wasn't near as heated as some had been.

Friends argued.

Then they made amends and moved on.

But it still didn't feel good I'd messed up.

I picked up my phone off the charging pad on my nightstand and saw I had a text from Valentine.

I should've ignored it.

Someone with stronger willpower would've.

I, however, was weak when it came to Valentine.

When you get this, call me.

I scrolled up to the last exchange from earlier.

How does this sound for a coffee shop tagline? Coffee is the key to a perky day.

Within minutes Valentine had replied.

Horrible.

Ugh.

Did you want me to lie?

No. But you suck at the gentle let down.

Sorry, baby, I didn't take you as a woman who liked it gentle.

After he'd sent that I'd reread the text no less than ten times trying to figure out if he was flirting or not.

I ended up sending a lame response.

It doesn't have to be gentle as long as I'm prepared.

It was a solid five minutes before he came back with...

Noted.

After that, I didn't know what to say so I stopped texting and went back to work on Hot Java's not-marketing campaign that included a rebrand. Thankfully I had a budget for logo design and a copywriter to come up with a catchy tagline and headlines for advertisements. Clearly, slogans weren't my strong suit.

Nothing from our previous exchange hinted at why he'd want me to call him. Which meant my good sense was overridden by curiosity. I needed to talk to Hayden, but that would take more than a couple minutes and Valentine never stayed on the phone long. At least that was what I was telling myself when I called Valentine first.

I hit his contact and waited. After the forth ring I figured I'd get his voice mail. At this juncture that should've been a relief. Everything about him was confusing and scary and made me feel anxious. Not to mention turned on. Maybe in a few months when I was over my crush we could be friends. I could drop by the Hope Center and watch him play basketball before I did my volunteer thing with the kids. Not that I'd called or emailed to ask about volunteering. I wanted to but if I did that now, I might come across as a stalker.

"Hey," he answered. "Hang on a second, let me go outside."

A few seconds later the sound of music disappeared.

"Sorry about that."

"No problem. What's up?"

"What's wrong?"

Good Lord, I couldn't catch a break.

"I got your text—"

"Sophie, what's wrong? Is your mom giving you a hard time?"

Why did he have to be so nice?

This would be so much easier if he was an asshole.

"No, I haven't heard from her since you put her in her place. So now you have my thanks, times two."

There were a few beats of silence and I was wondering if he was thinking about my fake blow job offer as gratitude.

Sweet Dolly P, I had to stop thinking about his penis and blow jobs and his face between my legs and what he could do with that big penis of his. My poor vagina had never been so well-acquainted with my vibrator.

"Did you want me to call so you could listen to me breathe?" I quipped.

"I wanted you to call so I could tell you, Ackerman's been locked up. But now I want to know why you sound like someone told you coffee has been banned for eternity."

Okay, so this would be easier if he was an asshole and *not* funny. And maybe if he was five steps down on the hotness chart and his penis was two inches and his hands were small and he'd admitted he hated going down on women because he sucked at it.

But this was Valentine and he was who he was and that included being funny. Which sucked. I loved funny people.

"I got into an argument with Hayden and was kinda a bitch."

"Kinda a bitch?"

"I said something uncool so yes, I was kinda a bitch, not a full-on one. Though if I'd been that he would've stayed and called me out. Instead, I just pissed him off and he left before I could tell him I was sorry."

"What was the argument about?"

You.

I didn't say that. I'd never say that. And besides, it was only sort of about Valentine. The rest was about me doing exactly what he said I was doing—hiding away behind the safety of my wall so I couldn't get hurt again. My mother caused enough ongoing hurt; I didn't need to invite more into my life.

"Nothing important," I lied.

"You're a shit liar, baby."

I'd heard that before.

"Whatever," I mumbled. "Everything will work out. It always does."

I crossed my fingers as an added signal to the universe to make that happen.

"I'm at Balls Deep. Come here and I'll buy you a drink."

"I don't need a pity drink," I said before I thought better of it.

"Come again?"

I hadn't come yet, but the way his sexy growl made my vagina involuntarily spasm was a good indication I might spontaneously orgasm despite my nightly vibrator regime.

"What I meant to say—"

"You said what you meant," he interrupted. "Is this

you thinking you're being kinda bitchy or is this edging straight to bitchy?"

My back shot straight.

"That wasn't nice," I snapped.

"Neither was you implying me asking you to shoot a game of pool and buying you a drink an offer of pity instead of what it was."

I really wanted to ask him what "it" was but I was too chickenshit.

"I think I'm gonna start my..." Thankfully I stopped speaking.

Regrettably, Valentine hadn't developed a rare case of temporary hearing loss and he chuckled.

"Uber over and come shoot some pool and have a drink. I'll get you home later."

I had no choice but to say yes or sound like a screaming bitch and a shrew.

"Okay."

"Yeah?"

God, he sounded...happy.

Down, Sophie. He's just being nice.

He's a friend.

A super sexy Hot Cop friend.

Nothing more.

"Yeah. And sorry for being kinda bitchy."

"No worries, baby. See you soon."

He disconnected.

I stared at my phone thinking I should feel relief that Ackerman guy was behind bars. And I did, but I'd barely given it more than a passing thought when I was more taken with Valentine's concern. I also should've called Hayden. But I didn't. I texted him, like the chickenshit coward I was.

Sorry. I don't know why I was so bitchy.

I had ordered an Uber and was putting on my wedges when Hayden texted back.

No worries, Huxley. And I know why.

See?

Friends argued then they apologized and moved on.

I was at the front door when I paused to text back.

Code Red inbound.

I'd have to check my calendar but I think that's in two weeks and you're never grouchy this early.

I laughed at that.

And it wasn't a lie; Hayden did mark my cycle on the calendar hanging in the kitchen. The first time I saw it I ranted and raged about it for an hour, explaining to him he was a jerk and he was lucky not to experience cramps and bleeding. It was three days before my period started when he circled the day on the calendar and in bold, upper-case letters wrote CODE RED. From then on, four days before my period started he always had my favorite salt and vinegar chips in the house, and three days before my period he made himself absent.

Since we were back to us, meaning he'd forgiven me and was back to teasing, I gave him more.

I'm going out. Don't wait up for me.

Tell Valentine I said hey and I won't be home tonight.

I rolled my eyes at the Valentine comment.

Be safe. Look both directions before crossing the street and use protection.

Yes, Mommy.

GROSS.

I got two laughing emojis and a sideways laughing emoji and a blue heart.

I sent back a middle finger and purple heart.

His next text came as my driver was pulling into the parking lot of Balls Deep.

Just be you. The Sophie I know and he'll fall in love.

If he doesn't he's a fool and not good enough for you.

In the meantime have fun. Get yourself some and be happy.

It's time, Huxley.

It's time, Huxley.

Butterflies took flight in my belly.

All my life I'd been a chickenshit. I didn't take chances and the one time I did and put myself out there I was royally screwed over.

Just so you know, when you find her, she better be perfect and if she hurts you I'll claw her face off.

Knew that already. Now stop bothering me I'm busy.

At least one of us was getting themselves some tonight.

Because it wouldn't be me.

I used my app to give my driver a tip, tossed my phone in my purse, and got out of the car.

With a big breath I readied myself to face Hot Cop —*my friend.*

11

I KNEW the second Sophie walked in the door. Ethan's partner and my friend Jase's attention went over my shoulder. His eyes fixated on something and did an up-and-down sweep. I focused my body to stay relaxed and my hand wrapped around my beer not to crush the can.

"Goddamn," Jase muttered.

Goddamn was right and I hadn't even looked at her yet.

"Be back." His ass slid off the stool, leaving me in a precarious position.

The irrational side of me wanted to body slam him before he got to her. The parts of me that were fighting the pull of her thought it would be great if they hit it off; then maybe I could get some fucking sleep and stop obsessing over her. The petty side wanted to watch him get shot down. My ego, however, worried she'd choose him.

I was fucked.

After a week of warring with myself and staying away that hadn't changed.

Six times in her presence and one kiss and I was hooked.

I turned on my stool and there she was.

Goddamn didn't touch how gorgeous she was, and when her eyes scanned the crowd she looked a little nervous, maybe a little lost. But when her gaze caught mine and her lips tipped up, swear to Christ she looked found.

I had no idea what I was supposed to do with that look or how it made my chest tight.

Jase said something to Sophie I couldn't hear. She shook her head and pointed. When he looked over his shoulder and realization hit, I almost felt sorry for the guy. He looked back and jerked his head. When he turned and gestured for Sophie to precede him I considered punching my friend in the face. My internal debate ended when his gaze stayed on me instead dropping to her ass and he mouthed *fuck you.*

A gentleman would've got his ass up and escorted her through the crush of people.

I stayed where I was for no other reason than I liked watching her walk to me. I liked knowing she was there for me. I liked that her eyes didn't unlock from mine and the rest of the bar had melted away. I liked that when she knew I was watching she added a little more sway to her hips. And I seriously liked she was getting off on me watching.

Christ.

I needed my head examined.

Or I needed to fuck her.

The first was an actual concern. The second was going to happen.

"Hey, baby," I greeted when she made it close.

"Hey—" If she meant to say more, I didn't let her finish.

I hooked her around the waist, pulled her close, and dipped in for a kiss. What was supposed to be a closed-mouth warning to all the assholes who'd watched her walk in, turned into something else when her tongue touched my bottom lip. The control I mustered up was award winning. With nothing more than a single swipe of mine I broke the kiss.

When I pulled back her lips were twitching.

"Glad you made it."

Those lips curved up.

"So am I."

A throat cleared. I glanced at Jase standing next to the stool he'd vacated. I shifted Sophie closer so she was standing between my legs.

"Jase, you met my girl, Sophie."

I felt Sophie jolt and not for the first time I wondered what the fuck I was doing.

"Yeah, brother, I introduced myself." He chuckled with a good-natured shake of his head.

"What do you want to drink, Soph?"

When she craned her head to look at me she was no longer smiling.

"A long neck of WTF with a shot of confusion."

It took me longer than it should've to comprehend what she meant.

"I don't know if Chelsea serves that here but I can ask."

"I heard it's called the Valentine Special," she quipped, and fuck me, I wanted to kiss her again.

I dipped closer and after a quick mouth touch stayed close to say, "I thought it was the Hot Cop Special."

"You think you're funny."

No, I thought she was hilarious and cute as fuck with her cheeks tinging pink.

"You guys doing alright over here?" Chelsea asked from behind the bar.

"What do you really want, Sophie?"

I saw her eyes flash. It was so quick, if I hadn't been close, staring right at her, I would've missed it.

But I didn't miss shit.

"Blue Moon, please."

"I don't know if I should fan myself, find my husband and take a break, or toss ice water on you two," Chelsea jibed.

"Tell me about it," Jase groused.

Fuck, we were in public.

I shifted Sophie, slid off my stool, planted her on it, and shifted again so I was at her back.

There. Gentlemanly.

"You look familiar," Sophie said.

"Yeah, I was there the day at the liquor store when you kicked that fuckstick's ass. Couldn't tell you then so I'll tell you now, that was epic." Jase paused, wiped the smile off his face, and asked, "You okay? I heard you were hurt."

Fuck!

I'd been too busy fighting whatever this was I felt for her, I hadn't asked about her injury.

Good God, I was an asshole.

"You're a cop, too."

I froze. Jealousy was a new and unchartered emotion for me. But there it was, and I wore it like a bad suit, wondering if Sophie would call him Hot Cop, too.

"Yeah, I'm Ethan's partner. We work out of the six-ten with V and his team."

Conversation was halted when Chelsea set down Sophie's drink.

"I'm Chelsea," she introduced herself as her husband Matt came up next to her. "This is Matt."

"Sophie."

Matt's gaze slid from Sophie to me.

I knew that smile and what it said. Matt owned Balls Deep with his wife but he worked at Triple Canopy and he'd been there the day I asked Dylan for the panic button for Sophie.

The thread of hope I had that he'd keep his mouth shut was cut.

"Heard a lot about you, Sophie. Good to meet you."

Fuck. Me.

"You've heard about me?" she asked Matt but had turned to look at me.

"Remember I told you I called in a favor to get that tracker? Matt works at TC," I explained.

"Right."

Was that disappointment I detected?

"I need to give that back to you, now that I don't need it," she continued.

Ethan and Jase had found Ackerman late last night and he was being held on a slew of charges including attempted murder. This after he was out on bail for attempted robbery. It was unlikely he'd be released again.

"Keep it."

"But—"

"Just for a little while longer, baby. Let's make sure he stays where he belongs."

I hadn't missed it before and I sure as hell wasn't missing it now when she read whatever it was she needed from me and relented.

"Okay."

And there it was again—that unnerving feeling in the pit of my stomach when she studied me. The woman saw far too much. The problem was I couldn't get a grasp on what she saw.

"Chels, need my tab, darlin'," Jase drawled.

"I've told you a thousand times, your money's no good here," Matt cut in.

"And I've told you a thousand times, my money's—"

"No good here," Chels finished for Jase.

Jase shook his head and slapped a fifty on the bar, which was triple what his tab would've been if Matt would have let him pay.

"I'm gonna hit it. Nice meeting you, Sophie, I'm sure I'll see you around. V, we'll catch up in the morning."

Goodbyes were exchanged with Matt and Chels then Jase was gone. Soon after that, Chelsea got back to work, leaving Matt behind.

"Heard about you kicking Ackerman's ass," Matt mumbled.

Soph glanced at me to ask, "Does everyone know?"

"Not every day a beautiful five-foot-six woman gets the drop on a man who's got six inches on her and seventy pounds, and beats the shit out of him. So, yeah, pretty much everyone knows."

"And approves," Matt threw in.

Thankfully Matt's underlying meaning went over Sophie's head. However, I caught it along with the pointed look he cast me.

"We're gonna hit a table."

"Don't let him bullshit you," Matt started. "The man can run a table."

"Eight ball or one pocket?" Sophie tossed out.

Matt blinked then a slow smile spread over his face.

"Oh, yeah, this is gonna be fun," he muttered and walked away.

He wasn't wrong.

This was going to be hella fun.

It was just that the real fun was going to happen later.

I offered my hand and when she took it and those small fingers wrapped tight I was reminded how perfectly her hand fit in mine.

"Tell me, Mr..." Sophie paused and looked up at me. "I don't know your last name."

"Malone."

"Valentine Malone." My name rolled off her tongue. I had yet to recover from the heat that hit my chest when she went on. "Tell me, Mr. Malone. Are you up for making a wager?"

I tugged her to a stop and spun her around. My arm darted around her middle and I yanked her close.

"Absolutely. But you should know, Matt wasn't lying. I can run a table, Soph."

I should've known I was screwed when her lips quirked up and she shrugged while admitting, "I'm not horrible."

"What do you have in mind?"

"If I win you take me home."

"I wasn't going to let you Uber—"

"To your bed."

Straight up, no bullshit, pure Sophie.

"If I win," I started, then leaned forward brushing my lips across her cheek to her ear. I paused to fully take in her shiver before I whispered, "I get you in my bed, at my command."

"So win or lose I still win," she mused.

"When *I* win, I get you in my bed naked, spread out, and at my mercy."

"So I win."

"No, baby, that'd be you giving me the gift of you so I'd win. But I promise you won't regret giving it."

I didn't let myself process her tiny jolt. Nor did I allow myself to ponder why she scared the hell out of me. Further from that, I didn't think about the small detail that once I had her in bed I wasn't giving her up.

Nope.

I shoved that all aside and led her to a table.

An hour later I learned she'd lied.

She wasn't horrible.

The woman was a goddamned hustler.

12

ALL I COULD DO WAS FEEL.

No, that wasn't true. I could feel and smell and taste.

I was completely surrounded by Valentine. Stripped down to my panties and spread out on Valentine's bed while he was fully dressed. One of his hands was cupping my ass, the other was lifting my breast to his mouth and his tongue was teasing my nipple. My hands were on a voyage of discovery, roaming his back under his tee.

I'd won.

Now I was cashing in on the spoils.

But I wanted more.

We'd been at this a long time. Touching, licking, nibbling, groping, stroking.

I tugged at his shirt and demanded, "I want this off."

His lips closed around my nipple. He sucked deep, and he shook his head.

"Please."

I was not above begging. Hell, I would get on my knees and worship at his feet if it meant he'd put me out of my misery.

"Not yet," he said as he moved to my other breast.

I forgot all about his shirt and got lost in what his mouth was doing. With my thighs clenched, I shifted under one of his jean-covered legs pinning me to the bed. My clit pulsed, pleading for friction. I was close and getting closer with nothing more than Valentine playing with my nipples.

His hand moved from my ass and over my hip, and his fingertips dipped under the lace of my panties.

Finally.

My pussy spasmed in joy.

No.

"Wait." I grabbed his wrist.

Everything stopped.

His hand did not move a millimeter. His mouth disengaged. His body was perfectly still when his head tipped back and he looked at me.

"You okay?"

No, I was not okay.

I was the very definition of not okay. I was mortified.

"Um..."

"It's all good, baby."

I could feel my face flame.

"It's just that..."

I trailed off again, wishing there was a way to travel back in time five hours, fix my mistake, and wind up right back here where I was without the embarrassment I now faced.

"Sophie, baby, you owe me no explanation."

My hand tightened around his wrist when he started to roll away.

"I didn't shave," I blurted out.

Valentine blinked.

The heat that had been concentrated on my face rapidly spread down my body until it felt like my toes were on fire.

He looked like he was now waiting for the explanation he said he didn't need. Though in all fairness that was when he thought I'd stopped the festivities for other reasons. And Valentine, being a good guy, had stopped immediately without question.

Now not so much.

Sweet Dolly P, I was such an idiot.

"As you know, I don't have a man and I wasn't planning on being here." My mouth was speaking words but my brain was praying for a meteorite to hit Valentine's house. "Here being in your bed with your hand getting ready to go into my panties."

"Yeah, baby, my hand's going down your panties." He smiled his confirmation. "And?"

Well, that was going to be embarrassing.

"And since I didn't know I was going to be here in your bed I didn't shave or...trim up."

Good God, that smile turned wicked.

His fingers skimmed the skin above my panties. His

other hand regained purchase on my breast and his thumb swept over my nipple. Both movements were slow and gentle but heady, nonetheless. My clit throbbed, uncaring I was in the middle of a horrifying situation.

"Are we talking full 1980's bush?"

"No." I meant to sound haughty but my answer came out breathy. "What's 1980's bush?"

"Don't worry, baby. I can find my way through the jungle."

Ugh.

"Valentine," I snapped.

Another smile, this one amused.

"Here's a tidbit of information for you; men don't care."

I didn't think that was true.

"Correction. I don't know what other men like but I don't care."

His thumb grazed over my nipple again and I was beginning not to care.

"You'll care when you're spitting out pubes."

Ohmigod, did I say that out loud?

Yes. Yes, I did. I was blaming Valentine's hand on my breast, and his earlier kisses, and what his tongue had done to my nipples for my fuzzy brain and big mouth.

"Don't worry, I've got a water pick."

I wanted to laugh and I would've if I hadn't been so mortified. Not that I would've had the chance because he was up on his knees, dragging my panties down my legs, tossing them aside, then Valentine was on his stomach between my legs. Before I could catch my breath his hands went to my ass and yanked me to his mouth.

My back bowed off the bed and my mind blanked out everything except his mouth sucking my clit deep. And when he added a thick finger I was lost to him.

"Spread wider." His demand vibrated against my clit and that, too, brought me closer to climax.

I spread as wide as I could. Valentine went in and *ate.*

He didn't nibble.

He devoured.

He sucked my clit hard and fucked me with his fingers deep.

My thighs trembled.

My muscles tightened.

On a long moan, I shattered.

And Valentine would not relent until I was groaning and begging him to stop, or never to stop, or to keep me in this place of perpetual mind-blowing bliss forever. My words were unintelligible, garbled, incoherent. His grunts and growls prolonged my pleasure.

Then he was gone.

In my haze of euphoria I vaguely watched him shed his clothes. Later I would kick my own ass for not pulling myself out of my daze. I was positive it was a sexy show but I was too blitzed out to do anything but to bask in the glow of the best head I'd ever had.

But I didn't miss that big dick of his when it sprang free.

Holy hell, how did I forget about that?

"Baby." He chuckled as he climbed back on the bed.

It must be said, that was sexy as hell—him climbing onto the bed, coming up over me, his dick bumping the inside of my legs as they opened for him.

Valentine said nothing more, but he did reach out to the nightstand. When he came back to hover over me, he hooked me around my shoulders and rolled to his back.

Nope, I was wrong. Me straddling his hips while his dick was hard between us, and his eyes blazed with need was sexy as hell.

He tore open the condom wrapper while issuing orders.

"This is how this is going to go. You're gonna take me —like this." He nudged me back to roll on the condom. "As slow as you need. When you're ready I'll take over."

I swallowed past the thick desire that had wedged in my throat and nodded.

"Hands on my chest," he bossed. *He didn't have to tell me twice.* I broke the land speed record I moved so quickly. "Take me, slow, baby."

I didn't have much say in how I took him, with one of his hands on my hip guiding me down and his other positioning himself between my legs. I hadn't realized how rigid Valentine was holding his body until I took the wide head of his dick inside of me. Then he turned to stone. His brows pulled together and his stormy blue eyes turned steely.

"Honey," I panted.

"Slow," he reminded me.

"I need more."

He slid his fist down his cock, giving me more room. I took another inch and puffed out a breath.

"Slide up, Sophie, then take more."

The up part felt good but the glide down felt amazing.

"Keep going, baby," he grunted.

Up and down I went, Valentine feeding me his dick an inch at a time. The stretch was the best kind of pain. The kind that made you crazy with need. The kind that made you feel insane with yearning and stole your thoughts.

I needed him.

All of him.

I slammed down, taking more, needing the pain so badly I cried out in a plea.

"Almost, Sophie, just a little more," he gritted out.

My excitement surged at his rough tone.

"More?"

There was more?

His hand tightened on my hip and I hoped he left bruises. I wanted to wear his mark of need on my skin. I wanted to remember the way he took excruciating care not to hurt me. I never wanted to forget the way his eyes held mine as my body welcomed him.

I wanted this moment forever.

"Sophie, baby, I *need* you."

Okay, *that*, I wanted to remember forever.

Slowly I glided up; even slower, I glided down, groaning as I took the last of him.

"God. *Fuck*. Christ," he bit out.

I panted.

"So goddamned beautiful."

I panted more.

"Prettiest eyes I've ever seen."

His hand skimmed over my thigh, went between my legs, and his thumb zeroed in on my clit.

My hips jerked.

"Stay still, Sophie."

I wasn't sure that was possible, but for him I'd try as long as he kept at my clit.

"Good, baby." His thumb pressed harder. "You're gonna come just like this."

Yeah, I was.

I rocked my hips and cried out when he pinched my clit.

"Be still, Sophie," he demanded.

Oh, God, that was hot.

Seriously freaking hot.

His thumb went back to circling. His eyes never left mine. The intensity with which he was watching me would've been frightening if it didn't make me feel so desired.

Right then it was just us. Me and him. There was no one else in the world. Nothing more important than us and the way we were connecting.

"You feel so good," I groaned. "I need to move, honey."

"Not yet."

I thought about disobeying him. I thought about how good it felt when he pinched my clit. I thought about how good the downward glides felt. The only thing that stopped me was the wave of pleasure that had consumed me.

"That's it, Sophie," he growled.

"Valentine." His name came out in three syllables.

My neck arched back. Valentine knifed up and demanded, "Tit."

In my fog I lifted my breast in offering. His mouth gladly accepted and pulled deep. My orgasm rippled through me when suddenly I was on my back but still connected.

"Wrap tight."

I hooked my ankles at his lower back and wrapped tight.

"Fuck, you feel gorgeous."

God, I loved he thought so.

"So do you," I whispered.

"Tell me if I go too far."

"I will," I lied.

I would take whatever he wanted to give me if it meant he got what he needed.

"I'm serious, Sophie. I don't want to hurt you."

"You won't."

"Baby—"

"Fuck me, Valentine. I want you to feel as good as you make me feel. You won't hurt me."

With a groan he dropped his mouth to mine and kissed me.

It was nearly as brutal as his thrusts.

It was glorious.

It was beautiful.

It was powerful.

Every grunt, every glide out and drive in, overwhelming.

My hands roamed his back, my heels dug in, my nails grazed. All of this without thought. There was no time to think—it was about touch.

Learning.

Memorizing.

It was the single most intoxicating experience of my life. Surrounded by Valentine's power went beyond sex, beyond pleasure and orgasms. In that moment, it was about being the center of his universe. And that was what it felt like. I was in control of all his dominance.

Me, Sophie, had Valentine at my command.

He'd deny himself pleasure if he thought I was hurting.

He'd stop at a moment's notice if I needed.

He'd give me really great orgasms and let me take him slow while it pained him to wait.

He broke the kiss. I felt his labored breaths on my cheek before I felt his lips brush there.

"Watch, baby."

I didn't know what he wanted me to watch and I wasn't sure I had it in me to concentrate on anything beyond what was happening between my legs.

Valentine shifted his weight to his elbow, allowing his other hand to skim up my ribs over my breast, up my chest until he gently used his hand at my throat to keep my face where he wanted.

That's when I saw it.

Steel-blue eyes unfocused with pleasure.

"Come for me, honey," I begged softly.

With a groan he drove his cock so deep, I fought to keep my eyes open.

Then I watched.

Oh, yeah, I watched as his eyes rolled, his lids went heavy, his face in rapture as he emptied himself inside of me. It felt like it went on forever. His cock twitched and jerked, his body above me stone-still, the grunts of relief filling the room.

I was well and truly addicted. I wanted to see that again and again and again.

Maybe for a lifetime.

I never wanted anyone else to ever witness the beauty that was him.

It was mine.

All mine.

I wanted that with a fierceness I'd never felt.

"Fuck," he snarled.

The severity of his tone had me blinking.

"What—"

His hand tightened on my throat. His features no longer held the vestiges of satisfaction; his eyes were still lit but anger was hedging out the desire.

Fear gripped my insides.

"Shh, Sophie." The softness of his tone contradicted his actions. "Did I hurt you?"

"No."

"Are you lying?"

"No."

"I took you hard, baby. You didn't stop me but I lost control."

He looked pained as he said the last part.

"I don't want you to keep your control," I told him. "I want you just as mindless as you make me. I want you with me, feeling what I'm feeling. So totally out of control all you can do is chase the pleasure."

His eyes flared in a sexy way that made putting myself out there worth it.

"Mission accomplished, baby."

That was good news.

"Then why do you still look pissed?"

He relaxed and dropped a kiss on my lips before he pulled back and gave me his undivided attention.

"I'm not pissed. I was scared I'd hurt you. I was worried I got so lost in you, I didn't have a mind to you."

"Well, you didn't."

His lips curved up and I didn't give the first shit his smile was arrogant. As far as I was concerned he'd earned it.

But I did note, "You look pleased with yourself now that you know you didn't hurt me."

"Yeah, baby, I'm pleased to know you can take a solid fucking and get off watching me blow for you. I'm also pleased to know that you go wild when my mouth's on your pussy. And I'm seriously fucking pleased to know that all it takes is you sitting on my cock while I play with your clit and you'll go for me."

I couldn't say anything about that, since it was all indeed true.

His thumb stroked the side of my neck as he asked, "Are you alright with this?"

"With the hand necklace?" I asked and he nodded. "I never thought about it. So I never thought it would be something I'd like. But yeah, I like feeling your hand on my throat. But more, I like knowing you want my attention. I also hope that I have your fingerprints on my hips so I can wear your bruises."

"Jesus, fuck," he growled.

His praise again made me safe to share honestly.

"Not now," he started. "But soon. When you're used to me and feel comfortable and safe with me you're gonna wear my marks on your ass."

That time I didn't verbally share how much I'd like that.

Yet, I still shared.

"Your pussy clenching mean you're down for that?"

That sex-rough voice was going to do me in.

"Yeah, Valentine, I'm down with that. But just to say, I'd like that to happen sooner rather than later."

"We got all the time in the world to play, Soph. No need to rush."

All the time in the world.

God, I hoped so.

"I'm gonna get rid of this condom," he said but didn't pull out. I knew why when he asked, "You sore?"

Since he was still close, therefore he'd read my lie in a heartbeat, I was truthful.

"Right now, no."

Those sinful lips stayed curled up in a smirk when he muttered, "Right."

"You know you once threatened to fuck my smirk off my face," I reminded him. "I think at this juncture I should warn you, I could rally and fuck that smile off your lips."

"Fuck, you're adorable," he groaned. "And tomorrow, you can try to make good on that threat."

"Try to?" I huffed.

"Soph, if you think you fucking me is a threat, you're wrong. If you think I won't be sporting a satisfied smile after your pussy milks me dry, you're again wrong. If you think I won't be anything but fucking thrilled after I wring a few orgasms out of you, you're seriously mistaken. But for tonight, we're done. Tomorrow after you're done fucking me we can discuss your disappointment."

As if I'd be disappointed.

Valentine's hand around my throat loosened and slid up to cup my face.

"That right there, that look you just gave me. So fucking pretty."

I had no idea what look I just gave him but I needed to know so I could give it to him again—thus giving it to myself—because the way he looked at me was the kind of expression I'd fight tooth and claw to keep forever.

"How am I looking at you?" I asked.

"Like you think I'm worth it."

I didn't like the way that sounded.

"You *are* worth it."

He abruptly kissed my lips and slowly pulled out. Meaning I lost concentration on our conversation and groaned.

Sue me, he was still hard and the outward glide felt good.

"Fuck, you feel good," he grunted.

"*You* feel good," I corrected.

"Let me toss this condom and start the bath. I'll be back."

Valentine shifted, rolled, and was standing beside the bed when I got a good look at his back. It was hard to focus on what I saw, with the acres of muscle my gaze encountered. But now that'd I'd seen them I couldn't not.

"Holy shit," I muttered.

I watched in morbid fascination as Valentine froze. Muscle by muscle he stiffened, his back ramrod straight. Woodenly, he looked over his shoulder at me.

"Sophie—"

"Oh my God, Valentine. I drew blood."

I was out of bed in a flash, stopping at his side long enough for me to tag his hand and pull him toward the bathroom.

"Do you have a first aid kit in here?"

"Sophie—"

"Why didn't you tell me I was hurting you?" I accused irately.

"Because you didn't."

"I drew blood, Valentine."

Good Lord, I knew I'd dug my nails in but I didn't know I'd clawed his back to shit.

How had I clawed his back? I'd never done that before. Though I'd never been fucked within an inch of my life.

I flipped on the light, gave him another tug, and tried my best to forget I was naked. I didn't have any hang-ups about nudity, it was just Valentine was perfect and I was not. Actually, maybe I did have hang-ups because suddenly I became very aware I had a poochy belly and my legs weren't toned. And while I had large breasts they were too big to be perky. And if all that wasn't enough, the mortifying no-shave issue reared back up.

Thankfully, Valentine turned to face me and pulled me close so our bodies were almost touching and I had to tip my head back to look at him.

"Listen to me, Sophie. I liked it."

"I liked it, too, but that doesn't mean I get to inflict—"

"No, baby, you're not hearing me. I *liked* it."

You didn't stop me but I lost control.

He'd said that like he'd committed a mortal sin.

"I'm hearing you, but I don't think I'm understanding," I admitted.

His face changed. That's the only way to describe what had happened. It became guarded, unsure, and hesitant. One of the things I really liked about Valentine was when you had his attention, you had it—period. But right then in the silence, his focus so acute, with him looking so uncomfortable, I wanted to close my eyes and forget I was seeing what I was seeing.

"I liked it," he repeated like a confession.

I still didn't get it. Especially the part that sounded like he'd admitted a deep, dark secret.

"I didn't hurt you?"

"That's the part I liked, Sophie."

Puzzle pieces shifted. But I wasn't fond of his tone.

"And you think I'll judge you for that?"

He blinked.

Oh my God. He did. He thought I was judgy.

"That doesn't feel good, Valentine," I whispered.

He remained silent and that didn't feel good either.

"I need you to talk to me, Valentine. I feel like I'm missing something here."

"I just told you I liked you tearing up my back with your nails."

So maybe the puzzle I'd worked out wasn't depicting the same picture as the one he was trying to lay out.

"Okay?"

Another blink.

"The pain of that, Sophie. I got off knowing you were so out of your head you were marking me. And fuck yeah, it hurt. I got off on that, too. The pain you were inflicting while taking my cock. I needed you mindless, I needed your nails digging in, I needed the control that gave me. Then I got so lost in you and it scared the fuck out of me."

Everything he said had been exactly what I'd been feeling. I had been mindless, so much so I hadn't realized I was hurting him.

"And here's more for you," he spat. "Those bruises you said you wanted? Careful with that, Sophie. You have no idea what you're asking for. I'll give you my mark. I'll sink my teeth into your tit and mark it as mine. I'll dig my fingers into your skin until you wear my prints. I'll smack your ass while I fuck you hard until you beg me to stop. Then I'll worship every inch of you so you know you belong to me and you'll beg me do it again. I'll work hard at it, Sophie. I'll make it so you'll never come again unless it's at my command. I'll wrap my hand around your throat, collar you, and make sure you know down to your soul that hand around your neck belongs to the man who owns every fucking part of you. And while I'm giving you that, you'll be mindless. You'll bite, scratch, draw blood, and I'll get off on that, too. I'll control every part of you while you're taking my cock, my fingers, or my tongue. Now, Sophie, do you understand?"

I understood my pussy was convulsing and excitement was leaking down my thighs.

"I understand," I confirmed.

Then because he was Valentine and he'd just laid it out and he'd made it safe for me to be me, I returned the favor.

"I understand that if you don't fuck me again right now I'm going to make you watch while I get myself off because I'm in desperate—"

I got no further.

Valentine bent forward, planted his shoulder in my belly, and hoisted me up into a fireman's hold. I grunted. He tore the spent condom off and tossed it into the sink before he carried me back into the bedroom.

He bent again, unceremoniously dropped me onto the bed, and demanded, "Spread wide. Knees bent. Feet on the edge."

I did what I was told with my eyes glued to the hand stroking the long length of his cock.

Valentine fell between my legs, one hand near my head holding himself up, the other jerking his cock.

"Hand between your legs, baby. I'm gonna watch you play with my pretty pussy while I jack off for you."

Yes! Please.

With anyone else I would've been embarrassed. But there was no discomfort with Valentine, not with his eyes on me making me feel like I was the most beautiful, precious thing he'd ever seen.

I jolted when my fingers grazed my clit.

Valentine's neck bent and he looked down between us where my hand was working.

"Fuck, that's hot."

He pumped his cock fast. I dipped my fingers into my pussy, getting them wet, then went back to circling my clit.

It wasn't going to take much more for me to go.

"Do not slow down."

Alrightly then, it would seem Valentine already knew my body as well as I did.

I rubbed hard. My breath came out choppy. My gaze stayed focused on the way Valentine worked his cock. The sight was primal, beautifully vicious the way he stroked, taking himself much harder than I would.

"God, you're beautiful," I rasped.

I could see a bead of come dripping from his swollen head and that was what sent me over the edge. Knowing he was getting off watching me. Knowing I once again had the control he'd claimed to desperately need. I vaguely wondered if he knew he gave it to me. It was my pussy, my hand toying with my clit, that was getting him off.

"Honey," I groaned and arched.

My empty pussy grasped at nothing but the heady goodness still washed over me.

"Knees," he growled and tugged me up. "Right fucking now."

I'd barely slid off the bed when my hands went to his thighs to stop myself from pitching to the side.

"Open."

I opened my mouth, then the tip of his dick was on my tongue. Hot jets of come splashed the back of my throat. I closed my lips tight, swirled my tongue around his head while he jerked off, swallowing until he finally finished.

My eyes tipped up and my lungs seized.

"Do not move."

With my lips still wrapped tight, his hand left his dick, went to my jaw, and gently, reverently stroked.

"I'll never forget how fucking beautiful you look on your knees." His hand slid into my hair. "I'll make it worth it, Sophie. I promise."

I could hardly answer with a dick in my mouth.

But I hoped he understood he'd already made it worth it.

And furthermore, I really didn't like how he'd mentioned the 'worth it' thing again.

I filed that away for a conversation for a different day. Right after I processed why the thought of Valentine owning my body had my stomach tied in knots and my heart thumping in my chest.

13

THE WOMAN in my arms slept like the dead. And there I was like a crazed weirdo watching her sleep, wondering what the fuck I was supposed to do now. I didn't have the first clue how to make a woman happy. I knew how to take her out for a good time, fuck her, get her off, then send her on her way. I didn't do sleepovers. I sure as fuck didn't climb into a bathtub with one and wash her hair. But I'd done just that—with Sophie. And worse, I'd made promises. I'd taken it too far. I'd lost control and abused the trust she'd given me. I used her body and her innocence against her. I knew after that kiss the worst thing I could do would be to fuck her, that the moment I got inside her everything would change. And it damn well had.

I should've kept it platonic, kept her safely in the friend zone where I could get my fix while keeping my dick in my pants and her safe from my dysfunction.

But those fucking eyes and the way she stared at me like she saw right through me and all I needed to do was open the door and she'd waltz her tight ass through it and heal what ailed me. But there was no mending what was broken. There was no magic cure.

I was who I was and I knew better than to allow myself to get close to a woman. Especially one like Sophie. A woman like her destroyed a man. And when the day came when she woke up and realized she deserved better than a man who was broken and she left, I'd turn into my father.

Alone.

Ruined.

Bitter.

Sophie shifted and her eyes fluttered open.

Christ. So beautiful.

"Hey," she rasped, her voice full of sleep.

"Morning, baby."

She stretched, arching her back, pressing her tits deeper into my chest. And if that wasn't torture enough, she shifted her naked body, rubbing down the length of me. But it was her pussy on my thigh that had commanded the attention of my already stiffening cock.

My hand resting on her hip slid down and around to cup her ass. More torture, but I needed her to stop moving. She'd been sore last night. She'd be sore this morning. On that thought, my cock twitched.

"Morning," she mumbled before she turned and kissed my chest.

Now that she was awake, I needed to get out of this bed.

Instead, I laid there, liking the feel of her pressed close.

I'd never been stupid about women. I was careful, controlled, every interaction purposefully impersonal. I always held back what I needed. But not with Sophie.

She was my lethal cocktail of stupidity.

The place where desire and lust mingled in all the worst ways.

A place where hope lingered on the sideline like a siren call waiting to edge in and destroy me.

A place I had no business dragging Sophie to, but fuck if I could stop myself. What was even more fucked was, I wasn't going to put a stop to it. I was going to do everything I'd promised. I was going to make her need me like I needed her with the same raw, archaic, primal cravings.

My fate was sealed.

I was destined to become my father.

Repeat his mistakes.

The pull of Sophie was greater than the lessons he'd taught me.

And it had started in the pasta aisle of a fucking grocery store when her gaze tipped up. She'd stumbled back and I'd tumbled headfirst into a pair of pretty eyes. It had happened so fast I'd been rooted in place, too stunned to chase after her.

"What time do you work today?" Her question

pulled me back to the present, reminding me I needed to get up before my dick forgot she was sore.

"We're on nights this week, so three. But I'm also on call."

"So we have time..." She let that hang.

We had more than enough time. Which was precisely the problem.

"Soph—"

"Let me, please." My warning stalled and my stomach muscles contracted as her soft hand traveled down toward my very hard dick. "I didn't get to touch you last night."

Last night I'd been more concerned with preparing her to take me than allowing her to explore.

Sophie's hand circled my erection and fisted tight.

"Is that too much?"

"No," I grunted my approval.

Slowly—excruciatingly, agonizingly slowly—she glided her hand down my shaft to the base.

"My fingers don't touch." It was impossible to miss the awe in her voice and when she went on I couldn't stop my smile. "I can't believe that fit."

"If you keep calling my cock a 'that' I'm gonna get a complex," I teased.

"Please," she scoffed. "I could call it Mini Valentine and you and your big dick would be just fine."

She was wrong about that.

And not because I cared about what she called my dick. There was nothing 'just fine' about me.

I opted not to speak when she slid her hand up and used her thumb to circle the tip.

"Is that sensitive?"

Jesus fuck, I was going to die.

"Yes."

"More than the base?"

"Yes."

"So you like it when I do this?"

Another graze with her thumb, this time adding the edge of her nail to lightly scrape.

"Yes."

"What about this?"

She didn't move her hand but her cheek slid down my stomach, her hair pooled over my chest, and when she made it to her destination her tongue replaced her thumb.

Good Christ.

"Yeah, baby, I like that," I unnecessarily confirmed.

I moved my hands up, threaded my fingers, and rested my head on top of them to stop myself from gathering up all that silky hair and using it to guide her deeper.

Her mouth was wet and warm and so fucking inviting I had to clench my ass so I wouldn't thrust up and fuck her mouth. The longer I let her play the harder it became—my cock and the need to take over.

My control snapped when on a downward glide with her tongue making magic, she took me deeper and I felt the tip hit the back of her throat, accompanying the sexy-as-all-fuck sound of her gagging.

I could take no more.

I freed my hands, used her hair to pull her mouth from my cock, shifted until I got my hands under her pits, and hauled her up my chest.

"Climb up, Sophie. I want you on my face."

Her eyes widened and for a moment she hesitated.

If I hadn't already fallen down the wrong side of hope with this woman, watching her tremble as she nervously climbed up would've sent me over the edge. It wasn't the apprehension she'd turned into lust. It was the absolute trust.

A better man would've put an end to the madness. I, however, scooted her higher, and when I had her cunt where I wanted it, I feasted on the insanity. I took everything she didn't know she was offering and devoured her pussy like the prick I was. I drank down her excitement. Desperate in my pursuit for her climax. Once again, I was thrust back into my frantic need to drag her under. Make her lose her mind, bend her, own her pleasure because I would never own her heart.

I didn't deserve her, or her trust, or her body.

But still I took her, until her thighs on either side of my head shook and she mewled her orgasm. One hand left her ass to reach for a condom. My other hand moved to tear open the wrapper and roll the latex down my aching cock. I slid out from under her, got to my knees behind her, gritted my teeth, and took everything.

Every. *Fucking*. Thing.

I took her scream as she took half my length in one thrust. I took her moan when I pulled out. I took her exhale, her full-body tremble, and her whimper when I gave her the rest of me.

"Brace on the headboard, Sophie."

I waited for her to curl her fingers over the top of the wooden frame.

"Good, baby."

Despite the war raging in my chest I set an easy pace. Slowly giving her more. Slowly working her up until she was meeting my drives. Slowly taking her with me—to the place I'd only been with her. Where reality couldn't creep in. To a place that was free of the garbage that lived in my head.

Mindless.

Just me and her.

This.

A place where I was not alone, lonely, and broken.

A place where I could breathe her in and hope like fuck she didn't see me for who I really was.

"Valentine," she groaned.

Her cunt was impossibly tight. I fought my way in and out. Held onto every ounce of control I had. She wasn't there yet. I needed more.

"Not yet."

"I'm gonna—"

"Not yet."

I slowed my strokes and kept her on the edge with me.

"Honey," she panted.

"Not yet."

My hands on her hips moved in opposite directions. One slid up to cup to her tit, using my finger and thumb to roll her nipple, the other down to toy with her clit. Purposefully not giving her enough.

"More."

I pinched her nipple but my finger on her clit slowed.

"Not yet, baby."

With my jaw clenched, I drove my hips forward, giving her one hard thrust.

"Oh, God. So close."

"I know you are. I can feel your pussy clutching—"

"*My* pussy?" she panted. "Last night it was *your* pussy."

Fuck.

There was no more doubt—Sophie Huxley was going to be my downfall.

"You giving me this?" I punctuated my question. I ground deep and rolled her clit.

"I can't give what's already yours."

Jesus *fucking* Christ.

"And these? Are they mine, too?" I gave her nipple a hard tug.

"Yes," she hissed.

The blood coursing through my veins heated. The left side of my chest started to burn.

More.

I needed more.

"And if I wanted more you'd give it to me?" I asked, knowing I was a motherfucking bastard.

"Yes."

"Cunt. Tits. Ass. They're mine?"

Seeing as I was already a world-class asshole and playing a dangerous game of moral gymnastics, I went for the gold and I pushed.

"And if I wanted more, would you give it? If I want all of you. Everything."

Too much of a coward, I didn't give her a chance to answer. I took her to the place I needed her to be, using my cock and fingers to drive her out of mind and behind the wall of pleasure where I knew she'd agree to anything.

"Yes!" she shouted as her orgasm took hold.

I rocked forward, planted deep, and let her sweep me under with her cunt pulsing and seizing, taking me away from my fucked life and pulling me into hers. With each rope of pleasure she pulled from me, I knew this was it; she'd leave and I'd turn into the very person I despised. Yet I did nothing to fight against it.

I might've laid claim to her body. She might've freely given it to me in return. But she'd stolen my soul, and in return I'd fucked her and given her my broken heart.

A heart that could never love her the way she deserved to be loved.

I didn't know how.

The man who was supposed to teach me had left me hanging.

14

SOMETHING HAD CHANGED.

It wasn't necessarily bad…but neither was it good.

It was just a shift in energy.

It was nothing more than a feeling, when Valentine looked at me searchingly. Like he was waiting for me to say or do something and he wanted to be prepared when I did.

I couldn't place it exactly but I knew.

This morning after Valentine had fucked me within an inch of my life and had given me the second-best orgasm in history, he'd scooped me up off the bed like he'd done the night before. But instead of the bath, he'd taken me into the shower. He'd gently washed every inch of me, including my hair.

When he was done, he didn't let me return the favor. He'd scooted me out and told me to get ready. Which was pointless because I was donning last night's clothes, sans already worn panties of course, and I had nothing I needed to get ready. So I'd dressed, pulled my tangled, wet hair into a bun that would take me approximately half a bottle of conditioner and two hours to work out the tangles when I got home, and headed to the kitchen in search of a coffee machine. I'd also done a bit of snooping since last night. I'd been more concerned about getting to Valentine's bedroom than I was about looking around.

Unlike me, he lived in a house. A nice one at that. Not too big. Not too small. Welcoming with comfortable-looking furniture that said 'sit and stay awhile.' Like his bedroom, the rest of his home was decorated in masculine colors—tans, greens, creams, browns. No pops of bright color. No placemats on the oval dining room table. No candles. No lamps on the end tables. No clutter. The whole place looked like a bachelor pad. Not a frat house or place a young man would live, but it was glaringly obvious a woman didn't live here. There wasn't even a potted plant in sight. Not that I had a plant at my place, but I did have candles and color and my apartment looked live in.

Valentine didn't have a home. He had a house.

I didn't like this. I didn't like what it said. I didn't like the feel of it.

Actually, I hated it.

I'll make it worth it, Sophie.

I'd hated that statement last night, too.

Actually, it wasn't the words I hated. It was the look in Valentine's eyes. The tone of his voice when he'd said it. It had been all wrong. Instead of rough from lust, his voice had been hollow. Raw. Tinged with pain and hued with isolation. I didn't understand how a man so beautiful, so self-assured, could sound...broken. How his beautiful eyes could look so haunted.

I didn't like it.

But I couldn't ask. Not yet.

And now that I was dressed and alone in his kitchen I couldn't stop thinking about his admission. He'd liked the pain of my nails. He liked dominating me in bed. I hadn't missed his dominance. Just like he couldn't have missed I'd gotten off on it in a big way. But he'd acted like it was a horrifying secret, like it made him weird or different and he was ashamed of it.

That, I needed to talk to him about. My problem was, I didn't know how to start the conversation and I had precisely zero experience with a man like Valentine. My last boyfriend was Oakley and he would've been happy if I'd topped him. And not because he got off on kink. He was lazy when it came to sex, doing the bare minimum needed and most of the time failing in that department.

"Find everything okay?"

I turned to watch Valentine enter the kitchen. His long legs ate up the distance between us, stopping close enough to kiss my temple. But otherwise he didn't touch me.

My nerves kicked up a notch. Not only had I been too busy snooping to hear him, I didn't know what to do with the no-touching thing.

With a scan of his kitchen, his gaze landed on the empty coffee machine, then came to me.

"You wanna drive through Jitters on the way to your place?"

No. But he obviously wanted me out of his house sooner rather than later and I didn't know what to do with that either.

"Everything okay?"

I wasn't proud of the way my voice gave away my nerves but there was nothing I could do about that. If I'd read more into what had happened last night and this morning or I'd wrongly assumed he felt the same connection that had been simmering between us I needed to know now. I was already in deeper than I should've been.

He didn't answer.

He stared.

My nerves kicked up a few more notches and I waited. In those seconds I felt more exposed than I had spread out naked for him. His study of me intense, his eyes guarded, his body stiff, none of his natural masculine grace was present. He looked as if he was holding himself back and having a hard time doing so.

When I could no longer stand the silence I broke it.

"What's—"

"Nothing's wrong," Valentine interrupted. After another eye-sweep around the kitchen, his gaze fixed on me and he continued. "I just didn't know how much I'd like seeing you in my kitchen." His admission was almost sheepish. "I've lived in this house for three years."

"Okay?" I prompted when he didn't go on.

"Not a single woman has been in this house."

For some reason that made me deliriously happy but I still didn't understand.

"Before that, I lived in a condo for five years. The only woman who'd ever stepped foot in the door was my teammate, Sunny, and that was only because I was sick and she felt it was her duty to load me up on meds and soup."

Suddenly I felt like I was intruding. Clearly Valentine didn't like people in his home.

"If you don't like—"

"Did you miss the part where I said I liked you in my kitchen?"

I didn't miss it, but the strange vibe I was getting didn't say he liked anything about the situation.

"I like you in my house, Sophie."

Okay. That was a little better but my stomach was still doing somersaults.

"Liked you in my bed. Liked fucking you there. Liked sleeping with you, liked waking next to you. Liked you in my shower. Bottom line, I like you here, in my space."

That all sounded good.

"And you don't like that you like all of that?"

"That's the problem, baby, I *like* it. I like it too much. I like it enough to forget all the reasons I should keep this casual between us."

"But you said—"

"I know what I said and I meant every word. I want

all of you. I knew before bringing you home with me, there was no way I could do casual with you. Last night proved what I already knew. Walking in here and seeing you standing in my kitchen after sleeping in my bed, proves I'm a selfish fuck because even though I know I'm wrong for you and you deserve better than anything I could give you, I'm not letting you go."

"I don't want you to let me go."

"That's good, baby, but I wasn't giving you the option."

Now the acrobatics were going on in my belly for a different reason.

"Then why when you walked in did you not touch me?"

The side of his mouth hitched and my Valentine was back.

"Are you sore?"

I will not blush.

I will not blush.

I was a grown woman who knew her body and what she liked and I wouldn't blush like a schoolgirl.

Yet I felt the heat hit my cheeks.

"A little," I admitted.

His right eyebrow slowly rose, calling out my lie.

"Fine. Yes. I'm sore."

"That's why I didn't touch you when I came in."

I must've shown my confusion because he explained.

"I was rough with you last night and I worked you over hard this morning. Seeing you standing here in my kitchen, in my space, knowing how much I loved what I was seeing, knowing you rolled out of my bed, remembering the way you come apart for me, if I'd gotten any closer and touched you I'd forget how sore you are and bend you over the island and fuck you again. I'd forget I need to get you home so you can get to work building your empire. I'd forget everything."

I wanted him to bend me over the island. I wanted to forget my responsibilities. I wanted him to lose control and treat me like I was his sole purpose for living. I wanted that more than I'd ever wanted anything.

But...

"Why do you think I deserve better?"

His eyes went stormy and I wondered if he knew when he was uncomfortable his gaze gave him away. The change was ever so slight, but it was there.

"You only deserve the best."

My phone started ringing. There was at least three feet that separated us yet I could feel Valentine's relief roll off of him.

"And you're not the best?"

His relief was short lived. Every bit of tension that had drained out of him when my phone rang came back full force. Steel-blue eyes stared through me, stiff shoulders, a tic of his jaw.

"Sophie—"

"That's bullshit, Valentine. Who told you you're not worth it? Who told you, you weren't the best?"

He blinked at my outburst and that pissed me off more.

"No, don't tell me. I don't want to know. I have mad internet sleuthing skills and I'll find the bitch and..."

Shit. I didn't know what I would do.

"And do what, Soph?" he teased.

Teased.

He was grinning.

"Are you seriously making fun of me right now?"

"No."

No?

Yes, he was.

"I don't find this funny, Valentine. More than once you've said you'd make it worth it. More than once you've talked about what I deserve, and now you've said I deserve better. That's not funny."

"I can see—"

"Can you, Valentine? Can you see how that's so totally absurd it would piss me right the hell off?"

His smile disappeared. So did the distance between us. Then his hand was on the back of my neck and his mouth was slamming down onto mine. My mind raced to catch up but it was too late; his tongue swept in and stole my thoughts. He didn't let me up for air until I moaned into his mouth, telling him I was ready for him to bend me over the island.

Valentine broke the kiss but unfortunately ignored my silent but obvious request.

"I couldn't see, but I do now."

Well, that was something.

"Who—"

"Give me time."

I wanted to push but with his gentle request paired with the pleading in his eyes I had no choice but to give him what he asked. Besides, asking for time when we were getting to know each other wasn't the same thing as denying me.

"Okay."

I knew I made the right decision when he brushed his lips over my cheek.

"Coffee here or Jitters?"

Jitters was my second favorite coffee shop after Hot Java.

"Jitters."

"You got it, baby."

Without further ado, Valentine was pulling me out of the kitchen into the living room. He nabbed my purse, handed it to me, retraced his steps, and we went into his small laundry room, then out into the garage.

"I like your Rover."

"So you said," he returned, holding open the passenger door for me.

My ass hit the tan leather and I looked up at Valentine doing that cool guy thing where they stand in the opening, one hand on the roof the other one on the frame of the door, and stare down.

"Was that your way of asking if you can drive her?" he asked, totally figuring me out.

"No, not if your answer is you never let anyone drive your expensive SUV. Yes, if you're considering letting me drive."

My answer garnered the Hot Cop smile I loved.

"I've never let anyone drive her. But if you want to take her out, she's all yours."

"Why do men refer to their cars as she and her?"

Hot Cop morphed into Sexy Valentine before my very eyes.

"Because men are smart and understand that, much like a woman if you want her to purr then you do everything you can to keep her tuned up and well-oiled."

With a wink he slammed the door.

I watched him round the hood. I did this smiling with butterflies in my belly. Not from nerves. These butterflies were telling me this was the beginning of something special. Something I'd been searching for but never thought I'd find. No, not something—someone.

If he needed space, I'd give it to him. If he wanted to know me better before he spilled his secrets, I'd wait.

At least that's what I thought I was supposed to do.

Unfortunately, I was wrong.

I should've pushed.

I should've asked.

But above all else I shouldn't have assumed.

My naiveté would prove to be heartbreaking and ugly.

15

I STARED at my phone and frowned before I tossed it in my purse.

"Who was it?" Valentine asked.

"My mother."

Valentine pulled into a guest spot near my building and put the Rover into park.

"Have you talked to her since that day at your apartment?"

"No."

"But she's calling you. You're just not answering."

"Correct, and texting."

If I'd had a different kind of relationship with my mother I would've felt guilty for not returning her calls or texts. But I didn't have a different kind of relationship with her. I had the one I had and I didn't feel like getting laid into.

When Valentine didn't say anything I turned my

head to look at him. He was staring out the windshield but I doubted he thought the cinderblock wall in front of him was interesting enough to study.

"I don't know what to say," he started. "I think I'm supposed to tell you she's your mother and you should call her and give her a chance to apologize. But from what I saw, I don't think that's what would happen."

"You're right. That's not what would happen."

"Right," he clipped. "Then stick to your boundaries."

"Are you close to your parents?"

The instant the question left my mouth the inside of the car became stifling. The air turned thick. And an unease like I'd never felt prickled my skin.

"My mom's dead."

Those three words ricocheted around the Rover and pierced my heart.

"I'm—"

"My dad's...not close to anyone."

I waited and when he offered no more I gave him a useless platitude since I didn't know what else to say.

"I'm sorry, Valentine."

"It was a long time ago."

He said the words but his statement didn't match the sorrow I heard.

Saying anything else at this point would've been cruel. Not that I had a choice in dropping the subject because he was out of the SUV.

Damn.

I collected my purse and gathered my thoughts

before I got out and joined him. When he grabbed my hand I felt marginally better.

"I shouldn't've—"

"You didn't know." He let me off the hook. "And like I said it was a long time ago."

I chanced a question.

"How long ago?"

"I was thirteen."

I didn't know exactly how old Valentine was but he had to be around my age, so indeed a long time ago. A long time to still be mourning the loss of his mother. As much as my heart hurt for him I was glad he had the kind of mom who he loved so much that still after all these years he sounded pained when he spoke of her.

Valentine jerked his head in the direction of the covered tent parking.

"Hayden's home," he noted.

I glanced at Hayden's truck parked next to my car and asked, "Is that a problem?"

"No. But before we walk in there hand-in-hand I wanted to give you a heads up in case you didn't want him knowing about us."

It was seriously hard remembering I'd agreed to give him time when I really wanted to know who had made him question himself.

"I want everyone to know I landed the hottest cop in Hollow Point. I want everyone to know how happy I am he picked me. I want to go get coffee holding your hand so I can sit across from you and dash the hopes and dreams of every single woman getting her morning coffee fix. I want to walk into a restaurant on your arm. I want you to know that I will make it *worth it* for you to put up with my irrational jealousy when it rears its head. And I'll make it *worth it* for you when you give me a choice of takeout menus and you have to wait thirty minutes for me to weigh my options. And I'll—"

Valentine tugged my hand, spun me, then dropped another soul-splintering kiss on my mouth.

I guess he was done with me blathering on.

And if this was how he shut me up when I was on a rant, I was A-okay with that.

"You're heard, baby."

I wasn't sure I was but I let it go.

"Irrational jealousy?" He chuckled.

"Totally."

His smirk would've been infuriating if it wasn't so damn hot.

"Looking forward to seeing it."

It was good he thought that, because I wasn't joking.

"For the record, I get to pick where we eat unless you have something specific in mind. No way in hell am I waiting half an hour for you to weigh your options."

"Works for me."

We were almost to my front door when he quietly muttered, "Just so you know, my jealousy won't be categorized as irrational."

I barely hid my smile when I said, "No? How would you categorize it?"

"Possessive and feral."

I tossed his earlier words back at him.

"Looking forward to it."

Valentine slipped his arm around my shoulder and chuckled.

I unlocked the door, stepped inside, and offered my normal greeting. "Honey, I'm home."

I heard Valentine grunt behind me.

"Possessive," he warned. It was probably against some rule in the woman handbook but I shivered. "And feral."

Our banter was cut short when Hayden appeared. His gaze danced between me and Valentine before a huge smile split his face.

"Huxley. Valentine, good to see you."

"Winslow..." I trailed off when a beautiful brunette materialized from the hall.

I felt Valentine's heat hit my back, his arm went around my waist, and he planted his hand on my belly, holding me tightly in front of him.

"Khloe, this is my roommate Sophie and her man, Valentine."

"Hi, nice to meet you both," she sweetly offered.

Valentine's fingers dug in and he stepped closer.

"Hey, Khloe. Nice to meet you, too."

The woman smiled.

Then it became awkward.

This wasn't the first time I'd met one of Hayden's dates. Some were nicer than others. Some gave me the side-eye because I was female and the roommate. Others didn't pay me any attention. A few I'd even watched a movie and scarfed down pizza with before I absented myself to my bedroom to give them privacy. It was rare but occasionally I'd walked into my kitchen in the morning and found a woman I didn't know helping herself to the fridge.

But that wasn't the reason it was awkward now. Khloe was staring at me with daggers in her eyes.

"Hayden. Khloe, it was good to meet you. If you'll excuse us."

Hayden, being none the wiser to his date's death rays, tagged her around the waist and pulled her into the living room.

"I'm making breakfast. Hungry?" Hayden asked.

I was starving but I was afraid if I said yes, the woman might spit in my food.

"No thanks."

"I'm good, brother," Valentine answered and propelled me forward, not letting me go until we rounded the corner into the hall. And I meant, *we*. It was like we were one as he shuffled us past Khloe.

The moment Valentine closed the door behind us I gave him big eyes and whispered, "You saw that, right?"

"Not gonna lie, Soph. I might've sized up Hayden if you brought me home and I didn't know him. But, yeah, I saw it. That chick was sending over-the-top death rays in your direction."

Wait.

"Hayden's just a friend. Nothing's ever happened.

The closest he's ever come to touching me is giving me a foot rub."

Valentine's eyes narrowed.

"My socks were on."

He said nothing so I went on.

"It only—"

"Sophie."

"Yeah?"

"I don't share."

Well, that was good news.

"I don't either."

"Right. I'll explain." He stalked across the small room and pulled me to his chest. "I don't share. Not even your feet."

I stared up at him and pinched my lips to stop myself from smiling.

"Are we clear?"

"Sure, we're clear, as long as we're also clear I'm answering in the affirmative assuming this is you being possessive and not condescending."

"And feral," he reminded me.

"And feral."

He kissed my forehead, then pulled back.

"For the record, I'd never be condescending."

"Good to know."

Valentine kept his chin dipped and held my stare. Something was working behind his steely-blue eyes. Even though I didn't know what he was working out, it was fascinating to watch.

"You gonna be okay here alone?"

I wanted to point out his question was one of the many things that made him worth risking my heart. He would whisk me away if I told him I didn't want to stay. That wasn't possessive, that was protection.

"I'll be fine. I can work in here until they're done with breakfast."

He stared at me a beat with his brows pulled together.

"Not cool you having to lock yourself in your room, baby. You wanna work from my house today?"

Again, worth it.

"It's not a big deal," I assured him. "And they won't be long."

At least I hoped not. At some point I had to shower and get ready to meet a new client for lunch.

He didn't look happy when he mumbled, "Alright, Soph. Kiss before I leave and let you get your day started."

I rolled up and kissed him. That lasted all of three seconds before he took over and kissed me.

His kiss was way better than mine.

"Damn, woman, you can fucking kiss."

"I was thinking the same thing about you."

I saw him smile. Up close the steely-blue looked like gun metal.

"Sucks I can't see you tonight. Lunch tomorrow?" he asked.

That's when it hit me.

Hot Cop.

I was dating a cop.

And not just a cop, a SWAT officer.

Tonight he'd be out with his team doing whatever the SWAT team did, which were things I knew I didn't want to think about too deeply or it would scare the hell out of me.

"Yeah, Valentine, lunch tomorrow."

"Would it fuck your day if after lunch you worked the rest of the day at my house?"

It absolutely would. I had very little faith in myself that I would be able to concentrate on work with a hot, six-foot...

"How tall are you?"

"Six-two. What does my height have to do with you working from my house?"

"Nothing. I was gauging my ability to concentrate around a certain hot, six-foot-two beast with the most beautiful eyes I've ever seen, who's possessive, feral, and bossy in a way that totally works for me. But really, those three things aren't about control and ego, they're protection and safety."

"Fuck," he growled. "Now I gotta kiss you again."

"Works for me."

"I know."

This kiss was nothing more than a tease. A stroke of his tongue against mine with a sweet peck to the corner of my mouth.

"What'd you come up with?" he asked as his lips brushed over my cheek.

"Huh?"

"Work. My house. Concentration."

Another lip brush. This one glided over the sensitive skin under my ear.

"Yes."

"Yes, you'll be able to concentrate?"

Not on work, I wouldn't.

"Yes," I lied.

"We'll see."

Valentine bit my earlobe and straightened.

Goodbyes were said that included me telling him to be safe and call me later. His included a smile and confirmation he'd touch base later.

Now I was standing in my room, my concentration shot, unable to think about anything other than Valentine—the way he kissed, the way he touched me, the way he smiled, the way his eyes gave away his every emotion, what he'd said about me in his kitchen, his mom...I couldn't stop thinking about all things Valentine. He was protective, strong, and confident. Which meant whatever it was that made him feel unworthy wasn't a woman. I was well-aware there were many ways a woman could scar a man, make him question himself, build walls, but this was different. This had rooted itself deep. This, whatever it was, had shaken the foundation of his life.

I hated that.

I wanted to pry. I wanted to beg him to tell me. Or

throw drama and break Valentine until he spilled his secrets. But this wasn't about me and for once I was going to be 'less Sophie' as my mother called it when I was being too much of anything and let this play out how it needed to play out.

On that thought, I needed coffee.

My affinity was such I would brave the kitchen and Khloe's obvious dislike to fetch a mug.

That was how I found myself tiptoeing down the hall, listening for voices, praying Hayden was feeling randy and aborted his mission to feed his date in favor of taking her to bed. I paused at the end of the short hallway and waited.

No voices.

Perfect.

I stopped dallying and rounded the corner to find Hater Girl in my kitchen alone.

Shit.

Her unhappy gaze landed on me and became less happy.

Double shit.

"Hey." I infused as much friendliness as I could.

Maybe she was a nice person and Valentine and I had caught her off-guard when we showed. Not everyone was great with impromptu meet-and-greets.

"Sophie." She all but snarled my name.

Nope.

Just a bitch.

I hated her for Hayden.

"Where's Hayden?"

"Why?"

Holy Hannah.

"Um...just making small talk."

No longer wanting coffee but also not wanting to allow this bitch to make me feel uncomfortable in my own home, I went straight to the cabinet and grabbed a mug.

I pulled the carafe from the burner but gave her my attention when she softened her tone and answered, "Someone from the clubhouse called and said a box had been delivered yesterday. He went to get it."

The woman was no longer shooting death rays in my direction. She almost looked excited. Her eyes went from me to the coffee machine then flicked back to me several times. It was creepy. She gave me the heebie-jeebies. I didn't like her at all.

But still I sucked in a breath and tried again.

"One of the great things about living here. Darrell, the clubhouse manager, keeps an eye on packages for us."

Her lip started to curl up but she caught herself, and fake as fuck, she smiled.

"That's great. Don't let me hold you up." She tipped her head toward the coffee pot.

Whatever.

This woman was strange and not nice and I hoped Hayden wasn't planning on keeping her.

I poured my coffee, doctored it up with cream and sugar, and didn't bother with farewells.

Fifteen minutes later, three emails answered, my stomach protested my coffee intake without food balancing the acid that was now swirling.

I should've grabbed a bagel.

I pushed through two more emails, finished my coffee, but could no longer ignore my stomach churning.

And that was how I ended up back in the kitchen with Hayden and Khloe. But I stopped dead when I saw her smiling at him. For a moment I questioned everything. She was very pretty but with her beaming a huge smile at Hayden I got what he saw in her. She looked like a fun, sweet, pretty woman. But when Hayden turned to do something at the stove and she caught sight of me, a flicker of hate flashed in her eyes. Maybe Valentine was right; it was that I was her man's female roommate. But Hayden would've explained there had never been—and never would be—anything beyond friendship.

Again, whatever.

I had shit to do to prepare for my meeting.

"Sorry to interrupt," I announced. "Just grabbing a bagel then I'll be out of your hair."

Hayden turned off the burner, plated the eggs, then glanced at me with narrowed eyes.

"Soph, if you're hungry I'll make more eggs."

God, he was blind.

"No time, Winslow, I got work to do."

And at this rate if I didn't get a bagel in my belly I was going to puke.

I didn't waste time toasting it and sloppily slapped

cream cheese on the slices. I was reaching for a paper towel when I noticed the empty coffee carafe.

"You know the rules. Whoever drinks the last cup makes a new pot."

With my bagel in hand, needing to make a quick escape because now my stomach was cramping, I barely stopped when Hayden returned, "There was a full pot when I left. How much—"

"Sorry," Khloe sweetly interrupted. "I drank the last of it. I'll make more."

"I got it, babe."

Barf.

With my back to the couple I rolled my eyes and immediately regretted it when a wave of nausea washed over me. I hustled to my room, not giving the coffee-guzzling-bitch another thought.

I took my bagel to my bed, shoved my laptop to the side, and ate with my eyes closed, hoping I didn't vomit with that woman in my house. I was what one would call a loud upchucker. It was a curse. It was never pretty. And it rarely happened unless I drank too many Bloody Marys.

An hour later I was praying for death and had to cancel my meeting with the bowling alley owner who wanted to revamp his marketing.

16

"THAT SHIT WAS WILD." Riddle choked back a laugh and slammed the door to his locker.

"Did you see the look on Valentine's face?" Chip added.

"Priceless," Shiloh joined.

This was not abnormal. Locker room talk after serving a warrant. What wasn't normal was I'd never been on the receiving end of the shit talk while I had dog piss soaking my boot and the ankle of my pants. Further from that I'd never had a high as a kite naked woman attack me before.

"She wrapped him up and humped his vest." Mereno shocked the hell out of me by getting into the riot act.

Christ.

I was tossing my plate carrier and sterilizing my magazines.

"Never seen a woman crawl up a man so fast." Riddle

lost the battle on his hilarity and busted out laughing. "V didn't know where to grab her to stop her from—"

"Shiloh, out. I'm undressing."

"Should I bring back a hazmat bag for your clothes?" she asked as she made her way to the door. "Or better yet, set up the emergency drench shower in the parking lot? I think I spotted a snail trail on your mag pouches."

There wasn't a chance in fuck I was looking at my vest in case she was right.

I stripped as fast as I could, not caring if Shiloh had bounced. I'd given her plenty of warning. We all did when she was in the locker room with us and someone was going to do so much as change their shirt. The reverse was the same with her; when she wanted the room we bolted and locked the door.

"Holy fuck, brother, you go head-to-head with a cat?" Chip announced.

Fuck.

Riddle whistled his comment as he passed me on his way to the shower.

I knew the drill, ignoring them was my best course of action.

"You got an extra set of boots?" Mereno mercifully asked.

"Yep."

"See you at the debrief."

We'd already debriefed at the scene but there was still paperwork to file. And an incident report to fill out.

I placed my sidearm and knife next to my phone in

my locker, shut the door, spun the combination lock, and headed to the showers without checking my cell. I'd washed my hands, used liquid sanitizer, but I still didn't want to contaminate my phone. I had dog piss, naked woman, and God knows what else growing on my skin.

I needed a scalding shower and a gallon of soap.

I stepped into the stall next to Riddle and got to work.

"All joking aside, you good?" my teammate asked.

I'd fucked up and let an occupant of the house get the drop on me. That shit was unacceptable. That was how people got hurt or worse.

"That shit will never happen again. You have my word."

"What are you talking about?"

I pumped the soap dispenser, uncaring I was using three times more than needed and before I was done I'd use half the contents.

"The woman—"

"The woman," he repeated in disgust. "You had her restrained. Not one of us would've predicted she'd turn on you the way she did. And not one of us would've done shit differently when she hopped up, with her bare breasts in your face and started..." he trailed off.

I didn't need him to finish. I knew what she'd done. And if it hadn't been me but one of my brothers I would've laughed my ass off.

"I know what she did. But I hesitated," I reminded him.

"Again. Naked woman. Where were you supposed to

grab her? You locked her down and contained her until Shiloh came in for the rescue. You know she's gonna hold that over you for the rest of your life, right?"

I owed Shiloh a bottle of liquor and whatever else she wanted in return for prying the moaning, humping woman off my chest.

"But that wasn't what I was talking about," he went on. "You've been...off for the last few weeks."

The ever-present tightness in my chest constricted into a ball of anxiety and anger.

"Everything's good."

Not an outright lie but still a gross exaggeration. The parts of my life that included Sophie were...mostly good. Except for the minor detail I was going to fuck this up and the best I could hope for was that I'd be the only one bleeding at the end. If Sophie could walk away unharmed it would be worth it. A few days. A few months.

I'd take all the goodness she was offering and drown in it. I'd drink it down like my father did with his booze and binge. I'd suck it back until the well was empty, then just like dear ol' dad I'd wake up one day in a mess of my own making and hate myself.

"So, are we gonna meet this one?" Riddle prodded.

The knot in my chest loosened at the subject change but the remnants of the guilt remained.

I was a selfish motherfucker.

"We're new," I evaded.

"Right."

With that, I heard the water turn off on his side of the wall.

I shoved all the unwanted thoughts of my father's latest bender and all the bullshit that went with it. Wondering when I'd get the call he'd dried out and couldn't find his car keys. I'd go by his house, "find" his keys, then we'd pretend he hadn't just spent a week stupid drunk and I'd take his keys to make sure he didn't drive anywhere while he was working through his demons with liquor. Then in a few months we'd do it again.

And again.

And again.

And again.

Over and over on repeat. It never ended and it never would until his body shut down from all the punishment he'd inflicted. I'd long ago given up on him getting sober. Rehab was not what he needed. Gus Malone needed therapy. He needed to deal with the death of the woman he'd loved and the death of the daughter he adored. Until he did that, rehab was pointless. And Gus refused to acknowledge my mom and sister had once existed so he certainly didn't acknowledge they died.

I slapped the spigot all the way to the left, letting the water heat as hot as the shitty regulator in the locker room shower would allow and I scrubbed.

Unfortunately the scrubbing wouldn't wash away my father's problems, and no matter how much soap I used, the trauma of his abandonment wouldn't rinse down the drain.

Life was life.

Shame and fear.

The shame I wasn't enough.

The fear one day my father would drink himself to death.

When I got back to my locker, my dirty clothes were bagged and someone had left a container of bleach wipes on the bench.

Logically I knew nothing could penetrate the High Abrasion nylon gloves I'd worn during the altercation, yet I still wiped down the combo dial and latch before I opened my locker.

Instead of dressing I grabbed my phone.

I ignored the three calls from my father. I would've done that regardless, but six missed calls from Hayden had my gut twisting. I didn't bother listening to the voice mails or reading the texts. I hit his contact and four rings later he picked up.

"Fuck. Finally."

"Is Sophie—"

"We're at the hospital."

Four words and I couldn't breathe.

"What the fuck for? Is she okay?"

I put the call on speaker and yanked clean clothes out of my bag at the bottom of my locker.

"She's fine, now," he clipped. "After you left she

stayed in her room working. Khloe left and I went to talk to her and she was curled up in bed with a stomachache."

I had my pants on and was pulling on a tee when I asked, "Stomachache?"

"Yeah. Stomachache. An hour later I'm getting out of the shower and hear her yelling for me. I go in, she's shaking and holding her stomach. I thought it was her appendix or some shit. I brought her to Memorial."

I tied my clean boots, grabbed my side arm and knife, and was heading to the door when I prompted, "Was it?"

"No. We've been here for hours. Blood test, urine test, ultrasound. No fever. The doctor can't find the source, but she's feeling better and they're gonna let her leave."

"No way they have the results of blood and urine this fast," I noted, stopping in front of my captain's office.

"You're right, they don't, but the stomachache has gone away. So she'll be discharged soon. Where are you?"

"At the station but I'll be on my way to you after I tell my captain I'm leaving."

"We'll probably be—"

"Do not leave that hospital until I get there, Winslow."

"Roger that."

I would've given him shit if he hadn't disconnected the call and my heart wasn't in my throat.

I needed to get to Sophie.

"Cap?" I called out and waited for his attention to

come to the doorway. "My woman's in the hospital, I need to bounce."

He looked shocked but to his credit he didn't comment.

"I'll call in someone from Bravo. Keep me posted. Go."

"Will do. Thanks."

I jogged through the station and out to my Rover, ignoring another call from my father.

Shame and fear.

Neither took a fucking holiday.

17

"WHY A COP?" I asked.

We were in my bed and I was curled into Valentine, doing my best to forget how embarrassed I was.

This was after he'd shown up at the hospital and stormed into my room like there was a bomb threat and he was there to clear the room. And that was after I'd spent hours in the hospital being poked—blood draws—and prodded—blood pressure, stomach ultrasound looking for appendicitis.

It was decided I hadn't been intoxicated—no, duh—appendicitis ruled out, no flu, negative for food poisoning, negative for pregnancy—again no, duh. Nothing. So I was discharged with a prescription to treat ulcers and the directive to reduce my stress level, curb my coffee intake, no spicy foods, and nothing fried even though the breath test that was administered came back negative for some bacteria I couldn't remember the name of. Bottom line was, the doctor couldn't find anything wrong and when the cramping and nausea went away I was fine.

Now I was mortified I'd gone to the hospital for a tummy ache. Though, in my defense when I'd agreed to let Hayden take me in I felt like I was growing an alien in my stomach and it was both fighting to escape and eating my insides at the same time.

"Being a cop was my backup plan," Valentine answered.

"What did you want to be before a cop?"

"A truck driver."

A startled laugh escaped.

"A truck driver?"

"Yup. I had this friend in the sixth grade, his dad was a truck driver. He owned his own rig, if he was home when I was spending the night he used to let us sleep in the truck. Mr. Shorty had these bumper stickers in the sleep area. There wasn't a space that wasn't covered. Every new place he hauled to he got a sticker. To me that truck represented adventure."

"And nine-year-old you wanted adventure?"

He was quiet a moment.

Then he confirmed, "Nine-year-old me wanted adventure. I knew I didn't want a job like my dad who wore a suit to work and sat in an office. I didn't want to do the same thing every day."

I thought back to when I was nine. I had no idea what I'd wanted or didn't want. I was too busy playing with my Barbies to think about important life issues. Hell, when

I'd gone to college, I hadn't concerned myself with a major. The thought of deciding what I wanted to do for the rest of my life at eighteen paralyzed me. At twenty when the time came to declare, I went behind my mother's back and chose marketing over her demand I get a degree in human resources management.

"Maybe my mother is right and I'm aimless," I muttered.

With my head resting on Valentine's chest, I couldn't see his face but I knew he was staring down at me. I could feel it, his attention. He was interested in what I had to share, and he'd wait and listen to whatever I had to say.

"I didn't know what I wanted at nine or eighteen or twenty-five or thirty. All I knew was what I was doing wasn't what I wanted for the rest of my life. My mother knew and the more she pressured me to find something, settle in, find a man, get married, be an adult, the more I pushed back. And now I'm wondering if I did that out of spite or rebellion or immaturity. All I know is the longer it went on, her hounding me, the more annoyed I became until I purposely did the opposite of what she wanted."

Valentine's arm resting across my back, holding me to him, tightened.

"There's a fine line between guiding and being overbearing."

He's right.

"I'm not disagreeing," I started before blowing out a breath. "But now I can't stop wondering how much of it I caused."

"Soph—"

"Hear me out. She's always been strict. A single mother who was raising a child on her own with no help while working full time to keep us fed and housed. When I was young, she used to tell me it was important to be self-sufficient. She wanted me educated with a good job so I'd never have to rely on a man. That was nonnegotiable. She'd struggled when my dad bailed. I get that. She wanted me settled and in a career. It wasn't until I hit thirty she started harping on me needing to find a man and get married. But before that, it was all about me and financial security. Which now has me thinking how sad it is that it was never about happiness. She never talked about finding what would make me happy."

"You need money to live, baby, but nothing's more important than finding your happy."

Was my mother happy now?

Nathan adored her. He worshiped her. I knew he cared deeply for me, he didn't hide it, and more often than not when my mother started in on me, he'd have a gentle, quiet word with her and she'd let it go. That was, until she felt like bringing it up again.

"She's married now. My stepfather Nathan is mellow. Nice guy, treats her like gold. I joke that it's a crime against the universe those two being together. I was happy for her when she introduced me to him. I was thrilled when she told me they were getting married. She seemed happy, but is it weird I never asked her?"

"Asked her what?"

"If she was happy."

Valentine didn't say anything, which I took as his confirmation it wasn't only weird, it made me a horrible daughter.

"I know when you met her she was behaving like a shrew. But she's my mother and I want her happy," I admitted.

His arm went impossibly tight around me.

"Of course you do, Soph, she's your mom."

I had a mom to complain about.

He didn't have a mom.

Damn.

"So a cop, not a truck driver." I moved us back to safer territory.

"Know what you're doing, baby, and you don't have to."

It was a long time ago.

His voice tight with grief.

Not only did I have to, I wanted to. He left work, rushed to my side, brought me home, tucked me into bed, then proceeded to crawl in next to me and hold me. Now was not the time for his mind to wander to anything that would cause him pain.

"I want to know about you."

He gave it a second, loosened his arm around me, and started skimming my hip with his fingers.

"I didn't stop wanting to be a truck driver until I was thirteen. That's when I met Officer Manning. My dad was so lost in shock he didn't notice I'd slipped out the front door. Officer Manning did. He sat next me on the porch. Neither of us said anything. He didn't offer me bullshit platitudes. He didn't treat me like a little kid and tell me to go back inside. He just sat there silently giving me strength on the worst day of my life.

"That's when I knew I wanted to be a cop. That's when I understood what it meant to be of service. Being a cop isn't about writing tickets, it's not about locking up criminals, it's not about kicking in doors or serving warrants. It's about that thirteen-year-old whose life has been irrevocably changed for the worse and sitting next to him in case he needs you. It's about humanity and decency. Knowing there is nothing you can do to bring a mother and sister back to life but still sitting with a grieving kid."

Mother *and* sister.

Grieving.

My broken heart started bleeding.

No, it hemorrhaged.

"Valentine," I whispered.

"Long time ago, baby."

Broken. Sorrow-filled. Distant.

I tipped my head back so I could see his face.

Jaw tight. Eyes focused on the ceiling. Caught in the past.

Shit.

I did that to him.

"It could be a lifetime, honey, and it wouldn't be long enough."

"Truth," he muttered, not looking at me.

I fell silent and settled back on his chest.

"Vienna was ten."

His sister.

Valentine and Vienna.

I blinked away the tears and fought to keep my body loose despite his rough voice.

When he said no more I slid my arm across his stomach and held on.

"She's been gone longer than she lived."

Oh, God.

"The mindfuck of that is, if I don't force myself to remember, I forget she existed."

I bet his idea of forcing himself to remember was merely thinking about her. And I'd bet he thought of Vienna and his mother every day.

There was nothing to say to that. So I just held on and gave him what I could while my soul wept for all he'd lost, for the young girl who never got a chance to grow up, for a mother who left her boy, for a husband who lost two out of the three parts of his world.

I felt Valentine take a deep breath, and when he let it out, he relaxed. Proof positive I needed to tread lightly. Go gentle and proceed with caution.

It was his story to tell and he'd give me more when he was ready.

18

NO. *No. No.*

This was wrong.

All wrong.

I didn't need to look over at Valentine to know.

The disheveled man stumbling out the front door holding a blood-soaked towel around his right hand said enough.

Explained enough.

"Fuck!"

His roar echoed throughout the Rover.

"Fucking hell."

The man pitched to the side but caught his balance before he fell.

Valentine got out of the Rover.

I disobeyed his previous order and got out to follow him.

I knew he'd be pissed but there was no way I was letting him deal with this alone.

I'd known it was going to be bad after he'd ignored the first two calls from his dad but picked up the third, and when he did everything about him changed. The change wasn't good, it was hideous.

We'd been on our way to lunch. It was three days after my hospital visit and I needed real food. That first night he'd stayed over at my house. The next two nights I'd stayed at his. Going to sleep without Valentine but waking up with him next to me. He'd fed me toast, grilled cheeses, pasta, and plain chicken.

I'd wanted real food.

That was the only reason I was here with him running this errand to his father's house.

He'd told me it wouldn't take but a few minutes and for me to wait in the Rover.

Thinking he didn't want his father meeting me had stung.

Now I understood.

Something was very, very wrong.

"Car, Sophie," he clipped.

His father stumbled, missed the first step down, and lurched forward. Valentine got to him before he could take a header. I quickly maneuvered around the men, opened the storm door, and held it open for Valentine.

The first thing that hit me was the putrid smell wafting out of the house.

I waited until Valentine cleared the threshold, found

the doohickey that held the pneumatic mechanism open, and slid it into place.

Then I watched in abject horror as Valentine looked around the living room. His face the picture of disgust and agony.

I swallowed down the sob threatening to break free.

"You coulda answer...two...ago," Valentine's father drunkenly slurred. "Called...yous fault."

Oh my God.

"Sit, Pop," Valentine demanded.

The man swayed and dropped his ass into a recliner.

"Let me see."

Valentine didn't give his father a chance to lift his blood-soaked hand before he reached down and grabbed it.

Not wanting to see what kind of injury would cause that kind of bleeding, I glanced around the living room. Old ratty furniture that needed to be thrown away ten years ago filled the living room. An old box TV sat on a stand. The walls were decorated in pictures. A huge family portrait hung on the wall above the couch.

No. No. No.

Valentine. His sister. His mom. His dad.

All of them together.

A family.

It was one of those professional studio pictures. The men in jeans and white button-ups. The girls in jeans and pretty white blouses. Valentine's mother was behind him. He was sitting on a stool, feet up on the rung, her arm around his shoulder, his arm bent at the elbow, his hand holding hers mid-chest. Vienna stood next to him, her father's arm around her, holding her hand in an identical pose as mother and son. Valentine was probably sitting because he was already taller than his mother.

It would've been beautiful, if it hadn't been hanging in a room that smelled like throw-up and rotting food. It would've been a lovely memorial to a beautiful family if I didn't suspect the man who lived in that house stared at that picture while he drank himself sick.

No. No. No.

"Jesus. Don't move."

Valentine stalked out of the room with none of his normal predatory grace. It looked like his legs were wooden, his steps heavy, his strides purposeful—if that purpose was to escape the trappings of the living room.

I moved to the window. After fiddling with the lock I finally got it to open. The windowsill was green and full of years' worth of grime, laying testament to the idea that the last time the window had been opened was probably the last time Mrs. Malone had opened it.

Gross.

"Don't bother, Sophie, we're not staying."

I turned to see him with a brown bottle of hydrogen peroxide in one hand and small first aid kit in the other.

"Fuck," he clipped. "I need paper towels. Don't move."

"I'll get them," I said and rushed into the kitchen.

Then I wished I hadn't.

Honest to God, there was nothing to clean the mess. It wasn't the dishes or the broken bottle of liquor that was on the floor, glass shards everywhere, which might explain the cut on Mr. Malone's hand. It wasn't even the trash and years' worth of debris on the counters. It was the filth. The mold. The stench that was so bad I gagged.

"Told you to wait in the fucking Rover," Valentine growled as he stomped by me.

"Valentine—"

"Not now, Sophie."

I clamped my mouth shut.

He nabbed a roll of paper towels from somewhere. I didn't dare tell him they were probably contaminated with a flesh-eating virus along with the rest of the kitchen, which should've been condemned as a health risk.

Valentine paused next to me. His mood was palpable, I could feel it choking me. His frightening, menacing, ominous energy slammed into me like a thousand needles puncturing my skin, plunging venom into my blood.

Venom I knew lived in him.

This was his father.

His reality.

I was an intruder.

He never meant for me to see this.

And suddenly I was pissed. Irrationally, insanely angry. If I hadn't been with him when his father's call of distress had come he never, ever, would've given this to me.

"Take a good fucking look around, Sophie. This is me. This is where I come from. You still wanna tell me I'm worth it, baby? You wanna tell me you don't deserve better than this fucking filth?"

"This isn't you," I chanced.

"This is where I grew up. This is my house."

I was right. He was going to keep this big, huge gaping wound hidden.

"This is your father's house. I spent the last two nights at *your* house."

He jerked back, his lips curled.

"Go out to the Rover and wait for me."

Oh no.

Hell no.

"No. Go clean up your dad. I'll wait."

"Sophie," he growled. "Now's not the fucking—"

I broke.

There was no other excuse. In that moment I understood the old adage about seeing red. I saw it—oh boy, did I see red. The room was hued, his face close to mine hazed, and I lost my ever-loving fucking mind.

"Shut. Up. Stop talking, Valentine. This is not your house. This is not you. So shut your fucking mouth and go help your father. I'd offer to clean up while you're doing that but short of calling in a demo team nothing's gonna put a dent in this mess. I'll need to come back after a trip to Costco and you find me gloves to withstand the acid I'll need to use to kill the germs. I'm not going outside. I'm not going to the Rover. I'll leave when you do."

"Soph—"

"We walk out of here together, Valentine. End. Of."

I didn't wait for him to argue. This time I was the one stomping. Unfortunately, I didn't do it as good as he did and I didn't have far to go. I stood next to the window sucking in as much fresh air as I could and waited for Valentine to do whatever he was going to do. A quick glance at Mr. Malone told me I'd been right. His gaze was fixed on the family portrait above the couch. The man had no idea I was in the house. He was either too intoxicated or in such a deep state of depression he was in a trance.

Probably both.

Valentine made quick work cleaning up his father's hand. He took the bloody towel and the rest of his kit back into the kitchen.

I stood there staring at Valentine's father.

I'll make it worth it.

Mr. Malone was the reason Valentine didn't feel worthy. It wasn't a woman. It wasn't anyone at work or his friends.

It was this man staring at a picture of his dead wife and daughter and ignoring the son who was alive.

I'll make it worth it.

Valentine came back into the room and his gaze locked with mine.

Shame.

That was all I could see in his beautiful, stormy eyes.

That was unacceptable.

Deplorable even.

"Are you ready or do we need to do something else before we leave?"

He blinked.

Big, strong, brave Valentine blinked—like he was unsure what to do or what he was supposed to do with me. It was a safe assumption this wasn't the first time he'd seen his father in this state. I'd bet it wasn't only frequent, it was most of the time.

It wasn't nice, but I loathed Mr. Malone.

He did this.

To my Valentine.

His son.

I understood grief. I understood there was no timeframe on when the sorrow of losing someone or the people you love lets you out of the death grip of anguish. What I did know was, a father never, ever should make his son feel unworthy.

And I didn't give the first fuck I was being insensitive and judgmental.

"Honey?" I prompted.

"Close the window."

I did as he said but not before taking in a huge lungful of outside air before I did.

Without saying goodbye to his father or wasting any time, he made his way to me, tagged my hand, and pulled me out of that hellhole of torture.

Valentine took care of the front door. I waited by the Rover and waited until he rounded the hood. But before he opened his door I announced, "If you think for one second you're taking me home and dropping me at my apartment you're mistaken."

"Soph—"

"I'm going to *your* house, Valentine."

He clenched his jaw so hard I hoped he didn't crack a tooth.

The lock bleeped.

"*Fuck.*"

An hour ago his frustrated growl would've made me back off. I would've been worried I'd pushed too hard or too fast for him to talk about things that were buried under layers of pain.

Now?

I was scared. I knew if I didn't tear this open right now while I had my shot, he'd sew it back shut and lock me out.

Then I'd lose him forever.

I'll make it worth it.

19

ANGRY DIDN'T TOUCH the emotion I was feeling.

Hell, I wasn't even *feeling* it. I was breathing fire. Every inhale burned. Every exhale felt like it scorched my throat.

She saw.

Sophie fucking saw. She saw him, the house, my neglect.

Fuck.

The drive home from my father's was silent.

I was positive that was a mistake, an even bigger one than not taking her back to her apartment and dropping her off. I needed to end this. And now I was going to have to do it at my house where she had no car instead of at hers where I could leave right after.

As soon as I shut the front door I ripped my own heart out, doing it fast.

"This needs to end."

Sophie tossed her purse on the coffee table next to her laptop and slowly turned to face me.

"Why?"

"You're not seriously asking me that after what you saw."

Since the very first day in the grocery store she couldn't hide her thoughts from me. Not the immediate attraction, not her interest, not her embarrassment that bled into the shyness that had made her flee. And every time she'd looked at me since then her eyes spoke before she did. And right then they were flashing with anger.

Her pissed off, I could deal with.

"I asked, so yeah, I'm *seriously* asking," she said.

"My father's a drunk who lives in a pit," I pointed out the obvious.

Calmly she moved around the table, putting more distance between us. My insides withered at the implication; Sophie always moved toward me, never away. She liked to be close and I liked her there where I could touch her, feel her body curled into mine, soak in all her goodness and use it to kill the pain.

"Not to be callous but I don't see what that has to do with you. Or me. Or us. Or why you're ending us."

"That's not the first time I've walked into that house and seen him like that and it won't be the last."

For the first time since I'd met her I detested her gaze on me. She saw too much. She always did and what had once been precious and cherished and brought me peace now felt like a noose. Either she was going to do it or I was, but I was under no illusion that by the time this conversation was over, I'd be the one hanging.

I'd be the one ruined.

She was it for me. The woman I'd never wanted. The one who I knew I should've walked away from immediately. The one who if I wasn't broken I'd spend my life with. Who I'd love and adore for the rest of my life. The one who would bring me to my knees.

I was a selfish asshole but I wasn't cruel. I'd tighten the damn rope around my throat myself if it meant she walked away unscathed. I had to cut her loose before she was in too deep. Before she fell in love. Before she wasted any more time on a jackass who wasn't worth it.

"I suspect as much."

Fucking hell.

"Then you know I'm a shit son. A total piece of shit who leaves his father to live in that."

Sophie tilted her head ever so slightly, kept her expression neutral, and like we weren't talking about my alcoholic father and the squalor he lived in, asked, "Is that what you think?"

"No, I don't think that. I fucking know it."

She nodded.

I was dangerously close to losing my shit. Her unemotional tone and gestures which contradicted the fire in her eyes pissed me right the hell off. I needed her to yell at me, tell me what a motherfucker I was. Ask me what kind of heartless dick leaves his father to rot away.

I needed it.

I needed her righteous fury.

I needed her to hate me.

"What exactly do you think you should be doing?"

Was she fucking crazy?

"I don't know, Sophie," I spat. "I suspect a son who wasn't such an asshole would figure it out. But, I'm not that son. I'm an asshole who allows his father to sleep in his own vomit."

"Does it make you feel better to call yourself horrible names?"

Fuck this.

Fuck it.

If she was too blind to see what was right in front of her then I'd force her to see it. I'd shove it down her throat until she had no other choice but to run away so she could breathe.

"I hate him, Sophie. Every day he wakes up and spits on my mother's memory. On Vivi. On the family we once had. Every day he puts that bottle to his lips he disrespects what we had and we had a good family. I had a great mom. A sweet sister. A beautiful life. The kind you see on TV. Nice house in a nice neighborhood. Clean, good food on the table, birthday parties in the backyard. You saw it now, what he's done, how he's desecrated the home he shared with his family. With his wife. The mother of his children. The mother who took me to baseball and football practice. The woman who shared his bed. Who took Vivi to ice skating and soccer. Who kept his home and loved him. Kissed him every morning before he left for work. Held his hand often. Sat next to him at my games, at Vivi's. I lost them, too.

"One day my perfect family, in a nice neighborhood, in a nice, clean house, with two parents who I knew loved me and a sister who idolized me, a family I loved, was gone. Vanished. Two of them dead. One of them forcing me to watch him slowly kill himself. And the fuck of it is, I understand him. I get it. The way he loved my mother. He didn't hide it. She came alive when she was with him, but he breathed for her. He loved me and my sister but he adored my mother. If it had been me and Vivi who died, he would've been able to go on. But not her. I wasn't worth it to him. I wasn't then and I'm not now.

"But that's not why I hate him. Why there are times like today when I see him, when I see what he's done to my home, to the memory of our family, when I don't wonder why God took my mother instead of him. I hate that I think that, so I hate him more. I hate he took the father I loved away from me. I hate he's making me watch him slowly kill himself. I hate that no matter how hard I've tried to get him help in the past it never sticks. I fucking hate I'm not worth it to him to get sober and stay that way so I can at least have my father in everything I lost."

I felt every millisecond of the breath I sucked in. It seemed frozen in my chest in direct contrast to the fire pumping through my body.

Hideous, toxic memories assaulted me like they

always did. Hatred and guilt fueled me to push on and give her the rest.

"I can't do this with you. I tried. I thought I could do it. But I've spent the last twenty-seven years of my life promising myself I'd never be like him. And all it took was you looking at me and I got lost in something I can't allow. I can't be him, sitting on that couch, day in and day out staring at a picture of the woman he lost drinking away the pain. This has to end before I lose myself completely. Before you get hurt."

The anger had leaked out of Sophie's gaze, but that wasn't to say she wasn't angry. I saw her hands shaking. Her body stiff and perfectly still.

I was so close to getting what I needed, the repulsion was leaking in. The silence was deafening—blood roared in my ears, my gut clenched, and the pieces of my heart that weren't already broken shattered.

As soul crushing as it was, I was doing the right thing.

I had to let her go. She had to be free. Sophie Huxley was a one-in-million woman, the kind who needed a good man who'd love her completely. And that was exactly what she was going to get.

"I'm not worth it," she whispered. "That's what you're saying."

Jesus *fucking* Christ.

"No, Sophie!" I shouted. "What I'm saying is you *are* worth it. You're worth everything. You deserve a man who isn't—"

"Call yourself a name again, Valentine Malone, and see what happens," she snapped indignantly.

Why wasn't she leaving?

"Fuck this," I snarled.

If she wouldn't leave I would.

I didn't bother looking at her when I got to the door.

"Don't be here when I get back."

"I'm not leaving," she warned.

Without fully turning I craned my neck to look at Sophie.

She'd never been more beautiful, with her pretty eyes boldly holding me captive.

"I don't want you here," I lied.

I watched her flinch before she rallied.

"I wish with all my heart your mom and sister were still with you. My heart hurts for you and I wish I could stop your pain but I can't. The only thing I can do is stand my ground and prove to you, you are worth it. You're worth everything. You're worth my dignity. You're worth the pain you just inflicted. You're worth my anger. You're just plain worth it. So you might not want me here, but I'm staying. I'm going to fight for this until I have nothing left. I'm going to fight for you even if I have to fight you to get it. You do what you need to do but know when you get back I'll be here. So come prepared to battle, Valentine. I won't give you up."

Fuck.

Her aim was true.

So when I walked out my front door I did it bleeding.

20

I WAS SHAKING.

My stomach was knotted worse than the other day when Hayden made me go to the hospital.

Everything hurt.

There wasn't a single inch of me that didn't feel like I'd been beaten.

My Valentine, so strong, so broken.

His perfect life torn apart by tragedy.

I wished I had my car here so I could go back to his childhood home and burn it to the ground. Of course, I'd get Mr. Malone to safety first. I might not like the man but I'd still save him even though he hadn't saved his son.

My mother wasn't loving or affectionate. But I knew in her way she did love me. She'd provided for me after my dad left. She hadn't sank into a bottle or lost herself in the grief of losing the man she loved. And she had loved my father deeply. She'd tried to hide it, but as I got older it was obvious. Plus I'd found lots of pictures of them from before I was born and a few of all three of us. I'd never seen my mother look as happy as she had in those pictures. It sucked but not even with Nathan did she look that carefree and blissful. She looked like a woman madly in love. Then years later that man had abandoned her.

Now I understood.

Standing on the precipice of losing the man I loved, I got it.

How that would change a person. Shape their future. Kill important parts of you.

It was strange how my mother could hold me distant while smothering me at the same time. How she could be cold while at the same time showing me how much she cared. Admittedly her delivery sucked, but she truly wanted what was best for me. Happiness didn't factor because she knew all too well happiness could be fleeting. There one day, gone the next. So instead she wanted to make sure I would never be unprepared for life.

But she didn't teach me how to love.

And now I was questioning myself.

You fought for the people you loved, right?

You didn't let them push you away, right?

I could love the pain away, right?

Gah!

I didn't know what I was doing. I swiped my purse off the table, dug through it, tagged my phone, then plopped down on Valentine's couch and called the only person I could.

"Yo," Hayden greeted, out of breath.

Unwanted thoughts of him with Khloe made my lips curl in disgust.

"You busy?"

"I was, but I'm not now. What's wrong?"

Gross!

"Never mind. I'll—"

"Sophie, I'm at the Hope Center playing ball. What's wrong?"

"If you're playing ball why'd you answer?"

"Because it's you and I always answer when you call no matter what I'm doing. Correction, I *almost* always answer unless I'm otherwise pleasurably engaged. You know that. Stop evading and tell me what's wrong."

I don't know what I did to deserve a best friend as good as Hayden but I was grateful. So grateful, I forgave Oakley for being such a monumental prick because he gave me this.

"Everything," I admitted.

"Where are you?"

Now he sounded like he was huffing, which meant he was running so he could come to me.

But he couldn't.

Not this time.

I'd started this. Now I had to see it through.

"I'm at Valentine's but—"

"On my way."

Shit.

"Hayden, you can't come here."

"Come again?"

"Just listen to me."

"I would but you're not talking except to tell me everything's wrong and I can't come to you."

I shouldn't have called him. Hayden was just as protective as Valentine. This could—and would—turn ugly fast if Hayden came here and Valentine came home. Likely Valentine would tell Hayden to take me and Hayden wouldn't like that so he'd gladly whisk me away, then I wouldn't be able to do what I needed to do.

"I think I screwed up and I need your help."

"How'd you screw up?"

"Valentine broke up with me and left. He told me he didn't want me here when he got back and I told him I wasn't leaving," I rushed out.

"Fuck that! I'm coming to get you."

God!

"Please don't. I need you to listen but I can't tell you everything without breaking Valentine's confidence. But I can give you a little so you understand the gist, then you can tell me if I messed up and how to fix it."

There was a brief pause and a car door slammed on his end.

"You can't come here," I hissed, panic rising to a fever-pitch.

"Start talking, Huxley, but I make no promises."

I started talking. I told him just enough without telling him things that I knew for certain Valentine wouldn't want him to know. Which meant I left out his father's drinking problem. But I did explain that Valentine lost his mother and sister and his father hadn't recovered. I also had to tell him that Valentine's father made him feel unworthy. I knew Hayden would never tell him anything that I said, but it still felt like a betrayal. But I needed him to understand so he could guide me.

"Did I totally screw up?" I whispered when I was done.

"No, Soph, you didn't screw up," Hayden said, then blew out a breath. "Did he say where he was going?"

"No."

"Do you want me to go and find him?"

He'd do that for me but also for Valentine. The two men were friends and Hayden was the type of friend who didn't allow his friends to suffer in silence. Case in point, now, when he'd put himself in front of Valentine's pain and make himself a target to help him see his way through it.

"No. Just talk me through this. He was really mad, Hayden."

"Fuck!" he clipped. "Can I come pick you up? We'll go someplace and talk then I'll drop you back at his place."

"I don't know how long he'll be gone and I have to be here when he gets back. I *have* to be here. Before he left I told him I'd be here, ready to fight to prove to him he's worth it. If I leave he'll never see what he means to me. He won't ever trust it. You didn't see him, Hayden. He was empty, haunted, totally destroyed. I can't leave this house until I either win or I have nothing left."

"Christ, you're killing me, Sophie."

"Help. Me. Hayden. Am I not supposed to stay and fight? Am I doing this wrong? I can't screw this up or I'll lose him. I saw it happen, the second he shut down on me. I have one shot at getting him back."

"You love him."

He wasn't asking yet I still answered, "Yes. I just need to know if I'm loving him the right way."

Hayden blew out a long sigh.

"This is gonna go one of two ways, Soph. He's either blowing off steam, working shit out in his head and he's going to come home and know he made a mistake, or he's somewhere shoring up his defenses. If it's the latter it's gonna be ugly and you have to be prepared to take some emotional hits. He's gonna be spun up, his pain is going to be close to the surface, and he'll strike out at you."

Damn.

That didn't sound good.

"Is there a third way this can go?"

"No, sweetheart, it's gonna go one of those two ways with no in-between."

My best friend didn't sound happy.

"I only know Valentine as a mellow dude. Great with the kids at the center. Good friends when they come around. Solid guy when we've hung out. But I only know what I've seen and all of that is surface, so I gotta ask, are you scared of him?"

"Scared of him?"

"Do you think he'd get physical?"

"Never!"

"You didn't—"

"I don't have to think about my answer. The answer is no. Am I scared? Yes. Very. I'm scared he's too far gone and I won't be able to reach him. I'm scared I won't be enough for him to want to face what's eating him. It's huge—so big he's hidden from it for over two decades. That's what I'm scared of. That's what I need you to help me with."

I glanced around Valentine's living room with new eyes, a clearer understanding. It was minimalistic and clean. No clutter anywhere to the point of boring. No daily detritus. Dishes were done right after we were done eating. Garbage was taken out daily even though the bag wasn't full. His bathroom was the same—clean, tidy, void of any kind of mess. He made his bed every day. I sniffed trying to catch a whiff of something but there was nothing.

Clean, sterile, barren.

I thought it was because he was a bachelor and didn't care about his environs. But he did care. He cared so much he'd rather live in a house completely devoid of any personality than live in a home with a speck of dirt or a full bag of trash.

How long had he lived in that filth before he got out?

"You still with me?" Hayden called out.

"Yeah, sorry. I missed what you said."

"I said, you're enough. And if you can't break through and make him see the woman he has on his hands, then I don't care what he's going through, he's not right for you."

"Don't say that," I whispered.

"Sophie, please listen to me," he said on a long exhale. "I love you more than I love my own blood. You're my best friend. You're the only person in this world that I trust. You're enough. More than enough. I like Valentine. I hope he doesn't end up being stupid and that's what he'll be if he shuts you out. He'll lose you, then he'll spend the rest of his life regretting it. That'll suck for him. But that will be on him.

"The last thing I can tell you is this. You're strong. You're a fighter. So stay and put up one hell of a good fight. Buckle up and let the bullshit he's probably going to spew bounce off you. But you're gonna have to know when to quit and walk away. And honestly, that might be the only thing that wakes him up, depending on how deep he is into his trauma. He might have to lose you before he can find himself. Then it will be up to you if you take him back or not."

God, I hoped it didn't come to that.

"So you think I did the right thing?"

There was a moment of hesitation before my best friend rocked my world. "I think he's the luckiest son of a bitch on the planet. I think he'll never do better than you. I think he's going to pull his head out of his ass and see who he has on his arm and in his bed and he'll know love like he's never known."

I was taking that as Hayden thinking I was doing the right thing.

"You know *you* only deserve the best, right?" I chanced telling him.

"And let me guess, you don't think Khloe's it."

There was a thread of humor in his voice but still I treaded cautiously.

"Um, no."

"Fear not, my love-sick friend. I am not in the market to settle down. Khloe knows what she's getting and what she's not getting from me."

Well, that was the best news I'd heard since I met the bitch.

"Your objections are noted. I won't bring her to the apartment anymore."

"Don't be ridiculous. She's not the first one who I'm not particularly fond of." *Understatement*. "It's your apartment, too. Bring home who you want. You know the rule; as long as they don't use my shampoo and conditioner it's all good. And if they steal my clothes it's immediate expulsion. Though we need another rule, seeing as this one's a coffee hog. I get right of first refusal for the last cup of coffee when I'm home."

"What are you talking about? I've never seen Khloe drink coffee."

"She drank almost a whole pot the other morning."

God, I did not want to think about that day or the medical bills that would soon be coming in for an ER visit and the useless tests the doctor ran.

"I know you said that, and I thought it was strange. Like I said, I've never seen her with a coffee."

"Just a warning, pal. Women like it when you pay attention to their preferences. That goes double for a coffee lover."

"Guess that's why I don't pay attention. Don't wanna send the wrong message."

I rolled my eyes to the ceiling.

"You good?" he gently prodded.

"No. I won't be good until Valentine comes home and we have this out."

"Rephrase. Are you better than when you called me?"

"Absolutely."

Thank God for Hayden. I don't know what I'd do without him.

"Right. Then I'm gonna let you go. Call me if you need anything. I'm always here."

"I know you are and I love you for it, Winslow."

There was a stretch of silence before he ended the call with, "There will never come a time when I won't be at your back."

With that, he disconnected.

I tossed my phone on the couch and rested my head on the cushion and waited for Valentine to come home.

Then I waited longer.

Night fell and he still hadn't returned.

So I sat there and readied myself for the battle I knew would come.

A battle I had to win or I'd lose everything.

21

FEELING like more of an asshole than I've ever felt in my whole life, I walked into my house.

My guilt and shame were no longer at war. After hours of sitting on my father's ratty-assed couch watching my father stare at a portrait of his dead wife and daughter, I snapped. The results of that were not pretty.

My father had a total and complete drunken breakdown—twenty-seven years too late—but he'd come apart, nonetheless.

The fallout was ugly, leaving more scars on my already mutilated soul. The only thing that was solved by having a front row seat to my father's trauma was the understanding I couldn't change him. I could spend the rest of my life feeling guilty, begging, pleading, wishing, wanting. Until he wanted to deal with the grief in a healthy way there was nothing I could do.

This wasn't the movies or the 1980's TV show I once

thought my life emulated, with a happy mom and dad and the perfect family who could weather any storm and everything would be fixed in a sixty-minute episode.

This was life.

Gus Malone was an irredeemable alcoholic.

I finally accepted it.

At some point during his break as I watched him throw everything he could get his hands on around the house I came to accept something else. I was not him.

I was me, the kid who had a great start at life. The kid who knew a bounty of love. A kid with a great sister who was sweet, and once I gave myself time to remember her I couldn't stop thinking about how funny she was. I'd had a mom who baked really great birthday cakes and always made her family feel special. Who loved me.

Then I became the teenager who lost what I'd been granted for a short while.

Nothing more. Nothing less.

Life. Loss. Tragedy. I was not special. I was not the only person on the planet who had bad shit happen to them. Neither was my father. Plenty of men tragically lost their wives or children.

I was not Gus Malone.

But I was a coward.

That realization was what drove me to a place I'd never been.

I wish I could say sitting with my mom and sister in a dark cemetery had given me peace, or even a sense of peace, but it didn't. What I found was closure. The day I watched their caskets being lowered into the ground was the last I'd been there.

Guilt.

I'd given my life over to guilt.

Guilty I was a shit son—I couldn't save my father from his drinking. I couldn't find it in me to visit my mom. I didn't love Vienna enough to put flowers on her grave.

The relief I felt when I found Sophie sleeping on my couch was a living and breathing entity that filled my house with hope.

I'd fucked up—huge.

I had one shot at making this right and suddenly the relief I'd felt turned to fear.

She was it for me.

Before I could decide if I was going to pick Sophie up and take her to my bed or sit on the chair and watch her sleep, her eyes came open.

The prettiest eyes I'd ever seen.

Intelligent eyes that held me hostage.

I knew she saw through me when her expression softened.

But then, she always saw, and I hoped she always would.

Still, I gave her what she needed to hear first.

"I'm sorry for every fucked-up word I said. I'm sorry I lied to you. I'm sorry I let you down. I'm sorry I hurt you and I promise you I will never do it again."

Sophie pushed her hair off her face and tucked it behind her ear.

"You'll hurt me again," she whispered.

Fuck. Fuck. Fuck.

"I won't, Soph—"

"You will," she asserted. "It's impossible not to spend time with someone, especially someone you care about, and expect to never hurt their feelings. It happens. It will happen. I will hurt your feelings, you'll hurt mine. That's just the way of the world."

Spend time with someone.

I held onto those words like a lifeline.

Before I could come up with something to say, she beat me to it. "Are you here to go to battle?"

Hell yes, I was.

We were battling it out until I convinced her to forgive my fool ass.

"Yes."

Sophie immediately untucked her legs, rolled to sit, then finally took her feet. And when she did, she squared up.

Magnificent.

So fucking beautiful in her bravery.

"Right. I'm not leaving."

"No, baby, you're not. And if I can state my case and you forgive me I'm never letting you go."

"I'm not?" She shook her head. "You're not?"

"Nope. Not ever letting you go."

That's when she broke.

This time it wasn't her hands that were shaking. It was her whole body. I was across the room scooping her into my arms just as her first tear fell.

"Please don't cry," I begged. "I'm sorry, baby. I'm such a motherfucker."

Without warning she pinched the back of my biceps.

Goddamn, that hurt.

"That's what happens when you call yourself a name," she growled.

The growl was sexy. The irritation on her face cute. The pinch would've also been cute if she hadn't been trying to tear the skin.

"Copy."

I remained silent all the way back to the bedroom and waited until I gently deposited her on the bed before I said, "Get comfortable, Sophie, I need to change."

No way in fuck was I crawling into bed with the filth of my father's house still lingering on my clothes.

I rushed to change, went to the bathroom to wash my hands, and scrubbed nearly as hard as I did the day I was cleansing the naked woman from my skin. That seemed to be a theme—me always trying to wash someone else's mess out of my life.

By the time I got back to bed, Sophie was on her side, watching the bathroom door.

Waiting.

Christ, I was a dick. I'd made her wait all day and into the night for me to come home.

"Did you eat?"

"No. But I'm not hungry and I swear if you try to force food on me when all I want you to do is get in this bed with me and talk to me, I swear I'll get creative in my violence."

I had no doubt.

With her pinch fresh in my mind, I let the topic of food go, hit the lights, and crawled in next to her.

"Turn, baby. I want to hold you."

"I want to see your face," she whispered and offered her hand.

When I took it, her other hand immediately came up to bracket mine between hers.

My sweet Sophie.

After everything I put her through she was offering me comfort when she should have kicked me in the balls and made me get to my knees and beg her for forgiveness.

"I went back to my dad's."

There wasn't enough light in the room for me to see her clearly but it looked like she was frowning.

"The first few hours we sat there in silence. I don't know if he knew I was even there. He was just staring at the family picture."

"The one above the couch?"

As fucked up as earlier had been I was now relieved she knew, that she'd seen him, and how he lived. No one else knew, just her.

"My mom was so excited the day that picture was taken. Our first professional family picture. I thought it was goofy as shit, all of us dressed in jeans and white shirts."

"How old were you?"

"Twelve." A year and a few months later and half that family was gone. "Vienna was just happy Mom let her wear lip gloss. Dad's decree was no makeup until Vivi turned thirteen. He used to tell her she was too beautiful to put that stuff on her face. He was always telling her how pretty she was, that God had blessed him with a daughter who looked like her momma. Before we left the house that day, he grabbed the back of my neck and told me I was the best son a man could have, humoring my mom, being cool about the picture even though he knew I was missing baseball practice. That was him. Always finding his times to tell us how much he loved us."

I had to stop as the bittersweet memories of a father I no longer had tumbled through my head. A man I was proud to have as a father. A man I wanted to be just like.

"It took like three months for Mom to get that big-ass print back from the photographer. It took her forever to get it just right on the wall. The whole time my dad stood there holding the frame to the wall, smiling. That was him, whatever she wanted. He smiled and gave it to her. And she returned the favor."

"Your mom's beautiful. So is Vivi," Sophie whispered.

Hearing Sophie call Vienna her nickname felt like a gut punch.

"They say a person experiences two deaths. The first

is when they die. The second is when they're forgotten. I can't remember the last time I heard my father say my mom or Vienna's name. I can't remember the last time I said their name out loud."

"Honey."

"I took the picture off the wall."

She was still whispering when she said, "Valentine."

"He freaked. Started yelling and cussing. He got out of that recliner faster than I'd seen him move in years. If I hadn't seen the empty bottle on the table I would've swore he was sober. He was moving around the room with purpose. Unfortunately, that purpose was to yell and break shit but he was vertical and walking without swaying. Tore through the whole house. Yelling, not making much sense, throwing shit around. He even went into Vivi's room. I don't remember the last time he's gone in there. The door's always shut and it's still a shrine to a ten-year-old. It looks like it did the day she left with Mom to go run errands. I don't know what he did in there, I stayed out in the hall, but he came out with the old bear and ranted about buying her a new one. That devolved quickly into him shouting about how it should've been him who died. That he wishes it was him and not my mom."

Sophie's hands holding mine tightened. She hitched her leg over my hip and brought herself closer. I hoped like fuck that meant she forgave me for being such a heartless prick.

"I never wanted you to see that," I admitted.

"I know."

"I wasn't ever going to tell you about him."

"I know."

"That's fucked, baby."

Nothing needed to be said, so she didn't. She knew it was fucked. I knew it was fucked so she let that lie.

"I knew it was fucked when I told you I needed to end things with you. I knew before I said it. I knew as I was saying the words. And I regretted them as soon as I said them. No excuse for me being a dick but you deserve an explanation."

I slid my hand between the pillow and her cheek, my thumb grazed the corner of her mouth, over her soft skin, and once again I was soaking in her goodness to drown out the ugly.

Taking more from her than I deserved.

"His drinking didn't get bad until I was about twenty. Before that he was just disconnected. He took me to school, went to work, I took a bus home, he came home, dinner was takeout or a frozen meal. Sometimes he cooked an actual meal. When I got older sometimes I'd cook. He didn't go to my practices. He made it to one or two of my games. When I started to drive, he never went to another game. I did the grocery shopping. He barely spoke to me but he wasn't drinking. He was simply hiding. No more fishing trips. No more batting cages. No more telling me he was proud of me or he loved me. No more tossing a ball in the backyard or watching a game on TV. My dad was gone. And I watched, all of it. I was a teenage boy who loved and looked up to his father and that's what he taught me. Love was a weakness."

Sophie nuzzled her face into my palm. I took a fortifying breath and rushed to get the rest out.

"I've never had a woman for more than a few weeks. I never wanted a relationship. A wife. Kids. None of it. Then I met you and I knew I'd go the way of my father if it meant I had you for however long it took for you to realize I was broken. I'd make it worth it until you saw me for who I really was. Today wasn't about me not wanting you. It was me being a coward and leaving you before you could leave me. Before I had to see the disappointment in the eyes I love so much. Before you could tell me what a piece of shit I was for leaving my father to live in the rat hole to drink himself to death. My mom and sister were taken from me and my father is forcing me to watch him slowly kill himself. That's all I know. The people who I loved the most left me. Then there's you."

She immediately stiffened. I fucking hated I did that to her. I made it so she braced for an emotional blow.

Christ.

"My Sophie. Brave. Strong. Standing toe-to-toe with me, not letting me get away with my bullshit. Being the strength we both needed because I was too weak to face my fears." I leaned closer to her, trapping our hands between our chests. "I need you to know, if I came home and you weren't here I was going to find you. I took your warning, baby, and I came home to battle. I wasn't going to let you leave me. I'll fight for this, for you, for us. But you need to decide if this is what you want. Twenty-seven years of grief and fear doesn't disappear after one night of facing it. I let go of some of the guilt tonight. Logically I understand I can't make my father do something he's not ready to do. But that doesn't mean it still doesn't feel like shit. It's gonna take time to work this out of me. And the choice is yours whether or not you stay for the ride or get off now."

Sophie still hadn't relaxed, not the way she was holding herself, not her grip on my hand, even the muscles in her thigh thrown over my hip was contracted.

I'd seriously fucked this up.

All of it.

"Baby, you don't—"

"How did you leave things with your dad?"

Oh, yeah, I'd fucked it so badly she was avoiding the conversation we needed to have about us.

"I put the picture back on the wall. He settled down. Tomorrow or the next day he'll run out of booze, sleep his bender off, then call me. I'll go over, clean up his mess the best I can, give him his keys, and wait for the next time he falls into a case of liquor."

"His keys?"

"Only thing I can do to protect him is take his keys so I know he won't drive to get more booze when he's like that."

"He doesn't drink like that all the time?" she sheepishly asked.

"He's an alcoholic. He drinks all the time, but like what you saw? No, that's an every-few-months treat."

And the benders were coming more frequently. What used to be a twice-a-year event—my mom's birthday and the anniversary of the accident—turned into adding Vivi's birthday. Then he added their wedding anniversary. Now, I had no clue what sent him spiraling, but it was more than four times a year.

"Do you think..." she trailed off.

I waited for her to finish. When she didn't, I told her, "You can ask me anything, baby."

"Do you think he wants to die?" Her question was so soft I barely heard it.

"Yep."

"Do you think he hasn't done anything permanent because of you?"

I blinked into the dark, rolling her question around in my head. The sentiment was nice, but the truth was I had no clue. I had no relationship with my father beyond me checking in on him. And during those times we barely spoke. At this point I wasn't sure he even remembered I was a cop. He'd never been to any apartment, condo, or house I'd lived in. He'd never been in my car. I hadn't been to a restaurant with him since I was a teenager and I couldn't remember the last time I shared a meal with the man. Maybe in my early twenties. I was nothing to him.

"Don't know."

I felt Sophie nod against my hand under her face.

"We need to talk about us—"

"We already did."

Panic assaulted until I was dizzy with it.

"Please, baby, listen to me—"

"I did. I heard everything you said, Valentine. Now you need to listen to me. You said all you needed to say about us when you told me you weren't letting me go. The rest is about you and getting you to a place where you don't see us and our future through the filter of your father's trauma. Like you said, that'll take time. You need to come to the understanding that your father's inability to see you through the loss of your mom and sister isn't a challenge of your worth. That's about him, Valentine."

"Have I ever told you how incredibly brilliant I think you are?"

"No."

Fuck, I was an asshole.

"I think you're brilliant, Soph. Way too smart for the likes of me." She lifted her head off my hand and I didn't have to see her to know she was giving me the evil eye. "But it's too late. I'm keeping you and I'll do my damnedest to be everything you need."

"You already are."

For the first time, I let that penetrate and didn't question it.

"I'm sorry, baby. So fucking sorry."

"I know you are. I knew when your dad came out of the house, everything was going to be bad. I put the pieces together and was ready when you turned. I just didn't know if I was doing the right thing pushing you while you were going through something so ugly."

It was a punch to the gut I made her question herself.

"Never let me get away with my bullshit. You're far from dumb so I'm not surprised you clocked that situation and knew what I was going to do. But what I did to you was total shit, Sophie. You didn't deserve any of that. I'm grateful you understand but, never again will I treat you to that."

"I won't."

No, she wouldn't. She'd call me out and put a stop to it.

She settled in and relaxed. Feeling that, I did the same.

Long moments passed. Us just lying there in the dark quiet. Grateful didn't touch what I was feeling holding her hand, listening to her breath, knowing she was giving me a chance to prove to her I'd do my part—I'd do the work to fix what was broken or find a new way to deal with it. If I didn't, I'd lose her.

"Can I ask you something?"

"Sophie, baby, you can ask me *anything*. Nothing's off limits. You need it all, so ask."

"The marks on your back," she started shyly but didn't finish.

"Are you asking about my GSW scars?" I asked, though the exit wound scars were nothing compared to the left of the center on my stomach.

"GSW? You've been shot?" she screeched and sat up.

Smooth, asshole.

"Few years ago. Took two to the gut, one to the neck."

"Valentine—"

I rolled up, tagged her around the middle, and pulled her back down. This time pulling her over my chest, with her cheek resting on my pec. She did the rest and curled into me.

This was where she was meant to be.

Her place.

"Though the neck was just a graze. And as you can see, I'm fine. So, what about my back?"

"We're not done talking about you getting shot," she groused. "But I meant my nail marks on your back. You said you liked the pain. You got off on it. Is that because you want to punish yourself?"

I tried. Seriously I did. I even locked my body tight so it wouldn't happen. But I lost the battle and shook with silent laughter.

"Are you laughing at me?"

Fuck.

I sobered immediately.

"No, baby, I'm not laughing *at* you. I get why you asked that, but no, I'm not trying to punish myself and using your nails as the tool to deliver it. Straight up, Sophie, it's about you. Only you. Not ever before did I get off on some chick tearing me up. It's about you losing control, being lost to the moment, me feeling that loss of your control in a visceral way. The kind of pain that heightens all your other senses. That's yours and only yours."

I felt her thighs squeeze together and shift restlessly.

"You okay, Soph?" I teased.

"Peachy."

"You need me to take care of that for you?"

"Do you need to ask?"

Normally, no.

"Right now, yeah, I need to ask. Before I take more of your body I need to know where you're at and I need you to know where I'm at."

"And where are you?"

It was time to buck up and lay myself out.

I rolled her to her back, came up on an elbow, and leaned in. Unseeing but still feeling her attention on me I gave her what she needed.

"I'm in deep. I'm falling in love with you and that scares the fuck out of me, but I'm not letting you go and I'm not running. We're in this. Together. Me and you fighting to keep what we got strong."

"You don't want kids."

I wasn't sure if that was a question or a statement. What I did know was my heartrate kicked up a few notches.

"I also didn't want a woman or a wife. Yet here I am with a woman, falling in love, hoping she doesn't wise up before I can get my ring on her finger. Do you want kids?"

"I used to. But I'm thirty-seven. I might've missed my chance."

She sounded pained and full of regret. She wanted kids.

"It's not too late. When the time comes we'll make beautiful babies."

"That's awfully presumptuous of you to think I'll be popping out mini-Valentines," she huffed.

I dropped my head and laughed. There she was, my Sophie, giving me shit.

Thank fuck.

"How soon do you want babies?"

"Before I'm forty."

That could be arranged.

"Tell me where you're at, Soph."

"I'm with you."

My eyes closed and three words I didn't know I needed so desperately seared through me.

"Then kiss me, baby, so I can get busy taking care of my girl."

Sophie lifted her head. I met her halfway before I forced her head back to the pillow and I kissed her.

Then I got busy taking care of my girl—slowly and methodically I worshiped her like she deserved.

And when I was done, I had a few new lines down my back.

22

WITH A PEP in my step I walked to my apartment door.

Valentine had taken me out to breakfast before he dropped me off at my house so he could go to work and I could get my car. I had appointments this afternoon I couldn't miss. But after my meetings I was going to go to the grocery store and get stuff to make dinner at his house. I was planning on something easy I couldn't screw up, like tacos. It would suck if after everything he broke up with me because he figured out my cooking was hit or miss. I could make the same recipe the exact same way and there was still a fifty-fifty shot I would mess it up.

I let myself in and my mood immediately plummeted.

Khloe.

I continued into the apartment toward the sound of Hayden and his bitch.

Don't judge me for calling his woman a bitch. A bitch

was a bitch. A woman was a woman. And Khloe, whatever her last name was, was a certifiable bitch. If her issue was jealousy, she could've taken a moment and assessed the situation between me and Hayden and she would've seen immediately we were nothing more than friends.

But she wasn't that kind of woman, she was a bitch.

"Hey, Huxley," Hayden greeted. "All good?"

"Yep."

"How good?"

"It was the former, not the latter. So, really good."

Hayden visibly relaxed and he smiled.

"Good."

My gaze went to Khloe to say hello. She wasn't smiling like Hayden. She was shooting daggers.

"Morning, Khloe."

"Sophie," she pushed out, trying to sound like she was happy to see me when she absolutely was not.

"Sorry to be rude, but I'm in a rush. I have meetings this afternoon."

"I forgot to tell you, your mother stopped by yesterday looking for you. And she came by this morning, too."

Before I could shift my attention to Hayden, Khloe's eyes flashed with pure hatred. Good God, what was this woman's problem? Did my mother's interruption bother her that badly? I lived there, my mother could stop by any damn time she pleased. Okay, that was a stretch, but the principle remained.

"Thanks. Sorry she bothered you."

"Bother? You know I'd rather deal with her than let her loose on you."

That was the truth. Any time Hayden got to turn my mother away was a good day for him.

Since I didn't want to air my personal business in front of Khloe—actually, I didn't want the woman knowing anything about me, period—I just smiled at Hayden and took off to my room.

When I closed the door, I looked around the room. Everything looked exactly how I'd left it with the exception of mail on my bed. I didn't bother sorting through it, all my bills were electronic. And junk mail made the save-the-environment side of me rabidly angry. I was in too good of a mood to get wrapped around the axles. Khloe's presence was enough. I didn't need anything else bringing me down. It was on that thought I went to my text messages. At first, I muted my mother's calls after she'd embarrassed the hell out of me in front of Valentine. Then when she didn't stop I blocked her completely.

I still wasn't ready to deal with her. I had to help Valentine work through everything with his father first. Once that was sorted, I'd deal with my mother. Set boundaries, stick to them, and attempt to have something healthy with her. I wasn't under the illusion it would be loving but it could be a relationship of sorts. I found Nathan's text string and sent him a succinct message explaining I was extremely busy with my new business and I would appreciate him running interference with my mother until I felt I was ready to sit down and speak with her. I didn't wait for his reply before I muted his text thread and tossed my phone back in my purse.

Since Khloe was there I changed my plans and packed today's outfit in my overnight bag. I'd shower and get ready at Valentine's. Hayden throwing cold water on me was one thing. Being stabbed to death through the shower curtain by a crazy girlfriend was another.

I had my overnight bag packed and my laptop totes stuffed with extra notebooks so it was time to scoot. Now that I was getting ready at Valentine's I had to hurry.

Extreme relief the kitchen slash living room was empty hit me harder than it should have.

"I'm leaving!" I shouted. "Have a good day."

A moment later my quick escape was foiled.

"Sophie, wait," Khloe called back.

Cheese and rice, this bitch.

"Yeah?"

"I know you're in a hurry. But I haven't seen you since you had to go to the hospital." She rushed into the kitchen and came out carrying a reusable plastic container. "Hayden said blueberry's your favorite. I'm really good at baking, so I made you some muffins."

I couldn't see my face but I was pretty sure my eyes were bugging out of my head, mainly because I felt them getting wide.

"You didn't have to do that."

Really, seriously she didn't. I didn't want *anything* from this woman.

Suddenly her face fell and her demeanor completely

changed. She almost looked nervous. There was no bitch in sight when she said, "I just really like him."

Damn.

What did I say to that?

"I hope you know, I have a man. But even if I didn't, I'm no threat. We've always *just* been friends."

She gave me a sheepish smile and now I felt like a total cow. A judgy cow.

"I know. Please take the muffins."

Khloe held out her offering.

Dammit all to hell.

"Thanks, Khloe. And I am really sorry but I have to run. I'm already late."

"Have a good day," she bid.

"You, too."

After that I was out the door and jogging to my car.

I made it to my first appointment with five minutes to spare.

I HEARD the garage door go up and something settled in my tummy.

Valentine was home.

He came through the laundry room door and stopped. When I glanced over my shoulder my smile died.

"Everything okay?"

"I love seeing you in my house. I love you in my bed. I

love waking up to you. But fuck, I love coming home to you."

The air in the kitchen grew hot, or was that my skin heating at his gruff declaration?

Holy Moses.

If he promised to come home every day from work and said those same words I'd vow to learn how to cook. I'd go so far as taking one of those cooking courses at the local college.

"Not as much as I like you coming home to me."

When he didn't move or say anything else I asked, "Good day at work?"

He tossed his gym bag on top of the dryer and came to me at the stove, kissing my temple before he asked, "Low-key."

Low-key for a cop sounded like a good day.

"Did you make these?"

I turned to see Valentine holding Khloe's muffins.

"No. Believe it or not, Khloe made them."

"Khloe?"

"Yep. Maybe I was wrong about her and she's a nice gal who just can't get over Hayden having a female roommate. Though since she's been around I've barely been there. But anyway, she seemed genuine today when she gave them to me. She even went as far as to ask Hayden what my favorite was."

I watched him pull the lid off the container before I went back to stirring the ground beef. This was normally my issue with cooking. I got bored and didn't pay attention, then I burned stuff or under-cooked it depending on what had caught my attention while I was in the middle of cooking.

"Jesus," he grumbled.

I turned down the burner before I turned and asked, "What?"

"This is the worst blueberry muffin I've ever tasted."

His face clearly conveyed his thoughts.

"She said she was really good at baking."

Valentine held a small piece out in offering.

"I'm not one of those people who has a compulsion to smell or try something when someone says it's gross. I believe you."

"This is so bad you have to take a bite to believe it."

"Hard pass."

Valentine tossed the piece in the trash, then dumped the others.

"Christ. If I didn't know any better I'd say she was trying to kill you."

"That bad?" I laughed.

"Worse."

He bent down, his intention clear. I put my hand over my mouth and mumbled from behind it, "Oh no. Go rinse your mouth out. I don't want residual nasty muffin."

His lips winged up in a smile.

"No joke, baby. I love coming home from work knowing you're home waiting for me."

I loved, he loved that.

So much so I dropped my hand, rolled up on my toes, and kissed him.

Residual nastiness be damned.

Luckily he tasted of Valentine—all yummy, sexy Hot Cop.

"Do I have time for a shower before dinner?"

"Do you want time?"

He glanced at the stove then back to me.

"Have you started the rice?"

"Damn. I knew I forgot something. Go, you have time."

See? I was not good at this cooking stuff.

"Be back."

He was halfway through the living room when I called his name.

"Yeah."

"I feel at this juncture I should be honest with you and tell you, if you're with me for my kitchen skills you'll be sorely disappointed."

"Then it's a good thing you're cooking doesn't have a damn thing to do with why I'm with you."

Well, that was a relief.

"Is it because I'm funny?" I joked.

"Are you fishing, Soph?"

Was I?

I didn't think so.

"Maybe."

"Right." He prowled back into the kitchen, yanked me to his chest, and dropped his chin so we were eye to eye. "It has a lot to do with how pretty your eyes are. But also your sense of humor, how smart you are, how gorgeous. And I'd be lying if I didn't tell you it also has to do with how perfect your ass is, how great your tits are, how phenomenal your pussy feels, how good you taste, and when you get your mouth on me I lose my mind. But mostly, it's about how you look at me. I want to be the man you see."

"You are that man," I whispered.

"Keep telling me that, baby, and one day I might believe it."

I was so telling him that every day right after he told me he loved coming home to me.

"Phenomenal?" I smiled.

"*Unbelievably* phenomenal," he countered with a smirk.

"I think that has more to do with you than with me."

His smirk turned devilish.

"We can test that right now if you want, Soph, but you have food on the stove."

Shit.

See!

"Damn. Go. Leave. Before I burn dinner."

He didn't go or leave. He pulled me closer.

"I'm never gonna go and I'm never letting you leave but I will go shower so I can come back so you can feed me. After that, I'll show you just how fucking beautiful you feel."

That caused a whole-body quake that could be probably measured on the Richter scale. Further from that, it made me want to jump to the after part of his statement.

He let me go, spun me around, and gave me a gentle shove.

"Stove. Cook, woman."

"You're lucky you're hot," I grumbled.

"Damn right, I am."

I listened to his footsteps as he left.

I did that smiling huge.

Everything was going to work out.

Phenomenally.

23

"I CAN'T BELIEVE you talked me into this," I grumbled and stared out the side window at a very nice, well-kept home.

I felt Valentine's hand on my chin. He slowly turned my face until I was no longer looking at the house belonging to his teammate, Shiloh, and her husband, Luke but, instead looking into steel-blue eyes full of concern.

"It's going to be fine."

I knew it would be. Valentine would never walk me into a situation where I wouldn't be fine.

But...

"What if they don't like me?"

"They'll like you."

Firm. Honest. He believed that.

"Okay."

Before we could get out of the car, my phone rang

and I grabbed it out of my purse. I saw it was Hayden and answered.

"Hey."

"You're alive," he returned. "I see how it is, you get a man and dump me."

Thankfully he was laughing, but the fact remained it was Saturday, a few days after Khloe's peace offering and tacos, and I hadn't seen or talked to him since then.

I looked at Valentine and said to Hayden, "Sorry, Winslow. I'll talk to Valentine. We'll spend the night at ours. We can have a pizza and movie night."

"Pass. You're finally gettin' it regular. Please do not bring that noise to the apartment. The walls are thin."

"No shit. I've heard you hundreds of times. I think you'll live or do what I do and sleep with earbuds in."

Valentine's lips twitched.

"I have ear sensitivity, that won't work. Besides, I was just giving you shit but an invite to Valentine's place wouldn't go unappreciated."

Ugh. Was it socially acceptable to invite someone over and tell them their booty call wasn't welcome?

"I'll ask Valentine his schedule this week and work out something, okay?"

"Good. I'm calling because your mom came by again. This time begging me to have you call her. She said it was imperative she speak to you."

Her idea of imperative and mine were two different things.

"I'll call her tomorrow. I'm getting ready to walk into

a cookout with Valentine's team. I don't want to go in there in a bad mood."

"Damn, Huxley. Meeting the friends. Nice."

"Yeah."

"Tell your man I said what's up and he's slacking. I haven't seen him since the last time I kicked his ass at the center."

"I'll tell him."

"Later."

I tossed my phone in my purse.

"Summary report: Hayden wants an invite over to your house for dinner. He says to tell you hi and you're slacking at the center. Also, my mother stopped by the house again and has upped the drama saying it's imperative I call her."

"Shoulda already said this; Hayden, or anyone you want for that matter, is welcome at the house anytime."

Hayden or anyone I want?

"What's happening?"

Steel-blue turned stormy when he leaned in closer.

"What's happening is we're falling in love. We're fighting for this. And while we're doing that I'm going to do everything I can to get you to keep packing bags and staying the night until you come to the conclusion it'd be easier to just hang your shit in my closet and clean out whatever drawers you need."

Easier to hang my clothes in his closet?

I was fighting against hyperventilating. We'd only

been together... I gave up mathing in my head when I started getting lightheaded.

"You want me to move in?" I whispered, not trusting my voice.

"Today if I could talk you into it."

Today?

Sweet Dolly Parton, was he serious?

"Are you serious?"

Did Valentine turn on the heater? Was I sweating? I was born and raised in Georgia; it took a lot for me to break out in a sweat.

"How'd it feel last night falling asleep next to me? What about this morning—did you wake up happy?"

He knew I did. I loved falling asleep in his bed just as much as he did.

"Yes," I muttered.

"Right. So did I. Can't remember a morning since my mom and sister died I've woken up happy. Truly happy."

Holy hell.

I was totally moving in with Valentine.

"I need to talk to Hayden."

"You know he won't care. Or he will, but the caring he'll be doing is being happy for you. The dude adores you."

I was so freaking happy Valentine understood my friendship with Hayden.

"He totally does. And the deal was, we moved in with each other so we could each save money for a down payment on a house. I know he's saved enough, and I know he's had the money for the last year but hasn't moved out because he worries about me living alone."

Suddenly Valentine looked over my shoulder. He never broke eye contact when we were in the middle of a conversation.

"Everything—"

"Didn't think anything about it until you just said you're saving up to buy a house. You got something in mind you want? A neighborhood? I don't want to go as far as Savannah, traffic to work would be a bitch, but something within an hour of the station."

An hour?

He was willing to make a crazy-long commute and move if I'd already been house hunting.

God, could this guy get any better?

"Your house is perfect with... some small changes," I rushed the last three words.

"You don't like my pad?" He chuckled.

"I do, it just needs..." God, how did I tell him he needed some color and personality infused into his surroundings?

"You, Sophie. It just needs you. Then you can chick the joint up and make it a home."

Holy shit. We were doing this. I was going to move in with Valentine and the decision was made spur of the moment sitting in his Rover parked in front of his friend's house. My mother would have a heart attack. She'd have a ready lecture about proper planning and other people's perception and whatever other negative things she could come up with. Her nagging would be done out of concern for my wellbeing but not my happiness.

However, I was choosing happiness.

One week, one month, a year or three.

Valentine made me happy.

I was shooting my shot and hoping for the best.

"Okay."

"You're moving in?"

"Yep."

"Today?"

"Well, I was already planning on spending the night."

Valentine's eyes turned warm and he smiled a smile I'd never seen him make. He looked happy. Joyful. Relaxed.

"If you keep smiling at me like that, honey, I'm gonna request you take me home to celebrate and I'll miss meeting your friends."

His happiness instantly transformed to desire. It felt great knowing he was just as attracted to me as I was to him. But, seriously sometimes a girl needed a break.

"Come on, Romeo, introduce me to your friends."

He waited a beat, then two, and when I thought he was going to break the silence he opted to kiss me instead.

A sweet, slow celebratory kiss.

A promise of good things to come.

Please and thank you.

"I'M SORRY WHAT?" I sputtered. "A dog peed on his boot?"

We were all sitting in lawn chairs in Shiloh and Luke's backyard. "We" being Shiloh, Luke, Riddle, Chip, me, and Valentine. Their teammates, Watson and Gordy, had left a bit ago after we'd devoured the burgers Luke grilled. Shiloh had a bunch of store-bought sides from the deli that were better than any homemade potato and macaroni salads I'd ever had.

My belly was full, I was relaxed and having a great time, everyone seemed to like me and I totally liked them. Especially Shiloh and Chip. Shiloh was my soul-sister—that was, if her being a badass and me not being a badass meant we could still be sisters of the soul. She was a straight shooter. She didn't waste time pretending to be something she wasn't. You took her as she was or you didn't take her at all. She was also watchful and obviously the little sister to all the guys. They gave her gruff and she gave it back ten-fold. It was fun to watch. And Chip was a riot. His real name was Alan but everyone called him Chip because his front tooth was chipped and had been for years. The story behind it was something about him taking down a suspect who was twice his size. The chipped tooth was his claim to fame. He was also the most soft-spoken out of all the guys.

Now Riddle was telling stories and this latest one was about Valentine and a dog peeing on him.

"You didn't tell her about the time you were assaulted by a naked woman?" Riddle asked.

"Jesus. Here we go," Valentine mumbled. "I need a beer, anyone else?"

"I bet you do." Luke chuckled.

"Sunny?"

"Thanks. I'm good." She held up her bottle of water in salute.

Valentine tipped his head then smiled at her before he looked at me.

"You good?"

"Yes, but I'll be better when I hear the story about you getting assaulted by a naked woman. When was this?"

His eyes did this funny thing where they got wide and twitched at the same time.

"Last week."

Last week?

"Oh, shit, he's in trouble," Chip put in.

"Please tell me you disinfected before you came home."

"I used all the soap in the shower stall at work and half a bottle of hand sanitizer, and I tossed my boots, and my vest has been dry cleaned twice."

"Your vest?"

The crowd dissolved in fits of laughter.

"I hate you all," Valentine grumbled.

"She didn't just assault him," Riddle said through his laughter. "She jumped on him and climbed him like a monkey. He didn't know what to do with his hands so he held them high and to the side like he was blessing the room. The naked chick took that as her opportunity to climb higher. Shiloh had to save his ass. Or actually his face, seeing as that's where she was headed."

I pinched my lips because I wasn't sure if I wanted to laugh or ask for this woman's name so I could beat her up. I was edging toward laughter but Valentine's unhappy grunt pushed me over the edge and I lost it and joined in the hilarity.

"And the dog?" I giggled.

"A puppy," Chip choked out. "He was sniffing around Valentine, jumping on his leg, but when the woman attacked the dog got excited and just started pissing."

I looked up at Valentine frowning at Chip and busted out laughing again. His attention came to me and his eyes narrowed.

"I thought you were irrationally jealous?" He actually sounded perplexed.

"Was she hot?"

"She was cracked out and didn't smell real good."

"Then she doesn't count."

"Woman, she was humping my vest."

At that I laughed so hard I couldn't breathe. This lasted too long for Valentine's liking.

"All of you suck," he grunted.

"I'd rather suck than have a snail trail on my vest," Shiloh put in.

I stopped laughing and went back to pinching my lips.

"There's a joke in there somewhere but I don't wanna be snipered so I'll refrain," Riddle said with a smile.

"Smart," Luke rumbled.

Eek.

"So, Sophie, what is it you do?"

"Thankfully, not a job where there's a possibility I'll get humped by a stranger."

The backyard filled with laughter again.

And there I sat in the waning Georgia sun, drinking a beer with my man and his friends.

Oh, yeah, I'd take happiness any day of the week.

24

I WAS A TOTAL CHICKEN SHIT! I'd circled the parking lot of my apartment building twice to check for my mother's car before I parked. It was Sunday. Valentine had to work so I thought this was the perfect opportunity to run back to my place, grab a few more things, and talk to Hayden about moving out. Part of my plan changed when I didn't see Hayden's car. I'd have to call him and ask to meet somewhere. Which was probably the safer thing to do if my mother was coming to the apartment. The less time I spent there the better.

I knew I needed to deal with my mother but I had important things to see to with Valentine, and moving, and work. However, I'd come to some realizations about her and our relationship and I needed to talk that out with her. I just didn't want to do that today or tomorrow. Maybe sometime next week and she should know that. I needed to stop being childish and unblock my mom and send her a text. I was being unfair. Before I could enforce the new boundaries of our relationship she at least needed to know what those were. Then if she over-stepped or didn't respect them and I limited communication she'd know why.

Those were my thoughts as I was gathering stuff out of the bathroom. However, by the time I was folding jeans into a suitcase I'd talked myself out of unblocking my mother. I didn't want anything negative screwing with my happiness. I'd text her after I was moved in and settled. Hayden was today's priority.

I didn't have a single concern about his reaction to me moving in with Valentine. Our lease was up in three months, I'd continue to pay my half of the bills, and he'd be free to do his own thing. I would never tell this to Hayden, because I knew he loved me and it would piss him off, but there were times when I'd felt guilty for holding him back. I knew he stayed my roommate so I didn't live alone. I knew he stayed even though he had the means to buy a house and start building his future. I knew there'd been times he'd canceled plans to stay home and binge shit TV so I wouldn't be sitting home on a Saturday night by myself like a loser. Beyond all of that I knew he'd be happy for me.

And that was what I needed—my best friend's excitement and encouragement, not my mother's misgivings.

Happiness.

I was finally happy. Truly happy with every part of my life and I wasn't allowing anyone to steal my joy.

So, I'd deal with my mother later—much later.

I shoved the last of what I needed in my suitcase. The rest would wait until after I talked to Hayden—it would be totally uncool for him to come home and see my room cleaned before I had a chance to tell him.

As I zipped up the case there was a knock at the door.

My insides immediately twisted.

Shit on a shingle. I should've waited, told Hayden what was happening, then begged him to pack my stuff and move it to Valentine's for me. Or better yet asked Valentine to do it. I loved my BFF but I didn't want him packing my undies.

Another knock came, this one louder.

Just in case it wasn't my mother, I tiptoed out of my room, down the hall, and as quietly as I could, made my way to the door. I chanced a look through the peephole. Not my mother. Worse.

It was Khloe.

I debated not answering. When she knocked again, she was staring at the peephole like she could see me.

Creepy!

Whatever, I could handle Khloe. I'd tell her Hayden wasn't here and she'd leave.

Easy-peasy.

I opened the door prepared to do that, when she stepped right in, forcing me to stand back or get run over.

Blueberry muffins were immediately forgotten and I was back to thinking she was a total cow.

"God, it's like you don't even live here," she seethed as she walked past me.

Um. What?

I closed the door and followed her into the apartment.

"Hayden's not here," I informed her.

For some reason I took in her appearance. Maybe because she looked so very different from all the other times I'd seen her with her hair and makeup perfect, cute outfit, and sandaled feet. Today her hair was in a messy ponytail, and she wore jeans, a t-shirt, sneakers, no makeup.

"I'm not here for Hayden."

Maybe that's why she wasn't dressed to impress.

Oh, shit, did he break up with her?

Yippy!

"I see that makes you happy," she snapped.

I guess I hadn't covered my elation at the thought my friend kicked her to the curb well enough.

"Khloe, you and Hayden aren't my business. I was simply telling you he's not here and if you're not here for him then why are you here?"

"We need to talk."

Oh, no, we didn't.

"We don't have anything to talk about. I told you, you and Hayden aren't my business."

"You just couldn't make this easy, could you?" she fumed.

I didn't understand the fury behind her statement

and I didn't have time to contemplate the pure hatred she had for me before she attacked.

I landed on my back, Khloe on top of me, pain licking up my back and hip. One second I was blinking in confusion the next instinct took over and I clawed at her neck and face while lifting my hips to buck her off. Her hand fisted my hair at my forehead my scalp screamed in pain then my head slammed onto the floor. I bucked again, twisted, grabbed at her clothes, arms, any place I could reach to get her off me. With her full body weight she pinned me, struggling underneath her. I finally got my hand wrapped around her ponytail and got ready to introduce her to the agony of a scalping. Unfortunately, I didn't get a chance to rip her hair out by the roots. I felt something stab me in the neck. I let go of her hair to cover my neck.

My hand didn't make it before it felt too heavy to lift and dropped to the floor beside me.

"Stupid bitch," Khloe grumbled. "I tried to do this the easy way."

She rolled off me. My brain screamed at me to move, to yell for help, to crawl into my room and get my phone. Nothing worked. I was numb. Awake but unable to get my body to do what I wanted.

"Be back."

I saw her stand but as soon as she moved I lost sight of her.

Think, Sophie.

Move.

Move.

Move.

I willed and begged my legs to get with the program.

Move, dammit.

I didn't move. What I did do was feel terror.

So much of it, I was having a hard time breathing.

Fear so immense my vision blurred.

"Good. You didn't move." I heard Khloe laugh.

Suddenly I was jostled, moved, lifted, and finally plopped upright. Throughout all of this Khloe huffed and puffed and bitched. During which I did not move.

My head lulled forward and I saw the small front wheels of a wheelchair. Khloe came into view when she shoved the footrest down and placed my foot on it.

Kick her in the face, Sophie!

I didn't kick her. I sat motionless. Neither did I move when she repeated the process with my other leg.

I didn't do the first damn thing to help myself as Khloe wheeled me out of the apartment.

If I hadn't been scared out of my brain I would've felt bad for Hayden, he was going to blame himself for this. I would've been thinking about how I should've called my mother; now our last words to each other were angry and not nice.

But I wasn't scared enough to know I had one regret —I didn't get a chance to tell Valentine I loved him.

25

"YOU GOT A MINUTE?" Sunny called out as I tossed my bag in the back seat.

I didn't have a minute, I wanted to get home to Sophie. I hadn't talked to her since she'd called me on her way to her apartment. She was wasting no time bringing more shit to my—our—house. She'd also planned on talking to Hayden and I wanted to know how that went, but with a barricade that took for-fucking-ever to clear and a search warrant I hadn't had time to call her.

But this was Sunny.

So I'd make time.

"What's up?" I asked and slammed the back door.

"I dig your woman," she started on a smile. "Luke does, too."

That was good to know but everyone had made that obvious yesterday. Sophie had been immediately accepted into the crew. Hell, Mereno hadn't shut up all day about me locking her down and wedding her before she wised up and found someone better-looking. He was more right than he knew, but I wasn't worried about her leaving me for someone better-looking.

"She's moving in," I told her.

"It's good to see you with someone who's actually worthy of you instead of the bar flies you usually pick up."

I ignored the bar fly comment.

"You got it wrong, Sunny. I'll never be worthy of Sophie."

Sunny's blue eyes roamed my face, the contrast between her study of me and Sophie's, blaringly obvious. Sunny had to *try* to read me. Sophie just did.

"You know, if any other man said that, I'd think that was cool. Him thinking his woman was too good for him. Implying he knew she was one-of-a-kind and he'd work his ass off to make it so she never turned her eye. But you actually believe that."

"Sunny—"

"I've known you a long time, V. But I don't know a damn thing about you. None of us do. We know what you want us to know. You're a good friend to all of us. You're excellent at your job. Always there if someone needs you. You didn't hesitate to get involved at the Hope Center with my brother and the guys from TC. But other than that—nothing. Don't know where your parents live. Don't know if you've got siblings. You steer any conversation that minutely personal away from you. I thought we were giving you what you needed, not asking questions. Now I'm seeing we fucked up. Friends don't let friends sort their shit alone."

Goddammit. I didn't want to talk about this. And not for the normal reasons. I wanted to get home to Sophie.

"Listen—"

"You listen. I'm gonna tell you something Gordy said to me when I was struggling. It doesn't feel real good to know you're the type of friend you are to all of us but you won't let us return that favor. You'll trust me to have your back when we kick in a door but not with anything else."

I blew out a breath and scrubbed my hands over my face, doing this to buy myself time.

"I get you. I do. And you're right, I guard my personal life. But that's not because I don't trust you or the team. It's because until very recently I was ashamed for anyone to know. I felt guilt and embarrassment—and a lot of both of those—but also I'd buried so much grief I didn't know how to let any of it out without fear of it exploding all over the place.

"I'll always make time for you. I appreciate you looking out for me. So don't take this as me being a dick when I tell you, I wanna get home to Sophie. My personal shit will have to wait for a time when we can crack open a beer and I can explain fully, but, I don't have parents. I have a father who lives fifteen minutes from here but is an alcoholic. I don't have siblings because my sister died in a car accident with my mother. I'm ready to tell those stories, just not when Sophie's been at her apartment packing and she should be home now, and that's where I want to be—at home with my woman so I can continue to convince her she made the right choice giving me a shot."

I'd been so hellbent to get my speech done and over with, I hadn't noticed the annoyance had leaked out of Sunny and now she looked gutted.

"Fuck, Shiloh, I'm sorry I—"

"Don't Shiloh me and don't you dare apologize for giving me that gift. I want to crack open that beer with you, V. I want to be the friend to you that you've always been to me. But I'm gonna have to settle on water while I listen."

She'd been drinking water yesterday, too.

"Are you..."

"Guess that test I took in the locker room was wrong. Echo thinks I should sue the manufacturer."

That sounded like something her big brother would say.

I didn't bother stopping my smile when I told her, "Happy for Luke. Seriously happy for your brothers. But I'm happier for you."

"I love that you understand what this baby will mean to my brothers, to our family. It'll make this next part easier. I'm quitting, V."

"Quitting, or stepping out of SWAT?"

"Quitting. I haven't told anyone yet. But I'm ready. I did everything I set out to do. I did my duty as a Kent to right the wrongs that needed to be made right. I believed in my brothers' mission. I set my sights on SWAT and I accomplished that goal. I set out to be the best I could be within the team and I feel I accomplished that, too."

"You did, Sunny. You know how valuable you are to the team."

She gave me a small smile and nodded.

"Now, I have a new mission. A new goal. I can't wait to be this little one's mom. I want to be everything to him or her that I didn't have. I know I could still be a cop and be a good mom. But that's not what I want. And since I have a husband who will give me not only everything I want but what I need, he'll give me this and do it happily."

She wasn't wrong. Luke was going to be thrilled to give his wife something she wanted.

"Like I said, I'm happy for you, Sunny. Really fucking happy."

"Thanks, V. And keep this between us, yeah? I haven't even told Luke."

The gravity of what she said hit me square in the chest.

I reached out, hooked her around the back of her neck, and pulled her in for a hug.

She stayed stiff for a second before she hugged me back.

"Honored, Shiloh," I muttered to the top of her head, then I let her go.

When she stepped back she tilted her head and

narrowed her eyes. "Don't go soft on me, Malone. Just because I'm pregnant doesn't make me less of a badass."

"Right." I smiled. "Are we done so I can get home to my woman?"

"We are as long as you promise never to hug me again."

"You're gonna be a great mom, Shiloh."

Her face softened and she lost the attitude.

"I know I will."

That was Shiloh "Sunny" Kent Marcou—nothing short of fearless and strong.

"I call dibs on babysitting duty."

"You're so full of shit." She laughed and started to back away. "You want to babysit and change dirty diapers about as much as you want two to the chest."

"Diapers?" I frowned. "I'm talking about when...what age are they potty-trained?"

"No clue." She shrugged.

"Do you know anything about babies?"

"Nope. Not a damn thing."

She busted out laughing. I didn't. I watched the miracle that I'd seen a lot since Luke had come into her life and smoothed all those sharp edges that used to slice anyone who got too close. Seeing that, seeing her, knowing the shit her life was growing up, knowing all she'd overcome to marry a good man, be happy, make a baby, and be able to stand in the parking laughing carefree, gave me hope.

Hope that I could do right by Sophie.

I WALKED INTO AN EMPTY HOUSE. I knew it was going to be empty because Sophie's car wasn't in the driveway or garage. I pulled my ringing phone out of my back pocket and frowned.

"What's up, Hayden?"

"Tell Soph she's lucky no one tagged my TV or I'd be pissed she left the door open."

What the hell?

"Come again?"

"Where are you guys? The club house?"

Something I didn't like raced up my back, making the hair on the back of my neck prickle.

"I just got home from work. Last I spoke to Soph she was going back to the apartment to talk to you. That was nearly nine hours ago."

"Well fuck, I've been out all day. Came home, door was open. Her car's here. Purse and phone on her bed. I assumed she was somewhere with you. Maybe she went down to get a package."

"On a Sunday?" I reminded him as I walked back out to the garage.

"Yeah. If something's delivered and it's too big for the mailboxes the guy who runs the club house stores them. I'll run down and see if she's there. Sorry to—"

"I'm on my way over to your place."

"I'll just take me a minute to run down there. I'll save

you a trip and have her call you when we get back upstairs."

He wasn't getting it.

"I'll be there in ten minutes."

There was a beat of silence.

"The door was open but not damaged."

I got what he was saying but it did nothing to loosen the knot in my gut.

"See you in ten."

I hung up, scrolled through my contacts, found Brady's number, and hit go.

He answered on the third ring.

"You're already calling for a rematch? I figured after the last time I smoked—"

"I'm calling in a marker."

"What do you need?" he asked, all traces of humor gone.

"I need you on standby. I'm headed to Sophie's place right now. Shady Brook Apartments off 15th and Marne. Her roommate got home, front door open. Car in the lot. Purse and phone on the bed. He's checking the club house to see if she's there."

"Fuck. That means her tracker is likely on her bed unless she carries it in her pocket."

"Correct."

"And you got a bad feeling."

"Every time we've left that apartment, she double-checks the door is closed. Even when her roommate is in the apartment. She still pulls on the handle. There's no way she walked out and forgot to shut the door. Either she didn't lock the door when she went down to the club house and someone let themselves in, but I reckon Hayden would've noticed if something was missing and her purse is on her bed, or something else went down."

It was the 'something else' I was trying to keep locked down.

"Copy that. I'm at home. I'll boot up now and be ready if you need me."

"Sorry about taking your Sunday."

"Fuck off with that. Out."

Brady disconnected and I drove.

I was parking when Hayden finally called back.

"I'm in—"

"She's not there. No one's seen her."

Fuck.

Fuck.

"I'll be up in a second," I told him and disconnected.

My chest started burning and that something became harder to lock down.

way she walked out and stood in the door. [illegible] She didn't lock the door when she went down into the house and someone [illegible] [illegible] [illegible] [illegible] [illegible] her [illegible] the [illegible] down."

"It was the something else I was trying to keep locked [illegible]"

"Copy that. I'm [illegible] now and [illegible] notify all [illegible]"

[illegible]

Back off with the [illegible]

Steadily disconnected [illegible]

I was [illegible] when [illegible]

[illegible]—"

She [illegible]

Fuck.

Fuck.

[illegible]

26

I SUSPECTED HAYDEN'S PATIENCE, like mine, was wearing thin.

Sophie's mother was a pain in the ass.

And I was done.

I stared at Hayden's cell sitting on the kitchen table between the two of us and wanted to reach through the phone and shake the woman.

"Listen to me," I belted out. "This isn't about you. This is about Sophie. We're not after a history lesson, a simple yes or no. Have you seen Sophie today?"

"No."

It was a long shot but fuck.

"Other than wanting to connect with Sophie has there been a reason you've come by her apartment?"

"Do I need a reason—"

"Yes or no?"

"I don't believe that's your business," Lorelai challenged.

The woman was dead-ass wrong but I didn't have time to waste arguing with her. Brady had already gotten to work checking traffic cameras in the area after finding out the only place the apartment complex had cameras were outside and inside the club house, the gym, and the pool. Nothing in the breezeways, halls, or parking lot. A huge fucking oversight on the owner's part.

"Lorelai, the other day you were here you said it was imperative Sophie get in touch," Hayden tried, and I had to hand it to him; he kept his tone even whereas I was ready to strangle the woman. "We need to know what was so important you speak to her."

"Why? Is it so strange for a mother to want to speak to her daughter after she's ignored her for weeks?"

Coming from a nice, kind, loving mother, yes, that would be strange—her repeated visits would come from a place of worry. For a pushy, overbearing one, probably not—she'd find it imperative to speak to her daughter so she could get her way.

"Why are you calling me instead of my daughter? Where's Sophie?"

It was about time she asked after her daughter.

"That's what we're trying to find out," I told her.

Any other parent, I would've cushioned that. But this parent? I didn't have the time or desire.

"What does that mean?" she shrieked.

Now, that was the first response I'd heard from the

woman that conveyed she actually gave one single shit about her daughter.

"It means her purse, phone, and car are at the apartment. But she's not. And we know the last call she made from her phone was to me before she walked into her apartment."

"I need to come over. I'll be there—"

"You don't need to come here," Hayden piped in before I could.

"I need to give something to Valentine."

Me?

What the fuck could she want to give to me?

And suddenly everything about Lorelai changed.

"I haven't seen or talked to her since what happened. But I got a letter in the mail from an attorney about...her *father*," she whispered the last part and there was more than a little pain when she said the word "father."

"What about her father?" I asked and opened my texts. "What's his name?"

"Milton," she continued to whisper.

"Huxley?"

"Yes."

I shot off a text to Brady asking him to run Milton Huxley.

"What's the letter say?" Hayden inquired.

There was a long stretch of silence.

Too long.

"Lorelai."

"I'll bring it to you. It doesn't say much. Just that Milton's estate is looking for Sophie."

Why would an attorney send a letter to a thirty-seven-year-old woman's mother's house?

"Why wasn't it sent here?"

"Apartment's only in my name?" Hayden guessed. "Soph uses her mom's address for registration and insurance because the rate is way cheaper. So her license has that address, too."

Well, fucking hell.

My phone dinged with a text from Brady.

Two words that had my blood turning to ice.

Office. Now.

"Do me a favor, Lorelai. Take a picture of the letter and the envelope and text me the pictures. If I need the original, I'll come by your house."

"I'll—"

"We won't be here."

"If you're going out to search, I want to help."

And fuck me, I didn't want to believe it because believing it would mean I had to admit I'd been a total cocksucker to a mother who loved her daughter deeply and just didn't know how to show it. Sophie had started to come to these conclusions. I, however, was reserving judgement until her mother showed me proof Sophie's theory was correct. But there it was, proof in a mother's voice wobbling with fear, wanting to help search for her daughter.

"Lorelai." I softened my tone. "Let me get to where

I'm going. Get briefed on the situation and I'll call you. I'll keep you updated as much as I can, but I hope you understand finding Sophie is my priority, reporting to you is secondary." I glanced at Hayden, lifting my brow in question. He got me and tipped his chin. "Hayden will also be in touch. If you need something, call him not me, just in case I'm busy."

The last part was throwing Hayden under the bus then backing over him for good measure. But there was only so much Lorelai I could take even if she was showing a side of her that stated plain she loved her daughter.

"Okay. I'll... okay...I'll just..."

"Text me what I asked for."

"Yes. I'll do that."

"One more thing. Milton, was he a dangerous man?"

She sniffed and cleared her throat. "I don't know, he left when Sophie was two and never looked back."

Yeah, Sophie and her mother had a lot to talk about, including her mother still loving a man who left her thirty-five years ago.

27

"I HATE YOU!" Khloe screamed.

I blinked, trying to focus. I had no idea where I was or how long I'd been there. My head was swimming and not just from Khloe's ranting. I'd been in and out of consciousness. But at no point had I regained the use of my extremities and it was getting harder and harder to swallow.

"You don't even look like me," she went on with her crazy rant.

"All my life I heard Sophie-this, Sophie-that. One day you'll meet her, Khloe, and we'll be a family."

A family?

Was I hallucinating?

"You should've eaten the muffins!"

Move.

I begged my brain.

Move.

Move.

Move.

Khloe was losing it. Every time she paced in front of me I saw the knife she was waving around.

The crazy bitch was going to kill me.

I should've called my mother. Now she'd never know I'd pieced together some things and I'd started to understand why she was the way she was. And I still loved her, even though she was bossy and complicated.

"Do you know how long it takes to find the right kind of mushrooms?" she asked.

I hoped she didn't expect me to answer, because she'd rendered me mute and unable to move.

Good God, this was torture. I wanted to move, to yell, to breathe without it feeling like something heavy was sitting on my chest.

"I picked those fucking mushrooms and dried them and ground them perfectly just like the instructions said, and all that happened was you got a stomachache. Hayden said you were a coffee fiend. You should've drank the whole pot, you stupid bitch."

Poor Hayden was never going to forgive himself for bringing this psycho home.

"I didn't want to do it this way."

I didn't want her to do this at all.

She stopped in front of me and bent down to look me in the eyes.

"You don't look like me," she told me something I was

well aware of, in an ominous tone that scared me more than anything else she'd done. "Dad was wrong."

Her hand plunged forward and searing pain tore through my abdomen.

My mouth opened to scream but nothing came out.

28

"SISTER?" Hayden snarled.

"Half-sister," Brady corrected.

I had to look away from Hayden's pain-filled, ravaged face.

He was wrecked.

Not that I blamed him, but the guy needed to get his shit sorted or he needed to go find an office to work through what he was feeling.

That was not me being heartless.

I got it.

I felt it.

But now was not the time to process that the woman you brought into your home was a lying, scheming bitch.

Brady had wasted no time digging into Milton Huxley. Not that he had to dig deep; the man lived open just as most normal, everyday, average citizens did. He didn't hide because he had nothing to hide. Widower. Homeowner. Paid his bills and taxes on time. He wasn't obscenely wealthy but he had a lot of money. And according to his trust, his eldest daughter was to inherit two-hundred-and-fifty thousand dollars. His youngest would receive the same. If one or the other were deceased before the inheritance was claimed it went to the other sister. They were also to split the remainder of a four-hundred-thousand-dollar life insurance policy after his final expenses were paid. And all property Milton owned was to be split equally. Unless one of them wasn't living, then the other would absorb all the assets. And the kicker...there was seventy-five thousand set aside for Lorelai Huxley. If Lorelai was deceased that money was to go to Sophie and only Sophie or her heirs. It would never go to the younger daughter.

The younger daughter—Khloe Huxley.

A Khloe Huxley no one could find currently.

Brady had sent Tucker, a new hire at TC, to the address on her license. He was told by the gentleman who answered the door he and his wife had moved in three months ago and didn't know who the previous renter was. The property owner was being tracked down.

But we needed answers now.

So it sucked I needed to push Hayden to answer questions, but I needed answers.

"Did you ever go to her place?"

"Yeah. She's got a house on South Maple by Cherokee Rose Country Club. I don't remember the street number but it's the first house on Maple next door to the liquor store."

Brady picked up his phone to make a call while I stared at the pictures of Milton, Sophie, and Khloe that had been printed out and taped to a whiteboard.

Those pretty eyes holding me hostage.

A thousand scenarios went through my head, from the innocuous to horrendous. Sophie wouldn't go anywhere with Khloe without calling or texting. Even if Khloe had come clean and told her they were sisters and their father had recently died. At the very least she would've called Hayden.

Close to half a million in cash and more than that in property was a damn good motive to kill.

If I didn't know any better, I'd say she was trying to kill you.

"Khloe was there the morning Sophie got sick."

"Hang tight, Tucker," Brady said into his phone, then looked at me. "Sick?"

"Sophie was in the hospital, unexplained stomach pain and vomiting. No fever. Nothing came up on any test. They discharged her with their best guess that it was an ulcer even though the breath test came back negative. Khloe was there that morning."

"Yeah," Hayden grunted. "Soph drank one cup of coffee, came out for a bagel about ten minutes later, and commented that the coffee pot was empty. But Khloe doesn't drink coffee so she must've dumped it."

"Did you drink any?"

"No."

"You're thinking Khloe tried to poison her?" Brady inquired.

It made sense. Unexplained stomach issues that came on fast, went away after vomiting, and hadn't happened since.

Maybe.

"What about the blueberry muffins? Did you eat any of those?"

"No. Khloe only made... *fuck*. I ate part of one, they were fuckin' disgusting."

"Do you still have them?" Brady asked hopefully.

"Nope. Tossed them and the trash has been picked up since then."

"You got that, Tucker?" Brady went back to his call. There was a pause then, "Yeah. House first. Then neighbors. I need you to go in, get all her electronics. We'll start there. If we need to we'll go back and do a full search."

When Brady set his phone on the conference room table his gaze came to mine.

"I'm calling in the rest of the team."

Fucking shit.

"Agreed."

"You know what that means, right?"

Exactly what I'd been trying to avoid.

If Luke got called in, he'd tell Sunny. Sunny would first call her brothers—both cops. Her next call would my team. Brady'd been holding out for the same reason I'd been. I wanted this under the radar. I wanted my woman back by any means necessary and I didn't want red tape and procedures to get in the way.

Fuck.

"Call the team. I'll call Shiloh."

"I can tell Luke—"

"Absolutely not. Shiloh pissed at me is one thing, but I'm not asking Luke to stick his dick out so his wife can chop it off."

"Right."

Brady grabbed his phone and made his way to leave the conference room to make his calls. On his way to the door he jerked his head toward Hayden.

It was debatable which one of us was more fucked-up.

Hayden's guilt was eating him alive.

But abject terror had taken root in my gut and it was taking every ounce of control for me to beat it back or it would consume me.

All it would take is for me to give in to the smallest thought of what was happening to Sophie and I'd unravel.

"Hayden?"

He didn't look up.

"We're gonna get her back."

Nothing.

"Right now, she needs you. She needs me. You've got two choices, brother—give into the shit swirling in your head or set it aside, lock it down, and work with Brady and the guys to help find where that bitch took Sophie. In ten minutes this place is gonna be swarming with the TC team and cops. As soon as we have a location, I'm getting her out. You can have no part in that or you can come with. But, Hayden, I need you in or out. If you're out, I'll get—"

"I'm in," he growled. "Never in my life did I think I'd want to beat a woman senseless. But goddamn, that's what I'm struggling with. What kind of man wants to put his hands on a female and beat her?"

I knew his struggle.

"One that's human. One that loves his friend and she's in danger and he's willing do anything it takes to get her safe."

"Right," he grumbled miserably.

Brady came back into the room just as I thought of something.

"I need you to call in Liberty Hayes."

"One step ahead of you."

Brady knew Sunny was pregnant.

It was arguable who was more badass—former Special Forces soldier Liberty McCoy Hayes or Sunny. Not that I'd actually argue the claim; either of them would give me and any man I knew a run for their money if not best the situation. I'd get in, get my woman, and unleash Liberty.

I pulled my phone out to call Sunny as it was ringing.

"Sunny, I was just—"

"We're on our way. Echo will be there before us. Phoenix is on his way to Tucker. He's going to search the house while Tucker gathers the electronics. Team's been briefed and they're on their way. What else do you need from me?"

I closed my eyes and bowed my head.

I should've called my team immediately.

"V? You holding it together?"

"Barely," I gritted out.

"We got your back, brother. Hang tight. We'll get her back."

Fuck.

That hold I had was slipping fast.

Panic like I'd never known was creeping in.

"We got this, Valentine. You know we do. This is what we do. We won't let you down."

Jesus fuck.

I'd seen this play out hundreds of times.

"We won't let her down."

Sophie.

"Copy that."

"There you are. Stone cold, six-twelve. This is textbook. We know this drill. We live this drill. We run it, train for it, we fucking own this, Valentine. Stay cold. Detach. We'll be there. Swear it, brother, we're bringing her home."

Home.

"We are. See you when you get here."

"Out."

I shoved my phone in my pocket. Three breaths later, I locked the fear, the panic, the dread down.

With my next breath I made a silent promise to Sophie.

She was coming home by any means necessary.

29

GORDY MADE THE CALL.

Riddle wasn't at one with the plan, Chip had ranted his disapproval, but Mereno, Sunny, and Watson agreed.

Triple Canopy would take the lead.

Fewer procedures and rules.

My team was three blocks away with the ACP at a staging area. Hayden was with my team. I was with Luke with strict instructions from my captain not to fire my weapon unless I was in mortal danger. I must've agreed though at the time I wasn't paying enough attention to know exactly what I was agreeing to.

I was going in with TC even if it cost me my job.

During Phoenix's search of Khloe's house he found an electric bill that was not for the Maple Street house. Brady ran it and it was an art studio Khloe rented. Phoenix did a drive-by. Khloe's car was parked out front but he had no visual inside the building. When we arrived I understood why; all the windows ran along the top of the building a few feet down from the eaves. You'd need a ladder to see in. Two doors in. The back door was steel with a metal security door in front of it. Without the ACP to pull that bitch off the hinges, we weren't getting through.

That left the front door, which would cause every door kicker's ass to clench. A fatal funnel of potential death with no windows to see where the subjects were inside. The point man couldn't go in guns a-blazing with no visual on the hostage.

We were working on the assumption Khloe was working alone. That could prove to be a deadly mistake within seconds of entering if we were wrong.

"You straight?" Luke asked as we approached the A-side corner of the building.

Tucker, Liberty, and Logan were on the opposite A-side corner. Drake and Brady were covering the back door. Trey and Matt were the entry team. Liberty would follow Matt in and subdue Khloe. Luke and I would be right behind Liberty.

"Valentine?"

"I'm straight. Just feel naked with my M4."

I eyed his MP5 and adjusted my grip on my Sig.

"This is over in three minutes."

He wasn't wrong.

It would be.

One way or another, in three minutes the world beneath my feet was going to shift.

I'd either come out of the building breathing or my life would be over.

"Setting charge," Trey said through the comms.

"Copy," Drake returned for the team in the back.

I took a breath.

We know this drill.

I exhaled.

"Standby," Trey announced, and Liberty made her way into position.

We live this drill.

"In three...two..."

We run it, train for it, we fucking own this.

The explosive detonated. Trey shouldered through. Matt rushed in, Liberty on his ass.

Luke took off in a sprint with me less than a step behind him. We hit the door, my left hand went to his shoulder, and as one we entered.

"Down!" Liberty shouted.

I cleared the right side of the room, sweeping to the middle, and my breath wheezed out of my body in one agonizing exhale.

"Get your ass *down*," Matt demanded.

I holstered my Sig and took off in a dead sprint.

There was blood everywhere.

Too much fucking blood.

"Take her!" Trey shouted as Khloe raised her knife.

Without thought I jumped the last two feet.

"No shot," Matt called.

I hit Sophie. The wheelchair she was in pitched to

the side and went down with us. I kicked it out of the way and folded myself over her.

Two shots rang out as I tucked her close.

"Down," Liberty announced. "Clear."

"Drake, medic," Trey called in. "Critical."

Critical.

"Get Logan in here," Luke demanded. "Roll off. We gotta check her."

Luke didn't wait for me to comply before he yanked me to the side.

Logan dropped to the other side of Sophie and tore her shirt open from neck to hem.

"Move, Valentine." Luke muscled his way in.

I moved to give the men room to move. Impotence like I'd never felt crashed over me.

Stab wounds.

At least three I could count under all the blood.

Jesus fuck.

I tore my glove off and wrapped my hand around her throat searching for her pulse.

Please, baby.

Be alive.

Be alive.

Nothing.

I heard the screeching of tires. Pounding of feet. All of it in a distant haze.

The thread that had been holding me together snapped.

I dropped my forehead to Sophie's.

"I love you, Soph."

"Ambo, one minute out," Drake called in.

One minute, Sophie.

Please come back to me.

I watched in horror as Logan and Luke put pressure on her wounds.

But the blood just kept on flowing.

And with it, my soul bled out.

30

"I LOVE YOU, SOPH."

I love you, too.

I wanted to open my eyes but they were too heavy.

"I LOVE YOU, BABY."

My eyes fluttered open and wooziness hit my stomach.

My hand lifted, warm lips pressed onto my palm, and the sweetest words I'd ever heard floated through the air.

"There's my Sophie."

I didn't know where "there" was, but wherever it was I never wanted to leave. I wanted to stay right there where it was warm and soft next to Valentine.

"I love you." My throat felt scratchy and raw but still I needed to tell him. "I want to stay where you are."

"Always, Sophie. Always."

Okay, good.

Always.

My eyes floated closed and the darkness pulled me under before I realized I hadn't seen him.

BRIGHT LIGHT ASSAILED my vision and pain blistered through me.

"Oh my God." I swallowed past the pain. "Hurts."

"Shh, baby, I'll get the nurse."

My eyes slid to the side and landed on a black t-shirt. It felt like it took a year for my gaze to travel to his face and when it did, my pain intensified.

The steel of his eyes a desolate, dull blue.

"What happened?"

With his jaw clenched, he leaned forward. The mattress under my shoulders depressed. Then all I could see was Valentine.

Bits and pieces flooded in. Khloe. The wheelchair.

Move.

I surged up needing to move, but I didn't get anywhere before a strong, warm hand gently stayed my effort.

"Relax, Soph. The nurse will be right in to give you something for the pain."

"Khloe," I whispered.

Valentine's stubbled jaw flexed.

"You're safe, baby."

I was safe.

"Can I move?"

"No, baby, you have to stay in bed."

"My legs? Can I move them?"

A sinister look passed over his features, so dark and dangerous it penetrated through the pain. Without warning he stood and yanked the blanket from the foot of the bed.

Cool air hit my feet.

"Your legs are fine, Soph."

He didn't understand.

"I couldn't move them."

More menacing vibes rolled off him.

"Lift your leg, baby," he demanded, staring at my feet.

I hesitated, too afraid of what would happen if my brain told the extremity to move and nothing happened. I opted to roll my ankle.

"Did my foot move?"

"Yes."

If there's a stronger word for relief, that's what I felt.

"Good afternoon," a sweet voice singsonged.

My gaze swung to the door. Pain ricocheted in my head, forcing me to close my eyes against the nausea that crept up.

How was it possible to hurt so badly?

"She woke up in pain," Valentine informed the woman.

"We'll fix that right up for you, young lady."

"Thanks," I croaked.

I heard a chair scrape against the floor. My biceps got squeezed by the cuff around my arm. Valentine's big hand engulfed mine.

I was safe.

The rest didn't matter.

Slowly, the pain started to recede. Then I felt nothing.

SOFT VOICES WOKE ME.

Valentine. Hayden. My mother.

My mother.

I kept my eyes closed to assess my pain. A dull, achy throb all over. From head to toe I hurt but it was bearable. Still, I wasn't ready to face the room.

"I'm not suggesting we lie, Valentine, but don't you think she's been through enough?" my mother asked.

Lie?

"Yes, Lorelai, she's been through enough," Valentine gently returned. Gently, not just quietly. *What in the world?* "But I'm still not withholding the truth."

There was silence, or at least the voices stopped. I could still hear the low hum of machines.

Then a sniff broke the quiet and my mother's broken voice replied, "You know her better than I do. Whatever you feel is the right thing to do, we'll do."

What in the actual hippopotamus hell was going on? My mother was backing down. Conceding to someone else's point of view.

I must be dead or dreaming or in a drug-induced alternate universe.

"If you think you have a better way to explain this all to her I'll listen," Valentine said.

"No. You're right."

That did it. I was dead and having an out-of-body experience. I had to be.

I slowly cracked my eyes open. Through the tiny sliver between my eyelids I saw Hayden sitting next to my bed. A deep frown instead of his normally cheery, carefree smile. His gaze was on me. He knew I was awake but he didn't move. I opened my eyes wider and took more of him in. The only way to describe the way he was staring at me was miserable.

No, worse—guilt-ridden.

I hated that.

"It wasn't your fault," I whispered.

He shook his head.

"It wasn't, Winslow," I tried again. "I can't lose you to her."

"You're never going to lose me, Huxley."

Before I knew it, my mother was standing next to my bed opposite Hayden. Her hand grabbed mine before she gentled her grip and slid our palms together, barely wrapping her hand around mine.

"Are you in pain? Do you need the nurse? What do

you need? Ice chips? Blankets?" My mother's rapid-fire questions made my head spin.

I shifted my head on the pillow and there she was. Not her normal, put-together self, she looked like she hadn't slept in days. And Valentine... my big, strong Hot Cop stood behind her like a bodyguard. Mine, not hers. I knew if she said one thing to upset me he'd carry her out of the room kicking and screaming.

My protector.

"I'm fine, Mother."

She frowned but quickly softened her face and nodded.

"What don't you want to lie to me about?"

My mother's face paled, Hayden picked up my other hand, and my gaze shot to Valentine.

I'm not walking out of here, is that it? I shifted my legs under the blankets. They moved. I twisted my arms the best I could with my hands being held but they moved. My body was no longer numb. I could speak again.

But something was wrong. Something bad.

"Someone please tell me, am I dying?"

"No!" My mother's firm answer made me relax. "The doctor says you'll make a full recovery."

That was good news.

But there was still something wrong.

"We need to talk to you about Khloe," Valentine explained.

Right.

The crazy bitch who stabbed me.

My eyes immediately went to my stomach. How had I forgotten?

"She stabbed me."

"Six times."

Six?

Six times?

"Six?" I screeched, and instantly regretted it when my throat burned.

"Two deep. Four superficial. Thankfully, her angle of attack meant she didn't do internal damage."

Well, thank God for that. But the crazy bitch stabbed me six times. Also thank God, I only remembered the first one.

"Where is she? Did you find her?"

Valentine waited until I dragged my gaze back to him before he laid it out. "She was killed during the rescue."

The rescue.

Khloe was dead.

I turned to look at Hayden. My head swam with the quick movement, but when I regained focus, Hayden was already shaking his head.

"Hux, I love and adore you, but if you ask me how I'm doing, I'm gonna be pissed."

"She was...you were..." I didn't want to say he was screwing her in front of my mother so I settled on, "Seeing her."

"Then she drugged you, kidnapped you, and stabbed you," he said, like that said it all.

And in a way I guess it did.

"Sweetheart."

That was not Valentine calling me an endearment. It was my *mother*.

Sweetheart?

I might not be dying but there was definitely something going on.

"Someone please tell me what's going on," I demanded.

I was still staring at Hayden when my mother asked, "Should we call the doctor first?"

The doctor?

"She doesn't need her doctor, Lorelai," Hayden spoke up. "Valentine?"

"Alright, Sophie, look at me, baby. Lorelai, go sit by Hayden, yeah?"

My attention went to Valentine—slowly this time to avoid the dizziness—but it was diverted when my mother squeezed my hand.

"Everything's going to be okay, Sophie Lynn, I promise."

With that she let go of my hand and did what Valentine had directed her do. Who was this woman and what happened to No-One-Tells-Me-What-To-Do-Lorelai? Valentine took my mother's vacated place and moved to sit on the edge of the bed.

"Did Khloe say anything to you before she took you?" he asked.

I cast my mind back to letting Khloe in. Her appearance now made sense. She had her drugging and kidnapping outfit on, complete with sneakers instead of heels.

"Um, she said something about doing it the easy way. She made a comment about me not being at the apartment very often. I don't know, I don't remember much."

Valentine slowly nodded but the small gesture contradicted his stiff posture.

"And when she had you, did she say anything?"

She said a lot of stuff. None of it made sense and I couldn't piece it together with big chunks missing. I had no recollection of leaving my apartment other than being wheeled to the front door. I didn't know how I got to wherever she'd taken me to. I remembered her screaming at me. I remembered being terrified I couldn't move. I remembered the pain of being stabbed.

I love you, Soph.

I remembered hearing Valentine. But that memory was nothing more than a whisper, like it wasn't real, something my mind had conjured up.

"She said I didn't look anything like her. She yelled about being a family. She just yelled and ranted about stuff I didn't understand. Something about her dad being wrong. I was more concerned I couldn't move than what she was saying. I remember begging my legs to work and them not working."

I paused to swallow down the tightness in my throat. "It was getting hard to breathe. I was scared I was going to die and Hayden would blame himself." I heard a grunt that didn't come from Valentine. "And I was afraid I wasn't going to live to call my mother back and work things out."

My mother's sob tore through the hospital room and I wondered why I couldn't stop my thoughts from spilling out.

Regret—that's why. I'd been drugged, kidnapped, and stabbed. I was terrorized with fear, made immobile, and during that time when I thought I was going to die I had regrets.

I held Valentine's gaze and told him the truth. "I was so scared I was going to die without telling you I loved you. That's what I thought about when she stabbed me. How much I regretted not telling you."

I watched his eyes slowly close. When they opened, his hand moved to my face, palm to my cheek. His touch was feather-soft—achingly gentle but excruciatingly sad.

I both hated and loved it.

"I love you, Soph."

I knew he did.

He'd already told me as the darkness took me. The last thing I'd heard was his voice.

31

"SOPHIE, YOU SHOULD SIT DOWN," my mother said from behind me. "Let me finish up lunch."

It had only been three weeks. I was not used to this mother who was more of a mom than a mother. Albeit a bossy mom, but not overbearingly so.

And she was right. So I pulled up my maturity and didn't fight it.

"Okay, Mom."

I caught her startled gaze before I slowly—since that was the only speed I had—walked out of the kitchen to the couch.

"Does Valentine like mustard on his turkey sandwiches?" she called from the kitchen.

"Yes. But no tomatoes for him."

"Got it."

My eyes caught on the mountain of legal forms on the coffee table then slid to my closed laptop.

A miracle of all miracles had happened and while I was in the hospital my mother had emailed my clients for me and explained I'd been in an accident and would be in the hospital recovering for a week. She'd also replied to the returned emails of well wishes and concern. Then she took it a step further and took over my phone, fielding calls and taking messages. Those were all miracles, but when I heard her on the phone with my new bowling alley client I listened to her reassuring him I was the best in the business and it would behoove him to be patient and wait for me to send him my marketing plan. Further from that, she offered to go to the bowling alley and personally record the footage I needed of the lanes that had been redone.

This freaked me out. And when she left the hospital to go home I asked Valentine if he was sure I wasn't dying.

"I think you being taken woke her shit up, baby," he explained.

"More like shook the devil out," I snarked.

"No doubt she loves you, Soph. Just somewhere along the way it got twisted in her head. She's untwisted it now."

And that was it.

My mother had untwisted it and become my mom.

She also loved Valentine.

Hayden was a work in progress, mostly because he had years of experience with Lorelai and it would take a lot for her to prove to him she wasn't going to turn back into a harpy. But also because Hayden had closed himself off in a way that worried me. Valentine promised he was working on Hayden and he wasn't going to allow him to sink too far into his guilt. But I hated he felt guilt at all.

My *sister* had played him.

I hadn't learned about the fullness of what Khloe had done until day three after I woke up. More of my memory came back and I remembered what she'd said about the mushrooms. It was then Valentine filled me in on what his friend Brady had found on her computer. She'd done a lot of research on deadly mushrooms, rat poisons, how to make arsenic, tasteless poisons. The bitch was insane and I no longer felt bad about calling her a bitch. First, she tried to kill me for our father's money. Second, she was my sister and sisters are allowed to call their sisters a bitch.

Our father.

The man who abandoned me and my mom when I was two. He'd started another family after he left us. I wasn't surprised—he'd been gone from us for over thirty years—but it was strange knowing about it now. Brady had given Valentine a whole workup on my father's life, everything he could find to build a timeline of the years he'd been gone. I hadn't read it and I didn't know if I ever would. I was curious but it just didn't matter enough for me to tear open old wounds that would have no impact on my future happiness. I offered the report to my mom to look at but she felt the same as me. Which shocked me, because I knew she still had some love for the man who was once her husband.

"Onward from here, Sophie Lynn. No looking back, my sweet daughter."

I nearly choked when she'd called me sweet daughter.

This new mom was freaking me the hell out. Valentine told me I'd get used to it. He was probably right, I would. In about sixty years.

"Have you thought about the furniture I showed you?" My mom's question pulled me out of my thoughts. "Nathan said the dark wood would suit Valentine. It was more manly than the whitewash, but if your bedclothes are dark it would still be manly."

Furniture again.

This topic was going to be the death of me.

"I don't think the nightstands will work, Mom, they're too bulky."

"You might be right. The room is spacious but the bulk of the furniture could close it in."

She was freaking me out again. Not only because she was considering my opinion but also agreeing with me. The furniture was a housewarming gift from her and Nathan, something she insisted on and wouldn't budge about. But since it was a nice gesture and something a mom would want to give her daughter, I hadn't balked. However, I hadn't known the process of finding a bedroom suite would be such a pain in the ass.

"We'll keep looking until you find something you

like," she said as she sat in the chair cattycorner to the couch.

It was time.

Before the guys got back from the store, I needed to tell her.

"I love you, Mom."

Long moments of silence passed with her just staring at me.

"I don't deserve—"

"Mom, please don't do that. You said we're going forward from here. Let's do that. Let's not rehash the past. Let's just be grateful we have this now, and keep it."

"I never told you how proud I am of you."

No, she hadn't, but that was looking back.

"You have now."

She gave me a soft, nervous smile I didn't understand.

"I'd like to work for you."

Say what?

Um. No.

There could only be one boss at Sophie Huxley Marketing and that was Sophie Huxley.

"Hear me out," she rushed on. "Your admin. I can answer emails, organize your client files, whatever you need so you can create. As little or as much help as you need."

I wasn't ready for an assistant yet, but hopefully in the near future I would be. And those were all tasks my mom had taken over while I was recuperating and she handled all of it with little input from me.

"Why? You don't need to work."

"Because I believe in you and I want to support you."

Well, fuck a duck.

"I could use your help. But, Mom—"

"You're the boss and my opinion isn't welcome."

That didn't freak me out. That, I didn't like.

"Okay, Mom, we need to have this out," I started and she sat up straight. I didn't like that either. "You're my mom, your opinion is welcome, and it's needed. But, Mom, I don't want you *telling* me how to live my life and when I don't follow your plan, you getting mad with me."

"I was very wrong to do that."

"It's not about being wrong." I hated to have to lay it out but it had to be said. "I want a mom who loves me. I want my happiness to matter."

Lorelai Stevens finally gave me something I'd been missing my whole life.

The truth.

"When I found out I was pregnant with you it was the happiest day of my life. The first time I held you, I felt real fear for the first time. I had no idea how to be a good mother. My mother wasn't...well, she wasn't nice. She always told me it was important to never depend on anyone but myself. Men come and go and if you can't support yourself you'd be destitute. I met your father and fell head over heels. I forgot everything my mother had taught me. I stayed in the US, followed him to Georgia, relied on him to take care of us, and then he left.

"And when he did, I realized my mother was right.

But it was too late. I had you and I needed to find a way to support you, so I did. But I promised myself you would never forget. You would never be in the position I was in. I was overbearing and imperious in my lessons. And even when I realized what I was doing and how damaging they were, I continued because I never forgot what it was like to be so poor I couldn't feed you and pay the bills at the same time. I never forgot what it was like to have the electricity shut off and come home from work only to find an eviction notice on the front door. Nathan warned me. For years, we've had disagreements regarding my continuing poor treatment of you. He thinks the world of you and has never agreed how I've mothered you.

"That said, he's stayed with me. And still I didn't see it. Or I did, I just didn't have the courage to apologize to you and do better. Be a better mother to you. Tell you I was proud of everything you've accomplished. The woman you've become. I stayed stuck in the past, in a time when I was a scared, young girl with a baby and no way to feed her. But at no time did I not love you. Sophie Lynn, you are my world. I love you more than I love myself and I'm truly beyond measure sorry for making you feel like I didn't."

Scalding tears burned down my cheeks. My stomach ached, and for the first time since I'd woken up in a hospital bed, it had nothing to do with the six stab wounds.

"I didn't know."

"I never wanted you to know." Her voice was barely above a whisper.

"Why not?"

"Because poverty and my failures aren't something I'm proud of."

Was she serious?

"I needed to know that."

"Why would—"

"Mom," I snapped. "I needed to know. I needed to know how strong my mother is. You didn't fail, you overcame. Those were the lessons I needed; how to fall down, get back up, and how to best any obstacle in my path. But beyond that, I needed it so I could share in that with you. So I could tell you how much I appreciate your sacrifice and hard work."

"You were never a sacrifice."

Okay, so maybe she had a point with that.

"Are you happy?" I asked.

"Happy?"

"Yes, are you happy? In general, with Nathan, are you happy, Mom?"

She relaxed back in her chair and looked around the living room.

"I'm happy with Nathan. He's always made me feel loved and safe and well taken care of. In general, outside of my marriage I was content but never happy. Not until I heard you call me mom again. You stopped calling me mom around the age of ten and started calling me mother. Having mom back, that made me happy."

I'd also told her I'd loved her but I understood. There was a difference; she'd been a mother to me up until that point.

"Are *you* happy?" she asked.

No hesitation.

"Blissfully, deliriously, crazy happy."

"Then that is what I am." She nodded. "Blissfully happy my daughter is crazy happy. Now, shall we continue to wait for the men to get home or would you like to eat your lunch? You need to take your pills and you cannot do that on an empty stomach."

There she was.

Our heart-to-heart was over. Not that I minded; I finally got everything I needed from her.

"I'm starving, so as rude as it is, I'm eating without them. I'm also eating on the couch. Sitting at the table feels like I'm being stabbed in the stomach. Oh, wait, my crazy bitch sister already did that."

"Sophie!" she gasped.

"This is me, Mom. Welcome to the crazy world of Sophie Huxley. It's drama-filled but amusing."

"You get that from me, you know," she huffed and stood. "Ask Nathan. I died twice yesterday because there was a spider on the ceiling."

"Only twice?" I gasped. "A spider on the ceiling is grounds for burning the house down."

"Yes, well, I did suggest that but Nathan informed me arson isn't covered under our policy. He felt it would be safer to get a ladder and kill it. Of course that meant I witnessed his kiss with death as he climbed on the death contraption. It was an ordeal I'd rather not re-live."

I watch my mom flounce out of the living room.

I did this with a newfound respect. The woman could flounce; I was totally adding that to my dramatic exit repertoire.

The unfortunate result of my mom being amusing meant I forgot I was still recovering from six stab wounds and my stomach muscles weren't ready for strenuous activity which most definitely consisted of me busting out a laugh.

Something I did right then.

And I didn't regret a moment of the pain it caused.

32

THREE MONTHS LATER...

"You know size matters," I mumbled.

"Are you speaking from personal experience?" Liberty asked from beside me.

"Please, for my sake do not answer that," Shiloh begged.

I watched as Phoenix easily blocked another ball from going near the rim.

The three of us were sitting on the bleachers watching the guys play basketball at the Hope Center. Phoenix's wife, Wren, had watched her husband and son play the first quarter but she had something to do in one of the computer rooms so now it was just me, Shiloh, and Liberty.

"I was speaking about Phoenix's height," I clarified. "But indeed, I have—"

"Stop right there," Shiloh grouched.

I kept my eyes on the court, or more specifically on Valentine and the sweat-drenched t-shirt molded to his chest and torso, leaving very little to the imagination. Not that I needed to imagine what my man looked like without his clothes on. Thankfully, those memories were all stitched together into one, long, continuous highlight reel of goodness.

Though it felt like an eternity since I'd had the pleasure to experience all that goodness.

Valentine's concern for my ongoing recovery would've been sweet if it wasn't to the point of torture. To say the sweet had worn off weeks ago would be an understatement.

"Is there a reason you're scowling at the court?" Liberty asked.

"I'm not scowling. I'm attempting to send subliminal sexy messages to Valentine."

"By scowling?"

"I'm concentrating," I corrected.

"You look constipated," Shiloh put in. "You should try smiling. It might work better."

She was probably right.

"I never thought I'd say this because my man is a master when it comes to his mouth but—"

"You've already said too much," Shiloh stopped me.

"Sorry. I'm used to blurting stuff out."

Where was Hayden when I needed him?

On that thought my gaze drifted to my best friend. After two months of actively avoiding me I threw a hissy fit to end all hissy fits and he started coming over to the house for dinner. It took another drama for him to stop pussy-footing around me. I suspected it was a show but things were back to normal, or a new normal, since we were no longer roommates. But he was at the house at least twice a week, and he and Valentine regularly played basketball together and on a few occasions had gone out to shoot pool without me. I knew those were the times when Valentine was pulling Hayden's head out of his ass.

"Not getting any?" Shiloh rightly guessed.

"I get plenty. I don't get to give and I don't get the main event but I get everything else."

I had no reason to be grumpy. Valentine was generous with orgasms. He stayed up late and talked me through the bad dreams. He held me every night. He loved me and told me often. He thought I was hot, sexy, beautiful, smart, and he gave that to me daily. But he would not let me return the favor. Not physically.

I needed more. I needed to get back what we had. I needed to give him what he needed.

"You didn't see what he saw," Liberty gently said. "You didn't see *him*. His whole world ended, Sophie. He couldn't find your pulse and I swear I saw him die right there. Your body needed time to heal. And maybe he needed distance from seeing you..." She stopped and shook her head.

She didn't need to finish.

He saw me covered in blood.

We'd talked about it. I made him tell me what

happened. It wasn't pleasant, he'd retreated and tried to stonewall. But he'd given in and given us what I knew we both needed.

But it had been three months. I wasn't healing, I was healed.

"Thank you for...everything," I whispered.

I knew she caught my meaning when she softly returned, "You're welcome, Soph."

Yeah, she knew I knew she was the one who shot my crazy-ass sister before she could stab me again. Or stab Valentine when he jumped on me, prepared to take the blade.

"GOTTA SHOWER REAL QUICK, baby, then I'll hit the store if you start the potatoes."

We were having grilled steaks and twice-baked potatoes later. The potatoes needed to be baked early so they could cool before I doctored them up into fluffy, cheesy, calorie-ridden yumminess. And our house was on the way to the butcher Valentine used so he'd stopped to shower.

I tossed my purse on the chair and watched him hit the stairs. Actually, I was doing more than watching, I was salivating. He was hot and sweaty and I was over him putting me off. I understood what Liberty had told me. He did need distance from seeing me covered in blood, but those images were never going to be completely wiped from his memory. The same as I'd never forget his dull, haunted eyes when I came to in the hospital. I'd never forget his pain as he sat next to me while I gave my statement to the police. Those things were forever embedded—they were a part of us. We'd never get rid of them, but I was not going to allow them to define us.

I needed my man mindless. I needed him to take me with him to a place only he could take me.

Before I followed him, I pulled my phone out of my purse and called Hayden.

Since we were back to normal he answered my call instead of sending me to voice mail, which had been annoying and frustrating.

"Yo."

"Change of plans. I need another hour. Come over at five instead of four."

"Everything good?"

"It'll be great when I hang up on you and join my man in the shower in the hopes I can seduce him and get myself a happy ending."

"You know when I used to tell you to go out and have wild monkey sex that didn't mean I wanted the actual details."

"Deal with it, Winslow. And for the record I'm *not* giving you details. But I'll confirm it's wild—"

"See you at five."

I smiled and tossed my phone on the couch.

Then I joined my man in the shower.

CHRIST, she was killing me.

How in the fuck had I let her talk me into this?

"Soph," I groaned.

Her wet tits pressed tighter to my back, the hand she had wrapped around my dick slowed, and her other hand cupping my balls rolled.

I was in hell.

She'd edged me to the brink twice.

"This is your warning, baby. Either you finish me off or I'm taking over."

We were nearing on four months. Four months of nothing but my hand alone in the shower after I got her off. I should've stuck to that and seen to her. Now my control was slipping. She needed more time before I took her with more than my mouth and fingers.

"It's my turn," she said sweetly and stroked faster.

That was how I'd gotten myself in this position. Sophie joining me in the shower, looking up at me with her pretty fucking eyes, telling me she wanted to give me a hand job.

"It's about to not be your turn," I grunted.

Her hand left my balls, grazed over my ass, went between us, and her hips jerked.

Good Christ.

"You playing with your pussy, Sophie?"

She was. I could totally feel what she was doing

behind my back. I was seconds away from losing what little control I had left.

"No, I'm playing with *your* pussy, honey."

That did it.

I pulled her hand off my dick, turned, grabbed her by the hips, and lifted her. I barely had the presence of mind to slap the faucet off before I carried her to the bed and unceremoniously tossed her on it. She scrambled back when I followed her onto the mattress and closed her legs.

"Open your legs. Spread wide for me."

"No. I want you on your back."

That worked for me.

"You wanna ride my face, baby?"

"No. I'm gonna ride *you*."

Before I could deny her request she attacked. My heart nearly stopped at her jerky movements, causing her to get the best of me and push me to my back.

"No thinking, Valentine." She straddled my hips. "Mindless, honey. Make me lose control."

Christ. My dick wept with excitement. But my gaze dropped to the scars on her abdomen, reminding me I had to let her heal.

"There are six of them," she drawled. "She tried six times to take me from you."

My gut churned at the reminder.

Sophie reached between us, fisted my cock, and stroked.

"But she failed."

My hands went to her hips to stop her, but my Soph was determined and she sank down taking the first few inches.

"Fuck," I grunted, holding my body absolutely still.

"I'm healed," she moaned and slid up. "And I need you," she panted on a downward glide.

Slowly she worked herself up and down until finally she had all of me.

Four months without feeling her. Three of those months tasting her, using my fingers to get her off, listening to her moan for me, but not feeling it the way I wanted. Only jacking off to take the edge off and stay the course. To let her body do what it needed to do.

She lifted herself up, slammed back down, and groaned, "So good."

This was not going to last. *I* wasn't going to last, not with her excitement coating my bare cock, her tight cunt already clenching.

"Lean forward, Soph, I want your tits in my face and your fingers toying with your clit."

I held her hips tightly until she gave me what I wanted. When I got her nipple in my mouth I loosened my hold. But I didn't give her much room to bounce. I needed her closer. I moved to the other nipple, toyed with it until she was squirming, trying go faster.

"Honey," she breathed, and dropped her forehead to the top of my head and started rocking.

Thank fuck.

"You wanna come, sweet Sophie?"

"Yes," she hissed.

"How bad, baby?"

"So, so bad, Valentine."

I rolled up, taking her with me, flipped her over, and drove back in.

"Wrap tight, baby."

She barely got her legs around my waist before I took her hard and deep with her back arching off the bed, her face shoved in my neck, and her nails scraping down my back.

Jesus fuck, she felt beautiful.

Her teeth sinking into my skin stifled her moan. Two more drives, I stayed planted, and poured myself into what had to be the longest orgasm of my life.

"I can feel you," she whispered.

I had no doubt.

"I love you, Valentine."

My dick jerked but my body froze and I closed my eyes.

"Say it again."

"I love you."

"Again."

"I love you, so, *so*, so much, Valentine."

Christ.

She'd given me the words a lot over the last few months. But never while I was inside of her. Never when she had me wrapped up. Now I had it all. Her body and her heart. Together, at the same time.

I lifted my head so I could catch her eyes when I gave her back everything she'd given me, "I love you, Soph."

Her lips tipped up into a smug smile.

"I know you do."

I gave her that. It was no secret how much I loved her. The brand-new bed her mother had insisted on buying us when I had a perfectly good mattress was proof. The new furniture was also proof. So was the addition of a shit-ton of toss pillows on the couch, and new towels throughout the house, and the pictures on the walls.

Whatever Sophie wanted, she got.

"Is me coming inside you without a condom your way of communicating you're ready to start trying for a baby?"

"Well, if it wasn't, we'd be in trouble since your dick's so big you hit my cervix, and I'm pretty sure your swimmers don't actually have to swim anywhere since you'll just inject them where they need to go."

I couldn't stop my chuckle.

"And don't take that as a complaint. A cervical orgasm can't be beat."

"Good to know."

"I'm ready when you are," she said softly. "But I just ended my period so I think we're safe. Maybe."

"Then I best find a time to give you your ring."

I leaned down, pressed a kiss to her forehead, pulled out, and rolled to my side.

Sophie yanked the throw blanket off the end of the

bed—this was a new addition as well—and covered herself as she pulled up to sitting.

"My ring?"

I smiled at her wide eyes.

"Yeah, baby, your ring."

"You bought me a ring?" she sang and bounced.

Fuck, she was cute.

"Yes."

"Can I have it?" she asked with another bounce.

"You can, when I find the right time to give it to you."

Sophie launched herself at me, came up on her knees, and slapped her hands on my chest.

"Now's perfect."

I started chuckling.

"I'm not joking, Valentine." She jostled over me. "Right now is splendid. Totally the right time."

Good God, her excitement was gorgeous.

"Soph—"

"Please. *Pretty* please."

Her still-damp hair was a stringy mess that fell over her shoulders, face clean from the minimal makeup she wore, cheeks still flushed from her orgasm, and she'd never been more beautiful than she was right then asking me for her ring. She didn't care about the jewelry or the perfect timing. She cared about what that ring said.

She wanted the promise.

The future that promise held.

"Open my nightstand."

The woman damn near kicked me in the dick when

she flung herself to the side to reach for the drawer. She came back with a black box in her hand, dropped back down, and held it in front of her.

"Open it," I grunted, still recovering from taking her weight.

"Yes."

"I haven't asked you anything yet, baby." I chuckled.

"Yes," she repeated. "A thousand yeses. Every day yes. Every day I choose you. Every day you're worth it. Every minute for the rest of my life, yes."

Everything she said hit me all at once. Then suddenly it morphed into 'six times she tried to take me from you' then 'I will fight for you.' And she had. She fought for me, for us, by lying on that floor bleeding out but fighting to stay alive.

"Marry me, Sophie."

"Hmmm. Let me think about—"

I didn't let her finish. I did an ab curl and kissed the correct answer off her lips. It tasted beautiful.

Like home.

Like the future.

Like forever.

Next up is TIM in Playing with Love...

ALSO BY RILEY EDWARDS

Riley Edwards

www.RileyEdwardsRomance.com

Hollow Point

Playing with Lies

Playing with Danger

Takeback

Dangerous Love

Dangerous Rescue

Dangerous Games

Dangerous Encounter

Dangerous Mind

Dangerous Hearts

Dangerous Affair

Gemini Group

Nixon's Promise

Jameson's Salvation

Weston's Treasure

Alec's Dream

Chasin's Surrender

Holden's Resurrection

Jonny's Redemption

Red Team - Susan Stoker Universe

Nightstalker

Protecting Olivia

Redeeming Violet

Recovering Ivy

Rescuing Erin

The Gold Team - Susan Stoker Universe

Brooks

Thaddeus

Kyle

Maximus

Declan

Blue Team - Susan Stoker Universe

Owen

Gabe

Myles

Kevin

Cooper

Garrett

Silver Team

Theo

Easton

AUDIO

Are you an Audio Fan?

Check out Riley's titles in Audio on Audible and iTunes

Gemini Group

Narrated by: Joe Arden and Erin Mallon

Red Team

Narrated by: Jason Clarke and Carly Robins

Gold Team

Narrated by: Lee Samuels and Maxine Mitchell

The 707 Series

Narrated by: Troy Duran and C. J. Bloom

The Next Generation

Narrated by: Troy Duran and Devon Grace

Triple Canopy

Narrated by: Mackenzie Cartwright and Connor Crais

More audio coming soon

BE A REBEL

Riley Edwards is a USA Today and WSJ bestselling author, wife, and military mom. Riley was born and raised in Los Angeles but now resides on the east coast with her fantastic husband and children.

Riley writes heart-stopping romance with sexy alpha heroes and even stronger heroines. Riley's favorite genres to write are romantic suspense and military romance.

Don't forget to sign up for Riley's newsletter and never miss another release, sale, or exclusive bonus material.

Rebels Newsletter

Facebook Fan Group

www.rileyedwardsromance.com

facebook.com/Novelist.Riley.Edwards
instagram.com/rileyedwardsromance
bookbub.com/authors/riley-edwards
amazon.com/author/rileyedwards

Made in the USA
Middletown, DE
08 October 2024

62171610R00199